✓ pu4

DATE DUE			
AUG 3 '00	OCT 12 '04		
AUG 11 '00			
SEP 21 00			
OCT 13 '00			
NOV 7 '00			
JAN 05 '01			
JUN 13 '01			
JUL 28 01			
AUG 04 '01			
DEC 14 '01			
JAN 02 '02			
FEB 14 '03			

7 / 00

JACKSON COUNTY
Library Services

HEADQUARTERS
413 West Main Street
Medford, Oregon 97501

D c

DESPERATE JOURNEY

DESPERATE JOURNEY

Cliff Farrell

edited by

R. E. BRINEY

Thorndike Press • Chivers Press
Thorndike, Maine USA   Bath, England

This Large Print edition is published by Thorndike Press, USA and by Chivers Press, England.

Published in 2000 in the U.S. by arrangement with Golden West Literary Agency.

Published in 2000 in the U.K. by arrangement with Golden West Literary Agency.

U.S. Hardcover   0-7862-1340-X   (Western Series Edition)
U.K. Hardcover   0-7540-4186-7   (Chivers Large Print)
U.K. Softcover   0-7540-4187-5   (Camden Large Print)

The text of this Large Print edition is unabridged.
Other aspects of the book may vary from the original edition.

Set in 16 pt. Plantin by Rick Gundberg.

Printed in the United States on permanent paper.

British Library Cataloguing in Publication Data available

Library of Congress Cataloging-in-Publication Data

Farrell, Cliff.
    Desperate journey / Cliff Farrell ; edited by R.E. Briney.
        p. (large print) cm.
    Originally published: Unity, Me. : Five Star, 1999, in series:
Five Star standard print western series.
    ISBN 0-7862-1340-X (lg. print : hc : alk. paper)
    1. Frontier and pioneer life — West (U.S.) — Fiction.
    2. Western stories. 3. Large type books. I. Briney, Robert E.,
1933– . II. Title.
PS3556.A766 A6 2000
813'.54—dc21   99-058962

Table of Contents

Acknowledgments

Foreword

Throughout a sixty-year career as a newspaperman and fiction writer, Cliff Farrell maintained an enviable reputation for both productivity and quality. During the 1930s and 1940s his stories were sought after by editors and enjoyed by a large audience of magazine readers. In the 1950s and 1960s, a period when Western fiction was receiving diminishing attention in magazine and newspaper review columns, Farrell's books were still favorably reviewed. In all, Farrell wrote more than six hundred magazine stories, twenty-three Western novels, and one non-fiction book of Western Americana.

Alfonso Clifford Farrell was born on November 20, 1899, in Zanesville, in the Ohio hill country, the same region that produced another popular Western writer, Zane Grey. By his early teens he had developed a fascination with newspaper work and, during his high school years, was given his first newspaper job, as a messenger boy at the Zanesville *Sunday News*. He loved the newspaper environment, but emptying wastebaskets, sweeping the floor, and carrying messages were not

9

enough — he wanted to write. His persistent entreaties paid off, and he was hired as a columnist and reporter for the daily Zanesville *Times Recorder*, where he worked full time in addition to attending school. On the day of his high school graduation he worked most of the day, took a couple of hours off to attend the evening graduation ceremonies, and then went back to work.

Farrell subsequently left Zanesville to work on newspapers in Columbus, Ohio, and in Canton where, still in his teens, he became a city editor. But he wanted to see more of the country than just Ohio, so he set out to work his way westward, going from one newspaper job to the next: first the *Indianapolis Star* and the St. Louis *Globe-Democrat* and then the cross-country leap to the San Francisco *Chronicle* and the Los Angeles *Record*. Finally, at the age of twenty, he was hired as a sports reporter at the *Los Angeles Examiner*, where he remained for many years, later serving in various editorial and executive positions. After several lengthy sabbaticals during which he devoted himself entirely to writing fiction, his last period of newspaper work was at the Los Angeles *Times*.

On June 1, 1927, Farrell married Mildred K. Raddon. The marriage produced a son, Clifford R., and a daughter, Mildred. The family settled in Mar Vista, near Los Angeles. Much later, after Farrell's retirement from the *Times*, the family moved to the San Bernardino Mountains. This mountain home was less than a mile from Lake Gregory, where Farrell could indulge his love of swimming and fishing. Another enthusiasm was foreign travel, and over the years the Farrells visited many parts of Europe, Asia, and South America.

In 1925 Farrell decided to supplement his newspaper income by writing fiction. Since he was then covering auto racing as part of his sports reporting, this was a natural choice of background for his initial ventures. His first story did not sell, but the second was purchased by Street & Smith's *Sport Story Magazine*. As many as a hundred other sports story sales followed over the next few years. His first known Western story, titled "Good Shootin'," appeared in *Cowboy Stories* for May, 1926. Farrell turned to Western themes more and more frequently as his writing career progressed. He also wrote stories of air adventure, such as "Air Speed Preferred" in the November, 1929 issue of *Air Trails*. When the editorial staff and policy at Street & Smith's *Sport Story Magazine* changed around 1930 and some of his stories were returned, Farrell was able to sell them un-

11

changed to Doubleday's *Short Stories* and its competitor, *Argosy*. These more lucrative and more prestigious markets continued to publish his work through the years. For *Argosy* he later wrote a few adventure stories with an Arctic setting.

In 1931 Farrell left newspaper work to write full time. In 1932, his first year as a full-time fiction writer, he wrote fifty-seven stories and sold fifty-two of them. Most of the sales were to Harry Steeger, publisher of the newly formed Popular Publications. In the late 1980s in a speech given at a gathering of pulp-magazine collectors at the University of Dayton, Steeger recalled that the only writer whose manuscripts he regularly took home from the office to read for pleasure was Cliff Farrell.

For the first few years Farrell used the form A. Clifford Farrell as his byline, switching to the more familiar shorter form in 1931. Some stories, however, also appeared under the Street & Smith house name Philip F. Deere, and for a few years the bylines Nels Anderson and Frank J. Litchfield were also used. But it was under the Cliff Farrell name that he built a major reputation as a prolific and popular writer. In *The Writers 1937 Yearbook* Farrell's name appeared, along with those of Max Brand, Erle Stanley Gardner, Walt Coburn,

Murray Leinster, and others in a list of "the tops among pulp paper writers." In his most prolific period he produced an average of four hundred thousand words of fiction a year.

From 1938 to 1943 Farrell returned to newspaper work, at first part time but later as a full-time sports editor for the *Los Angeles Examiner*. In 1941 he made the first of many sales to *The Saturday Evening Post*, a Western story called "Fiddle Footed" in the March 1, 1941 issue. Throughout the 1940s, while continuing to write for the pulp magazines and now the front-line slick-paper magazines as well, Farrell branched out into markets as varied as *Liberty*, *Woman's Day*, *Farm Journal*, and *The Country Gentleman*.

In the 1950s, his production of magazine stories decreased markedly, although occasionally stories continued to appear for another decade. Farrell wrote his first book-length story, *Follow the New Grass*, in 1952. After being rewritten twice during the next year, the novel was published by Random House in 1954. An abridged version of this novel also appeared in *Zane Grey's Western Magazine* (8/53) under the title "The Pitchfork Boss." Farrell's second novel, *West with the Missouri* (1955), was also published by Random House. His next two books were published as paperback originals by Popular Library. His fifth novel, *Santa Fe Wagon Boss* (1958), was sold to Doubleday, which remained his publisher for all of his subsequent books. In all, Farrell averaged a book a year for the last twenty-three years of his life. Some of the books were chosen as book-club selections, and almost all of them were reprinted at least once in paperback form.

Cliff Farrell died on November 5, 1977, after a brief illness, just two weeks before his seventy-eighth birthday.

As would be expected from such a large body of work, Farrell's fiction, both magazine stories and books, includes examples of all the traditional Western plots and perils: cattle rustling, land grabs, outlaw gangs, gunfights, Indian attacks. The protagonists are working ranchers, rootless wanderers, lawmen, outlaws, frontiersmen attempting to tame their corner of the wilderness, cowboys trying to establish a permanent place for themselves. A recurring character in Farrell's work is the unjustly accused loner, attempting to prove his innocence and make a new life for himself. The stories are told and the characters depicted in a smooth, economical prose. Farrell is especially good at distinguishing a character quickly through speech and small details of appearance and manner. Even the most breathless action is clearly set forth, and suspense expertly maintained, although not all the stories are action-oriented. Some are quieter and smaller in scope, dealing with personal relationships and crises, small victories and gentle satisfactions rather than large triumphs. But in almost all of Farrell's stories, one feature stands out — the author's emotional investment in his characters, which evokes a corresponding reaction in the reader.

Before his death, Farrell and his agent had begun planning a collection of his magazine stories. Several of the stories intended for that collection are included here. The remaining stories have been chosen in part to display the wide range of time and settings in the author's work. The locales range from the Ohio frontier in the early 1800s ("He Knew All About Women") to sheep ranches in Wyoming in the 1930s ("The Lady Was a Dude"), from riverboats on the Mississippi ("Fire in Their Stacks") to isolated settlements in the Arizona desert ("Thorns for Johnny Spring"). The people are equally varied: experienced frontiersmen, a gawky teenager on the verge of manhood, a sheltered picture bride, working cowboys, a schoolteacher who views the West initially as a quaint curiosity, gamblers, farmers, an unlucky new cavalry lieutenant, confidence artists, and a tomboy. The main characters' goals, which drive these narratives, include avenging a past wrong ("The Pay-Back Race"), helping a disaster-plagued group of travelers reach their goal ("Five Aces West"), breaking out of a constricted life into a world of larger possibility ("I'm Going to California"), taming a small piece of wild land to establish a home ("River Ambush"), foiling a gang of thieves ("The Day the Outlaws Came"), and simply performing an unselfish but dangerous act to help ease a child's pain ("Desperate Journey").

Let Farrell introduce you to his West and its people, and you will care what happens to them.

R. E. Briney
Salem, Massachusetts

River Ambush

Summer's warmth had again brought the northwestern tribes to raiding down upon the thin Kentucky settlements. A band of Shawnees had passed by Kaine's stockade three days previously, leaving death and burning cabins in the raw new clearings, and the men from Kaine's had been trailing them ever since, bent on ambush and vengeance. There were only eight Border men in the pursuit — nine, if you counted Homer Kaine — and the trick was to avoid walking into an ambush themselves in case the Shawnees became aware they were being followed. For the odds would be three to one.

The Indians had taken to canoes and pirogues at the Ohio River, and Jeffrey Kaine was of the opinion they were heading back to their villages by way of the Scioto. The men from Kaine's had crossed the Ohio on makeshift rafts before daybreak, and by noon they were moving silently through swampy brush, with the main river close at hand on their right and the mouth of the Scioto not far ahead.

Old Casper Dawson was scouting ahead, and their nerves were set on a hair-trigger, for

17

they expected to pick up some sign of their quarry at any moment. Therefore, when the signal came — the call of a catbird twice repeated — every man froze in his tracks.

Homer Kaine froze, also. He was next to last in line, being followed only by his father who had chosen that position in order to keep an eye on him. Unfortunately the alarm caught Homer in the act of crossing a swamp hole by way of the fallen trunk of a small tree. Homer halted midway on his slim footbridge. And that was his undoing. He began to sway. He futilely tried to balance himself with his long rifle. The wet bark skated beneath his moccasins, his long legs gyrated wildly, and he hit the brackish water flat on his back with a splash that echoed through the hot silence of the forest.

He found footing in the waist-deep, mucky bottom, and emerged. Everybody was glaring at him. His father glared right back at them, daring them to say anything. So they held their peace.

"Homer!" Jeffrey Kaine breathed in the strained voice of a father who had endured about all a man could stand.

Humiliation shriveled Homer. He stood rigidly motionless in the water. Throbbing silence came again. Presently Casper Dawson emerged soundlessly from the brush. He gave

Homer a critical look and said: "Lucky 'twasn't the Shawnees. They'd heerd that racket half a mile. It's only a flatboat party of settlers, headin' downriver. They're tied up on this shore a little piece ahead."

The buckskin-clad men relaxed and began moving. Homer waded through cattails, pulled himself to dry land, and fell gloomily into line, his wet buckskins clinging to his legs, his moccasins squishing water. He dried his rifle and renewed his priming. Lanky, freckled, with a tangle of sun-bleached, tawny hair and eager gray eyes, he had just passed his seventeenth birthday. He had shot up to nearly six feet lately, and was still growing. He had to fight back tears now, for tears would have been the ultimate disgrace.

He was aware of his father's discouraged silence. And he had been trying so hard to justify his parent's confidence in him. His mother had opposed his coming on this venture in the first place. So had some of the men. Homer, the men conceded, was bringing in his share of game to the stockade, now that he was growing up. But hunting deer and stalking Shawnees were vastly different matters.

Only his father had seen the appeal in his eyes and had ruled against the objectors. "Homer's no longer a boy," Jeffrey Kaine had said. "It's only right he share the danger with the rest of us."

Right from the start Homer, aware that he was on probation, was all thumbs and feet. Whenever a dry twig snapped on the trail, it seemed his luck to be the one who had caused it. In his anxiety to be helpful he had spread Casper Dawson's bed blanket on an ant hill in the first camp. Casper hadn't yet forgiven him. He had left his sheath knife at the second stopping point, and his father had lost a night's sleep, backtracking, to retrieve it. And now this new disaster. . . .

Even the sight of the flatboats that were tied up to the river shore did not dispel his despondency. There were two flats — thirty-footers — roughly made, one with a deck and deckhouse, and powered by six sweeps each. The party numbered some thirty settlers, including a dozen or more women and children.

They were Tidewater folk, their leader allowed. "Jersey and Maryland," he explained. His name was William Marlowe. He was a mild-voiced, bearded man with the strong hands of a farmer.

They had floated down the river from Pittsburgh, and there were four head of horses and pens of squawking chickens on the undecked trailer flat. They were hunting land.

"You're more likely to find yourselves chained to a torture stake if you tie up to this northwest shore without knowing what's back in the timber," Homer's father said. "Where are you bound for?"

"Up the Kentucky River, most likely," William Marlowe said. "We've been told there's likely land to be had around Harrodsburg or Boonesboro, or close by there."

Jeffrey Kaine stiffened. This part would be a welcome addition to the settlement around the stockade he had built on the Licking. "Harrodsburg an' Boone's are all right," he said a trifle deprecatingly. "But there's good farming to be had up the Licking, also. Better, if you ask me. Soil so rich the grass is blue. And not near so far to go, either."

That led to questions. Jeffrey Kaine enlarged on the advantages of settling on the Licking, and particularly at Kaine's stockade. The settlers listened eagerly.

"We wouldn't take it kindly, if this place didn't measure up to descriptions," one of the Tidewater men said. He looked to be in his early twenties. Husky, with a big jaw and a bigger voice, he said his name was Walt Stapp. He had been asking most of the questions and had edged Mr. Marlowe into the background.

Homer's father frowned, but Walt Stapp

21

wasn't the kind to be easily abashed. "And if we decide to take a look up the Licking, how would we know when we got to it?" he demanded.

Jeffrey Kaine turned. Homer, appalled, suddenly realized what was coming.

"Why," the father said, "my son, Homer, will travel with you to make sure you don't miss it. The mouth of the Licking is only about three days' float from here."

Homer stared tragically. His father would not meet his eye. Homer swallowed hard. Jeffrey Kaine had jumped at this chance to send him back to the stockade in the company of women and children.

Walt Stapp appraised Homer disparagingly. "I'd prefer a grown man," he stated.

"You can depend on Homer," Jeffrey Kaine said sharply. "And I'd advise you to heed what he says. You can't be too careful on this stretch of river."

"I reckon Indians would think a second time before tacklin' a party as big as this," Walt Stapp said positively.

Mr. Marlowe called for a vote, and the decision was to investigate possibilities on the Licking. Homer listened numbly to his father's final instructions. He shook hands, and watched forlornly as Jeffrey Kaine picked up his rifle and moved off into the woods with the others.

"You'll be safer with us, lad," Mr. Marlowe said consolingly.

Indignation aroused Homer. Now that his father was no longer around to watch every move he made, he felt at least more at ease. "You folks better get moving," he said. "Indians could board you mighty easy here."

Walt Stapp laughed. "We'll see that the Injuns don't get you, Homer," he said.

The settlers began preparing to shove off.

Mr. Marlowe looked around. "Louisa an' Jenny ain't back yet," he said.

Homer turned.

"Louisa's my daughter," Mr. Marlowe explained. "Jenny's the cow. Louisa took Jenny off up the bank to look after her as she grazed."

"*Alone?*" Homer exclaimed. "A child and a cow? Why. . . ."

The peaceful moo of a cow echoed from the timber.

"I'll fetch them," Homer said.

He leaped ashore, climbed the flood bank, and hurried into the brush. He heard the cow again. He leaped a small rivulet, then came to a rigid stop, staring at something at his feet, a freezing, sinking sensation in his stomach. In the sandy margin of the rivulet were moccasin prints. And they toed in. The marks were so

23

fresh the seep of water had just started to blur them.

Homer swung up his rifle, trying to look in all directions at once. Wild grapevines festooned the trees in the background, and he expected to take an arrow any instant from that gloomy cover. But nothing came.

He raced frantically ahead, and burst into a dry, grassy clearing. A hippy brown cow stood there, gazing with wonder at a girl who stood before it, bowing and twirling, one arm arched gracefully above her head, the other holding the hem of her calico skirt high enough so that Homer glimpsed a slender, unstockinged limb above her tiny slipper. Homer pulled up, disconcerted. She seemed to be performing a version of the minuet, with the cow as an imaginary partner.

She discovered him. The dance ended. She stared, petrified, at his damp buckskin garb, hastily releasing the hem of her skirt.

Louisa Marlowe was no child, and she wasn't a grown woman, either. She was outrageously comely. Her thick dark hair was caught at the back with a ribbon. She had young and slim and impetuous features. Her eyes were big and snapping black — and, also, very stormy.

"You . . . you sneak-peeper!" she exploded.

"Shush!" Homer cautioned fearfully. "Head

for the boat, miss. Hurry! There might be Indians around."

"Indians?"

Homer caught her arm, trying to get her moving.

She resisted. "But . . . the cow!"

"Drat the cow!" Homer whispered frenziedly.

She wrested from his grasp. "Who are you? I'm not going to leave the cow here unless. . . ."

Homer was in no mood to reason with a headstrong slip of a girl. He still expected an arrow to come momentarily from the brush. So he picked her up bodily, slung her over his shoulder, and ran toward the river.

She began kicking like a colt. "You . . . you . . . !" she panted. "You . . . you kidnapper! You let go of me!"

She caught him under the chin with a knee, snapping his teeth together with a jolt. Homer tightened his grip on her squirming weight, stretching his legs to the limit. He tore bodily through grapevines and brush. With vast relief he burst into view of the flatboats.

He set Louisa Marlowe on her feet on the gangplank. He said apologetically: "I hope I didn't upset you, miss."

"Oh, you . . . you!" And she kicked him with great energy on the shin.

25

That hurt. It hurt about as much as the one she had handed him on the chin. But Homer refused to give her the satisfaction of even wincing.

Walt Stapp came racing, his fists knotted. "What's this?" he demanded, advancing on Homer.

"I spotted a track of an Indian," Homer explained. "I fetched her here the quickest way I knew how."

"You sure you wasn't imaginin' things?" Walt Stapp scoffed. "Did you see any Injuns, Louisa?"

Louisa said she certainly had not. She glared down her small nose at Homer as she would at a worm.

William Marlowe explained the circumstances of Homer's presence. "Homer meant well, dear," he said. "He just got a little excited. His paw told him to go back home with us."

"But there are Indians around!" Homer protested. "Better get away from this place. Right now!"

"But the cow!" Louisa exclaimed.

"I'll get the cow," Stapp said.

Mr. Marlowe and two other men got their guns and joined Walt, although he allowed it wasn't necessary. Homer reluctantly went along, although he was of the opinion that a

26

cow wasn't worth the risk. He had seen those scalped bodies back at the settlement, but these people had never looked on the handiwork of Indians.

Walt Stapp wanted to see the tracks Homer had sighted, but Homer couldn't find them. The stream had erased them, no doubt.

Walt said: "Better quit tryin' to be a hero, young feller."

They led the cow back to the boat and prodded her aboard. "There's your Indian scare for you," Walt told the others.

Homer endured the tolerant laughter of the party. Louisa gave him a pitying look. That rankled, also. In spite of her superior ways he judged she wasn't as old as he by a good many months. But it was evident that Walt Stapp regarded her with considerable favor and treated her like a grownup. He kept showing her his best smiles as he took his place at the bowsweep in the pilot boat. He had his sleeves rolled high and took pains to flash his brawny muscles. He gave a lot of unnecessary orders in an authoritative voice.

It was Walt who assigned Homer to a sweep in the trailer boat, where he found himself in the company of the livestock and chickens. The flatboats, connected by a thirty-foot line, lumbered into the current. Homer guessed that by this time his father and the others had reached the Scioto.

He swung the sweep listlessly. Then he aroused. He plainly saw an Indian, peering out at the boats from the willow brush a hundred feet abeam — a Shawnee by his yellowish skin. He leaped to seize up his rifle. "Indians!" he yelled, his voice running up the scale humiliatingly.

Startled men dropped the sweeps and stumbled for their guns. But the face had vanished on shore.

Homer's knees were shaking. "Swing farther out in the river," he croaked.

A child began to weep. Others joined in the wailing.

Walt Stapp came striding, his biceps swelling. "If you upset the young ones again with your Indian nightmares, boy, I'll take you in hand, an' I won't be gentle," he vowed.

Women glared indignantly at Homer. Louisa uttered an audible sniff. But her father, at least, gave Homer the benefit of the doubt. Over Walt's outraged objections, he ordered the boats to midstream, even though the faster channel current hugged the Ohio shore along this stretch.

Homer watched that gloomy shore until his eyes ached. But he saw nothing more. His back began to ache, also. The twenty-foot sweep was bringing unaccustomed muscles into play.

An eddy brought the two boats together, and Louisa stepped aboard the trailer, ostensibly to look after the cow. She was as lithe as a willow. She had changed to a dress with a gay blue-and-white striped overskirt and wore a little ruffled sun cap to match. She stroked the cow's nose. "You could take it a little easier with the rowing, Homer," she said. "You'll raise a terrible crop of blisters."

Homer already had blisters on his hands, but he didn't care to admit it.

"Are there many young ladies of my age at this Kaine's settlement?"

"Three or four," Homer said.

"Are they pretty?"

Homer considered. "Regular stunners," he said. He was stretching the truth considerably, but he had to be loyal to his home settlement.

"I'm very glad to hear it," Louisa said a trifle stiffly.

Homer couldn't take his gaze off her. She had the liveliest dark eyes he had ever seen, and the nicest mouth. "But they can't hold a candle to you, Louisa," he blurted out, and blushed a tomato hue.

"Well, now . . . ," Louisa murmured. She was coloring faintly, too, but she was pleased. Homer guessed this was what she had wanted to hear.

Walt Stapp was glaring back at them, his

jaw jutting. "Don't let the youngster skeer you with his Injun talk, Louisa," he bawled derisively.

Then Homer was sure he had caught the reflected wink of sun reflection from the shore. It might have been the shine of a riflestock, or maybe a shell ornament. He did not see it again. This time he said nothing. He kept watching, but there was only the forest and the willow brush.

Miffed at his sudden abstraction, Louisa presently returned aboard the pilot boat, and took a place near Walt Stapp.

The afternoon wore along, and Homer's blisters increased. Toward sundown Walt and Mr. Marlowe began peering ahead for a likely stopping point. The Ohio shore was attractive, offering occasional natural clearings on the bank. The Kentucky bank along this stretch was flat and marshy and girded by swamps of reeds and cattails.

"It would be safer to anchor across the river off the Kentucky shore," Homer said. "They couldn't very well get to the boats through the marshes."

"How about the stock?" Walt Stapp demanded angrily. "They need graze."

"The stock won't suffer by losing a feed," Mr. Marlowe decided. "Maybe Homer knows best."

And so, with Homer responsible for it, they dropped anchor off the gloomy marshes. After dark the mosquitoes, riding a breeze off the Kentucky shore, descended on them in voracious swarms. None of the settlers got much sleep. They gave it up long before daybreak, pulled up anchor, and manned the sweeps again, tired and angry.

The worst of it was that the mosquitoes hadn't bothered Homer much. They had never seemed to care for his type. He felt guilty about it. He had slept soundly, when he wasn't on watch.

"Next time," Walt Stapp vowed fervently, "we'll decide our own stoppin' points."

Walt and his big voice had taken charge of the boats. The settlers rebelliously followed the main current during the morning, letting it carry them where it willed — and this was often very close to the foreboding Ohio shore.

Each time Homer fearfully scanned the background of willows and sycamore and sumac. Once, far ahead, he saw a buck and two does race wildly away from a sandbar where they had been rolling off ticks. They had winded something in the forest.

Homer judged that they must be nearing the mouth of the Little Miami River, which joined the Ohio from the north. Walt Stapp began looking for a nooning spot. He presently sighted a feasible place and gave orders to work the flatboats nearer the Ohio shore.

Homer didn't like it. There was a small stretch of sloping, open bank, but brush and forest masked the surroundings. His rifle slung in his arm, he boarded the pilot boat at first chance.

Louisa sat with her knitting basket in the scant shade of the deckhouse. Homer had that choking, throat-grabbed sensation again. She was as pretty as a spotted fawn. She regarded him a trifle aloofly. She hadn't forgiven him that mosquito siege.

Homer walked to the bow where Walt Stapp was directing the oarsmen. The flatboats were swinging out of the current toward an eddy which would drift them to the landing point that was still a hundred yards ahead and off the beam.

"It might be better to wait for a safer place," Homer said hesitantly. "Lots of thick brush there, too close to shore."

Walt evidently had been expecting something like this from Homer. He swung around. "Homer," he said, "can you swim?"

"Why, yes," Homer said. "But what's that . . . ?"

"Well, then, it's time you cooled down!" Walt exploded. He placed a heavy hand against Homer's face and gave him a shove.

Homer tripped over the foot-high gunwale as he went toppling overboard. He managed to flip his rifle to the deck, when he felt himself going, so that at least the gun wouldn't be lost. Then, for the second time in his recent experiences, he hit the water flat on his back, and went under. He came to the surface, raging and blowing water. Walt was looking back at him, howling with laughter. Louisa was staring, frightened.

Homer was in the current, and both flatboats had slid into the eddy before he could get to them. He saw that he would have to make for shore farther downstream. He was a hundred feet below the landing point, and the pilot boat was pushing its blunt prow into the fringe of willow brush on shore when an eerie screech, savage and utterly bloodthirsty, drifted from somewhere. It was taken up in the next instant by other voices.

Then guns opened up. Homer lifted himself high in the water, horrified. The brush on shore had spawned Indians. They were Shawnees, and they were swarming upon the two boats through the thigh-deep water in an evil, squirming mass. Homer saw it all, and he couldn't do anything about it, for the current was too strong to swim against.

Men were fighting the Indians hand to

hand on the decks. Powder smoke gathered above the boats, and that screeching never ceased. Beneath that he could hear the screaming of women and children. It went on and on while Homer futilely fought the current. He saw the glint of tomahawks through the thickening powder smoke.

Evidently the settlers began to give a good account of themselves after paying the price of the first surprise. The fight suddenly tapered off. Homer saw the Indians racing ashore again and into the brush, brandishing trophies. They had given up the attack when it became too costly to them.

Homer swam ashore, landing well downstream. He dragged himself over a cutbank, then ran desperately through the brush to the scene. The two flatboats were adrift in the shallow water, and women were still screaming. He pulled himself aboard.

Walt Stapp sat in the prow, his eyes rolling whitely, an egg-shaped lump on his forehead and a knife scratch on his cheekbone. Mr. Marlowe was leaning sickly against the deckhouse, an arrow jutting from his thigh. There were others down, and some of them, Homer saw, were past help. Three had been scalped. A dead Shawnee dangled over the gunwale, and another lay aft. But, all in all, the settlers had escaped lightly.

"Louisa!" Homer shouted. He raced quickly aft. "Louisa!"

A wounded settler looked up at him dazedly. "They ketched her," he said, speaking with great effort. "Two of 'em carried her with 'em, when they skedaddled."

Mr. Marlowe came reeling aft, and Louisa's mother appeared and began screaming. Walt Stapp got to his feet, staring wildly.

Homer's voice was shrill. "We got to follow 'em."

Mr. Marlowe mumbled — "I'll go. . . ." — and he crumpled on the deck, the shock of the arrow wound having its way. Other faces only stared vacantly.

Walt Stapp looked at the forest on the Ohio shore and muttered: " 'Tain't any use."

Homer's rifle lay on the deck, undamaged. He picked it up. His powderhorn had remained watertight in the river.

The uninjured settlers were calming a little now and beginning to look after the wounded. Homer, so pale his freckles stood out, slid overboard into the waist-deep water and went ashore.

He looked back, hoping Walt or someone would decide to come with him. But no one offered. So he entered the hot gloom of the forest alone. He soon found the trail of the Indians. They were heading northwesterly, away from the Ohio. The Little Miami lay in that direction. Wary of a possible ambush, Homer traveled slowly, carefully, calling on all the skills he had learned in stalking deer.

It was two hours before sundown when he reached the Little Miami. Two canoes and three bigger pirogues were just rounding a bend nearly a mile upstream. He caught the flash of striped calico in the hot afternoon sun. Homer ran through the forest, cutting off the necks of the curves in the river until he got a closer view. Louisa was in one of the canoes with two golden-skinned Shawnees. There were at least twenty more Indians in the crowded pirogues and the other canoe. Evidently the Shawnees had been trailing the flatboats, both by river and land, and had gone ahead the previous night to the Little Miami to hide their craft for a possible surprise attack by water, but the easier chance by land had presented itself.

Homer kept the flotilla in sight. The Indians camped before dark on the west shore. From the brush on the opposite bank Homer saw Louisa, sitting huddled in the firelight. She seemed to be unharmed.

The war party was camped well up on the flood bank, with the canoes and pirogues drawn up on the sandy margin of the river. A freezing realization of what he should do reached into Homer's marrow. He half lifted the rifle time after time. Once he drove himself to the point of laying a sight on that faint shine of calico in the firelight. Louisa, he knew, would want him to trip the trigger, but he could not bring himself to it. Then the fire was extinguished, and that ended his awful responsibility — for the time, at least.

He tried to think of a way of matching his strength against twenty, but his only hope was that the Indians would split up. That seemed futile. Abruptly he arose and moved upstream until he found a ripple nearly a mile above the Indian camp. With only the shine of the river beneath the stars for light he tied his rifle and clothes to a small dead log and waded and swam the river to the west shore. He cached his clothes and rifle beneath a giant sycamore. Naked, except for his sheath knife, he entered the river again. Clinging to the length of log, he drifted downstream, keeping to the deep darkness of the overhang of trees. It seemed an eternity before he made out the yellowish glint of the sandbar, and the vague shadows of the drawn up pirogues and canoes.

He drifted upon the sandbar, stroking soundlessly beneath the surface. The river was low, with little current at this point. His feet touched bottom scarcely thirty feet from the boats. His danger now was that a Shawnee might be on watch, but the only sounds were those of sleeping Indians from the blackness of the tree shadows higher up on the shore. He was silent.

He abandoned the log, moved in, a step at a time, sinking lower as the water shallowed. Finally he was on his stomach, pulling himself ahead an inch at a time. Then he was beneath the curving stern of the canoe, which barely dipped the margin of the river. Lying flat, he drew himself almost clear of the water. His fingers explored the bark sheathing until he found a pitch-covered joint. With infinite caution against sound, he worked the keen point of the knife into the joint until he had opened a tiny puncture. He repeated the damage at a second point. Then he slid back into the river and drifted downstream until he was clear. He left the river, circled the Indian camp, and returned to his cached clothes and rifle.

He waited there until daybreak. The river, mirror-smooth in the windless dawn, telegraphed the sounds of the camp breaking. Soon the Indians were in the boats, and the splash of poles and paddles came nearer. The pirogues, followed by the canoes, came in sight, paralleling this west shore, heading for a bend upstream. Louisa and two Shawnees were in the canoe that Homer had damaged.

He watched, his eyes red-rimmed with a forgotten weariness, a throbbing tension roaring in his ears. The flotilla moved steadily past, and his hopes began to fade. Then a Shawnee said a disgusted word. A guttural discussion followed. The pirogues slowed. Homer wriggled to a new vantage point. The canoe, carrying Louisa, was turning toward shore just above his position. The two Shawnees were waving the others on, their voices sharp.

It was plain enough. They had a leaking canoe, and they were going ashore for repairs. They needed no help. The girl was their prize, and they wanted no one else to have any claim on the glory of taking her to their village. They would overtake the others shortly.

This was what Homer had hoped would happen. The canoe was making for a sandy opening in the underbrush just above his hiding point. He worked his way silently through the brush and was crouching back of the massive, tangled roots of a flood-toppled tree when the canoe grounded, not thirty feet away.

The Shawnees were disgruntled by their luck. Homer heard Louisa cry out as she was roughly dragged from the canoe. And then he chanced to look. Louisa, her hair down, her calico dress torn, her eyes big and blank with lost hope, huddled scarcely a dozen feet from him. The two Shawnees were dragging the canoe from the water, heeling it on its side to inspect the damage. On the river the pirogues and the second canoe had resumed their paddling and were rounding the bend upstream.

Homer sank back, waiting until the main party was well out of sight. When he ventured another look, the river was vacant. The two Shawnees, speaking occasionally, had gathered twigs to build a small fire in order to remelt the pitch and caulk the punctures. One of them was spilling a few grains of powder on the fire set and had his flint and steel in his hand. Both had their backs to Homer. He started to draw his knife. Then he saw a three-foot length of stout, broken driftwood at his feet. That was even better.

He came from cover silently and was upon the Shawnees in long, desperate strides, swinging the club. The sound was solid and complete as the weapon thudded on the skull of the Shawnee who was standing erect. This one took a step forward, groaning, and began to fall.

The second Indian turned, the flint and steel poised. Homer was upon him. The Shawnee tried to launch himself at Homer's knees, but the club caught him a glancing blow on the head, deflecting him. Homer whirled it again, and this time it landed, square and true, on the Shawnee's coarse, roached, black hair. The warrior was driven back on his haunches, and then he rolled on his side with a thin moan.

Louisa came to her feet, her eyes great black pools against her chalky cheeks. "Oh . . . oh!" she gasped.

"We'll take the canoe!" Homer panted. "Help me . . . and be quick!"

He seized up the flint and steel from the Shawnee's hand, knelt over the fire set, and worked with shaking fingers. The powder flamed, and Homer and Louisa fanned it into life. Homer tore bunches of dead grass, igniting them, and held them against the pitch seams until the resin softened. He worked it swiftly into the punctures, hoping it would hold. Then he shoved the canoe into the water.

"Oh, Homer!" Louisa choked, and her knees caved in.

He lifted her into the prow.

The two Indians were showing signs of reviving. One wore a small silver locket around his neck that Homer remembered had belonged to Ira Wills's wife at Kaine's station. In the canoe was other loot that had been taken from his neighbors' cabins. These were the very Shawnees his father and the others were vainly hunting on the Scioto!

Homer tapped the Indians with the club again. They had hard skulls. Then he dragged them to the canoe, dumped them in amidships in a tangle of arms and legs. He climbed in with his club and rifle, seized up the paddle, and dug it deep into the river. He sent the canoe downstream. Louisa was now completely aroused. She seized the other paddle and began helping. The same question was in both their minds. How soon would the main party become suspicious and turn back to locate the two missing warriors?

Homer had to take advantage of the current, except when it was necessary to rap the reviving foes on the heads from time to time. He judged they had traveled ten miles or more, that the junction with the Ohio could not be far away, when he saw the resigned terror show in Louisa's eyes as she glanced back.

He turned. The pirogues, with poles and paddles flashing, had rounded into sight far upstream. Then they emerged from the Little Miami into the full sweep of the Ohio. Homer croaked. "Look the other way, Louisa! There . . . across the river."

The two flatboats were moored off the Kentucky shore, directly opposite the mouth of the Little Miami. Men were moving on deck, shouting. Their canoe had been sighted.

Louisa saw her father on a makeshift crutch. And Homer saw other figures — men in buckskin — aboard the flatboats. He made out his own father's lean length. A surge of pride suddenly rushed through Homer.

Louisa quavered again. "Oh, Homer!" And, knowing now they were safe, she began to sob like a small child.

Homer drove the canoe across the Ohio. The Shawnees in the pirogues were drifting now, giving up the chase.

Jeffrey Kaine steadied the craft as Homer brought it alongside. He looked at the two Indians. Then he glanced at Casper Dawson and the others. Jeffrey Kaine's pride was vast, but he was trying to act as though this was what was to be expected of his son.

"Looks like you bagged yourself a couple of Shawnees, Homer," he said. "We'll keep 'em hostage against any more raids on the settlement by the others. We never found any sign of 'em, so we headed back. They gave us the slip, when they began following the flatboats down river. We came across the party anchored here this morning. I guess this thing is about all over."

Louisa clung to Homer as he lifted her on deck. "Oh, Homer," she said again. Her voice was trembly. It was meek, but it was purposeful, too. She continued to cling to his arm.

She looked now like a prospective wife, sizing up a claim.

Homer saw Walt Stapp, looking at them disconsolately. Then Walt moved somewhere out of sight without saying a word.

Old Casper Dawson's leathery face was grinning. He said to Jeffrey Kaine: "You was right about Homer growin' up. He caught himself more'n a couple of Shawnees today. Looks like he's caught himself a gal who don't aim to let him git away for a right long spell."

Homer looked down at Louisa, who was coloring now. "I don't figure to try to get away," he said very softly.

I'm Going to California

The prairie wagons had made a brave picture when the company headed out of St. Joe five weeks in the past, with bullwhips popping and women waving kerchiefs and banjos strumming. Now the varnish was peeling from the rakish hulls, the clean yellow paint on the wheels was only a memory, and the canvas tilts were weathering into the buff-colored hue of the land. The oxen were beginning to show their ribs.

Louisa sensed that the first real doubt entered the minds of the men after the wagons had climbed out of the valley of the Little Blue into sight of the loneliness of the plains, but it was another week before anybody put that doubt into words. It was Alonzo Coakley who finally took the bull by the horns.

They had been pulling through heavy sand all morning, double-teaming some of the worst stretches. When they wearily nooned in the treeless glare of the June sun, Alonzo sleeved sweat from his forehead and looked around to make sure Jason Blue was not within hearing.

"Any man," Alonzo said explosively, "that

lets himself be stampeded into starting by wagon for California ought to have his head examined! I've had durned near my fill of it!"

Louisa saw the way they all glanced at one another, and she knew it wouldn't be long before they'd be turning back to St. Joe. Well, she reflected practically, she could ride the wagon now, and even Jason Blue couldn't shame her into walking to save wear and tear on the oxen. This Jason Blue had figured it out in what he called ton-miles. Louisa didn't recall exactly how many tons she would weigh on the trip to California, according to his calculations, but the total was astounding, considering the fact she measured only five feet two and the scales said one hundred and four pounds.

Louisa's aunt held different views. "It's scandalous," Aunt Tansy Whipple had said. "You a-paradin' along barefoot like a squaw just because that Jason Blue's tongue is set on a loose swivel. My land, whatever is 'Lonzo going to think?"

Aunt Tansy was a forceful woman, and Jason also had a mind of his own. Between the two, Louisa had found matters a little trying. But now there would be no object in saving ton-miles if they were to return to Illinois. Louisa could ride like a lady and wear her suede slippers, print dress, and chip bonnet on occasion, thereby dazzling Alonzo Coakley into popping the question in short order.

It had seemed such a bother, in the first place, having to travel all the way to California in order to marry Alonzo. But Aunt Tansy was determined. Alonzo was husky, with a mane of thick dark hair. He knew he was handsome. And he was a Coakley. He knew that, too. His father owned the bank in Wabash City and the biggest farm in the county. Back home, Alonzo could have had his pick of the field, and even Aunt Tansy had been at her wit's end as to how to snag him for her niece. Then Alonzo had got the California fever after listening to the returning 'Forty-Niners. His father had fitted him out with a four-yoke team and a Pittsburgh-built wagon.

Aunt Tansy had jumped at the chance to work on him, when there was no other competition around. Uncle Chet, who was the brother of Louisa's dead father, was still a little bewildered at finding himself on the California trail, whacking a bull team, with his wife issuing orders from the moored-down rocking chair she occupied in the bow.

The Snyder family and the Andersons had come with them from Wabash City. This Jason Blue, who owned a two-yoke team and a rebuilt wagon with a patched top, had joined up somewhere before they crossed the Big Blue River.

Chances were they would have turned back before this if it hadn't been for Jason Blue and his talk about California, his everlasting, questing eagerness to push ahead and see what lay beyond the next skyline. A person would think he was Lewis and Clark and Kit Carson all rolled into one, the way he expounded on the lore of the Great Western Desert. But Louisa happened to know that Jason Blue's knowledge of the trail amounted only to what was printed in a dog-eared guidebook he had bought in St. Joe and which he was continually consulting.

The moment they threw off for this nooning, he had hurried ahead on foot to scan the country from the crest of the next swell. He was returning now, traveling in his usual hurry-up manner. He sprouted lankily from cowhide boots. He had sandy hair and eager blue eyes, and was always brushing impatiently at a cowlick that dangled on his forehead.

"The Platte ford, ladies and gentlemen," he announced with the pride of an original discoverer. "I sighted it ahead. We'll be there by mid-morning tomorrow, if we shove along."

Alonzo cleared his throat. "I've been told," he said reflectively, "that it's a dangerous

48

crossing. I'm wondering if we can make it."

"Plenty of other outfits have crossed the Platte," Jason Blue asserted. He added with finality: "There's no other way to California." He lifted his banjo from the gate of his wagon, struck a string, and began to sing:

Oh, Susannah, oh, don't you cry for me,
I'm goin' to California, some gold dust for to see.

He ended with a flourish before Louisa. "In California, Miss Whipple," he said grandly, "the trees grow as big as mountains, and the mountains look down on the clouds."

What could you do with a man like that? Even Alonzo didn't have the courage to ram his head against the wall of Jason Blue's enthusiasm.

"The man's a fool," Alonzo told Louisa as he inspanned without enthusiasm for the afternoon haul. "He'll learn. He'll see enough before he goes much farther."

Defiantly Louisa climbed into her uncle's wagon, when they got under way. Jason Blue, whose long legs spurned the miles, pointed imperiously at her with his goad.

"If you were a hard-working ox, you'd appreciate any help you could get along this

49

stretch," he said accusingly.

"It's very enlightening," Louisa stated, "to be compared to an ox."

Aunt Tansy also flew to the attack. "I'm remindin' you, Jason Blue, that you're talkin' to my niece!" she blared from her rocking-chair throne. "Please be respectful."

Jason Blue was horrified. "Good gawsh, I didn't say anything like that. Why, Miss Whipple's prettier than any ox that ever. . . ."

"Thank you," Louisa said frigidly. "I understand . . . perfectly."

For once, he didn't know what to say. But Louisa couldn't avoid the criticism in his eyes as he watched her there in the wagon. Finally, to Aunt Tansy's disgust, she couldn't stand it any longer, thinking about those ton-miles she was adding to the burden of the team. She removed her slippers to save shoe leather. Ignoring Jason Blue, she alighted and began walking.

Jason Blue's whip popped a salute. He was walking the clouds again and hurrying eagerly to peer over each swell they surmounted, as though he expected to sight gilded spires in the distance.

Louisa, also, had got in the habit of gazing expectantly as each new vista unfolded, but the remainder of the company toiled stolidly along. Louisa could not help feeling a little sorry for Jason Blue as she pictured what a disappointment it would be to him when Alonzo finally made up his mind to turn back. The others would follow Alonzo's example. Being a Coakley, they looked to him for guidance.

"The man's a fool," Alonzo repeated to Louisa when they camped at sundown. "Him and his talk about California. There's no reason why the folks can't turn back, if they decide it's best for them."

Alonzo was asking in that roundabout way for her to encourage him to announce his decision. Louisa knew then that she had Alonzo firmly hooked, but she decided to let him dangle a while, now that she held the upper hand. He had been courting her in entirely too assured a manner.

"It must be nice in California," she said perversely, "the way Mister Blue talks about it."

"We've got to get rid of that idiot," Alonzo snapped.

Louisa got the buffalo-chip fire burning, and she and Aunt Tansy cooked the meat. They had used the last of the firewood they had brought from the Platte forks, and Louisa hoped she'd never have to cook over buffalo chips again. It was a nuisance trying to maintain even heat.

She made a point of denouncing the quality of the fuel in Jason Blue's hearing. He was carrying a big bundle of dry cottonwood poles in his wagon, and Louisa had her eye on them. But he, too, was burning chips. Louisa gave him a look that told him what she thought of a man who would miser firewood when she was having so much trouble with the biscuits over a chip fire. But Jason Blue was telling the Snyder children about a spring somewhere along the trail ahead which gushed real soda water that tasted mighty nice when you flavored it with raspberry preserve.

She learned the real purpose of those hoarded poles when the wagons heaved through the last stretch of sand the next morning and they halted, staring at the Platte ford. Louisa more than half expected Alonzo to speak his mind then. For this was a frightening prospect. Her brown eyes were shocked as she looked at this primeval thing that was called a river, rushing along in a bleak, treeless channel through the emptiness of the plains. The water was the color of lead, and its voice was metallic, too. Her gaze lifted to the opposite flat shore, and she felt like hiding back of Aunt Tansy's skirts, for that shore seemed terribly far away.

But Jason Blue gave them no time to nurse

their apprehensions. Carrying a bundle of the poles on his shoulder, he mounted his saddle mule and rode boldly into the shallow river. They watched him stake a wagon route across the Platte, driving the poles into the bottom here and there to mark the holes and rock chains.

When he came back, his face was ashine. "Guide upstream above the stakes, folks," he said. "There are only a few stretches of swimming water. We'll double-team, so some of the stock, at least, will always have bottom under their hoofs. There're some soft spots. The trick is to keep the wagons moving, so they won't bog."

He was a buzzsaw. He had his wagon double-teamed with the Anderson oxen and lurching into the water before Alonzo could make up his mind to speak against it. Then it was too late.

The wagon dwindled across the flat expanse of river and lurched ashore in the distance. Jason Blue and Hoke Anderson came riding back with one of the teams. Jason Blue looked challengingly at Louisa, and she found a high pulse of excitement beating in her throat. In spite of herself, she nodded, and he swiftly swung the dripping oxen around and hooked them ahead of her uncle's team.

Aunt Tansy screamed, hanging grimly to

the stakes, as the wagon lurched into the stream. But Louisa braced herself in the bow, facing it. She felt the strength of the Platte against the wagon, seeking to yaw it toward disaster. The roar of the sand-laden current through the wheels brought her heart up into her throat, and she was breathing hard. But with Jason Blue and Uncle Chet and Hoke Anderson prodding the team, the wagon never stopped moving. The north shore crawled nearer, and at last the wheels climbed to dry land. Jason Blue was singing some exultant and bold song of the gold camps. Louisa listened as she held the smelling salts to Aunt Tansy's nose, and that pulse in her throat seemed to keep time with the words. The other wagons followed safely. The occupants were white-faced, shaken as they emerged from the river, and Louisa felt a little guilty because she knew her own cheeks were rosy, her eyes bright with excitement.

It was a silent camp they made beyond the Platte ford. For the first time, Jason Blue must have sensed the way things were going. He outdid himself at the supper fire with his stories of the wonders that lay ahead — Courthouse Rock, Fort Laramie, South Pass, Green River, the City of Rocks, Thousand Springs Valley. He tried to enchant them with those names as he was enchanted with them.

When they did not respond, he seized up his banjo and began beating out "Pop Goes the Weasel."

"Swing your partners," he urged. "Everybody dance."

But they didn't stir. Jason Blue swung his heels energetically, plunking madly away. He came dancing to where Louisa stood.

"May I have the honor, miss?" he challenged.

Louisa hesitated. Then she was dancing, whirling around in the glow of the wagon fires, her fingertips on his shoulders while he played. She was laughing, even though she was aware of Alonzo's scowling disapproval and Aunt Tansy's scandalized silence. They ended it, Louisa with an exaggerated curtsy and Jason Blue with a heel-cracking leap in the air.

"I declare!" Aunt Tansy told her helplessly. "What'll 'Lonzo think?"

It was plain what Alonzo thought. He went stamping out of camp, kicking an inoffensive wagon tongue that got in his way. That dancing business had squelched any idea Alonzo might have had of bringing up the matter of turning back — for tonight, at least.

When the first morning call to turn out sounded, four of the oxen were missing. They were Jason Blue's cattle. Somehow they had wandered off the bed ground in spite of the stock guard's vigilance. Alonzo had been on late guard, and Louisa could imagine why it happened that only Jason's cattle were missing. Alonzo was taking steps to discourage Jason Blue and silence his flighty talk. Alonzo insisted that the wagons shove ahead, leaving Jason to overtake them, if and when he found his cattle. Louisa prevailed on her Uncle Chet to help Jason in the search.

When her uncle and Jason overtook them at noon, driving his wagon and the oxen, which they had rounded up after an hour's search, she suddenly had to sit on a neck yoke until her knees quit shaking. All morning she had been imagining them lost somewhere or scalped by Indians.

The wagons were now toiling through country that grew increasingly rough. These hills leading to Ash Hollow loomed like mountains before the eyes of men and women who had lived their lives in the flatlands. Louisa had heard stories of Ash Hollow and Windlass Hill. It was said that this place was a dizzy precipice.

"Not even that nitwit will have the ambition to tackle such a risk," Alonzo assured her. "Not after what we've been through already."

He patted her hand. He had been showing

her marked attention all day, giving her courtly assistance over the worst ascents. Aunt Tansy was all abeam at this evidence that Alonzo was as good as in the family. She was taking all the credit for herself, when Louisa knew that Jason Blue was responsible for bringing Alonzo firmly to heel.

It was Jason Blue who sounded the call late in the afternoon. "Ash Hollow, ahoy!"

Everyone went hurrying ahead on foot. Mamie Snyder shuddered as she peered. Hoke Anderson's wife closed her eyes tight, and made her husband lead her back to a safer distance. But Louisa was a trifle disappointed. It wasn't exactly a precipice. True, it was a fearsome place, littered with the scattered skeletons of smashed wagons. The bluff broke abruptly, dropping sharply to a valley dotted with stunted cedars five hundred feet below. In spite of the evidence that many had met disaster here, it was plain that others had conquered Windlass Hill. Someone had set a strong snubbing post at its brink, and the post was grooved with rope burns.

"We'll put one team on each wagon to keep it heading straight," Jason Blue's eager voice aroused them.

"You going down that thing?" Alonzo challenged scornfully.

Jason Blue stared. "Of course. Why not?"

Alonzo spoke to the others. "Let him try it," he shrugged. "We'll think it over."

Jason Blue soon had his preparations completed. Alonzo volunteered to take charge of the snubbing rope. Jason Blue locked both rear wheels of his wagon as a further precaution.

Louisa held her breath as the wagon lurched over the rim and tilted sickeningly downward with its bow pointed at Ash Hollow below. The rope screeched on the snubbing post, and the locked wheels wailed as they slid down the steep.

The wagon was a third of the way down when it happened. Alonzo uttered a yell of warning, and the rope became a live thing, spinning around the post unchecked. Alonzo had released the snubbing rope, letting it run free. He was making a pretense at trying to regain control of it, but that was impossible now. Louisa knew he had done this deliberately. This was how he was finally discouraging Jason Blue from continuing on a trail that he had decided to abandon.

Louisa was screaming. She saw Jason leap clear. The wagon slewed sidewise, capsizing and throwing the oxen. Then the vehicle went rolling over and over, strewing its contents over the face of Windlass Hill. The coupling broke, freeing the oxen, but the animals tumbled almost to the bottom, also.

Louisa watched Jason Blue. He ran first to the oxen. One had a broken leg, and he searched among the wreckage until he found his rifle. A shot sounded, and the ox was out of its misery. Jason Blue walked about, his shoulders tired, retrieving a few of his scattered belongings. Presently he climbed back up the hill and looked at Alonzo Coakley.

"You did it on purpose," he said.

Alonzo began to bluster and deny it. With the same expression with which he would step on a spider, Jason drew back a fist and hit Alonzo in the mouth.

Alonzo squared off, but Uncle Chet and Hoke Anderson got between them. "It was an accident," Hoke Anderson said. "There's no call for starting a ruckus with Alonzo."

"It was no accident," Jason Blue said bitterly. He looked at them all, his glance pausing longest on Louisa. "You folks don't want to go to California," he added slowly. "You've made up your minds to turn back." He spoke wonderingly, as though it were beyond his power of understanding.

He turned his back on them. Rounding up his other yoke of oxen, he started down the hill toward his wrecked wagon.

"Where you goin'?" Hoke Anderson demanded.

Jason again gave them that wondering look. "I'm going to California," he shrugged.

"Don't be a fool!" Alonzo shouted after him. "We're turning back! You better come with us!"

Jason Blue only shook his head and didn't answer.

"Let him go," Alonzo scoffed. "He'll think better of it before morning."

Louisa stood there, watching Jason begin salvaging his supplies. The popping of whips and the crunch of wheels aroused her. Alonzo beckoned. The wagons were turning, heading back toward the Platte.

Louisa climbed into her uncle's wagon. There was no need for saving ton-miles now. They camped at twilight. Afterward, in her bed in the wagon, she lay sleepless, looking up at the vague outline of the canvas-covered hoops above.

It was long after midnight, when she arose. She dressed silently in the chill of the plains night, without arousing Aunt Tansy. She managed to assemble a few belongings she would need. She alighted and awakened Uncle Chet from his blankets beneath the wagon.

"Good bye, Uncle Chet," she whispered. "Tell Aunt Tansy what I've done."

Uncle Chet was an understanding man. "I seen it in your eyes as you watched that Jason

Blue," he chuckled. "I never was any too keen about having one of them stuck-up Coakleys in the family, anyway. Don't worry about Aunt Tansy. She'll paw the air, but she'll be proud of you afterwards."

The morning star was burning in the sky as Louisa headed toward Ash Hollow. Big daylight was at hand when she reached the rim of the bluff. Jason's cook fire lifted a thin streamer of blue smoke as she descended. It was a wood fire. She saw that he had already started jacking up the wagon bed to begin repairs. The hoops were smashed, and the front hounds were broken, but she guessed that Jason would make it sound enough to reach California with a little work.

He turned and discovered her there, carrying her bundle of clothes.

"It'll be nice," Louisa said, her voice shaking, "seeing places like the City of Rocks, and this Soda Springs, and South Pass, where you cross to the Pacific slope."

He stood looking at her with the awe of a man watching dreams come true. "I never figured I was lucky enough to . . . ," he began.

"Yes, you did," Louisa told him. "You knew it for sure that night we danced. We both knew it."

Then his arms were around her. "There'll be somebody at Fort Laramie who can marry people," he was saying wildly.

"That same thought," Louisa admitted, "occurred to me also, Jason."

And, as she kissed him, she could almost hear Aunt Tansy's shocked voice: "What will 'Lonzo think?"

For that she had no answer. She was going to California.

Thorns for Johnny Spring

Empty-handed after a week's pursuit of Natchez and his Apaches, two weary troops of United States Cavalry emerged from the thorny Dragoon Mountains at mid-morning, and followed their back tracks across the sun-baked bench toward Parmelee's ranch, where water and feed for the stock were available.

Some of the younger cavalrymen brightened at the sight of the ranch and began furtively slapping dust from their uniforms, but Johnny Spring, whose commission as second lieutenant was scarcely two months old, wished the earth would open and hide him. Riding into a cannon's mouth, he reflected, would be child's play in comparison to having to meet Felicity Parmelee after the way he had disgraced himself on his first field of action.

Johnny Spring did not have even the spirit to resent the smug cat-and-mouse expression on the handsome face of Rick Hollister, who was a first, in command of K Troop. Shuffling hoofs kicked up a drifting fog of hot, stinging dust. Johnny rode heavy in the saddle. He was young and square-built and sunburned. The eagerness and intensity had been beaten out of his brown eyes. His nose was red, and his head felt like an overstuffed pillow. He knew another sneeze was coming and tried to smother it. He failed.

Colonel Burns's beet-colored, beet-shaped face glared back at him. "So it's you again, Spring?"

"Sir," Johnny said miserably, "it's the dust, I guess."

The colonel spoke in a strained voice: "Perhaps you haven't noticed that the wind is carrying the dust right into you, now that we've come out of the *malpais*. You'll find it more comfortable on the opposite flank, Lieutenant."

A stir of sour amusement ran along the column. Burning with this new humiliation, Johnny shifted position. Lost in his thoughts, he hadn't noticed his error. Everything he did, he thought morosely, branded him deeper as a greenhorn and a liability to the outfit.

He sneezed again, explosively. The adjutant, whose expensive breeches were ripped from belt to boot top, said: "Bless you." But the adjutant didn't say it kindly.

During the previous night, Johnny, in his zeal to be an alert officer, had mistaken a rock shadow for an Apache, pointing a rifle. He had shoved the adjutant aside in a vigorous attempt to save his life. The adjutant had

64

rolled into a patch of catclaw cactus where he ruined his temper and his forty-dollar pants. Previous to that, Johnny had got himself and the rear guard lost when he took the wrong fork in a dark cañon.

Then, to top these and other mishaps, he had sneezed penetratingly in the dawn silence just as the skirmish line was creeping in to surround the renegade Chiricahuas in the *malpais* where the civilian scouts had located their camp. Johnny hadn't mentioned that he was contracting a head cold, for he feared he would be detailed to remain with the horse guard. The Indians, warned by his outburst, had scattered like quail into the dawn. All the detachment had to show for days of hard campaigning was a new crop of blisters and ragged dispositions.

The colonel beckoned Johnny to join him. "You can locate Parmelee's, I trust, Lieutenant?"

Puzzled, Johnny peered at the ranch, whose 'dobe buildings and pole corrals and hayfields were plainly visible only two or three miles ahead. "That's it right in sight, sir."

"Then you're sure you won't go astray?" the colonel said mercilessly. "Good! Please proceed and present my compliments to Mister Jubal Parmelee. Request his permission to bivouac the detachment at his place."

Appalled, Johnny framed a request to be excused. Riding into Parmelee's with the detachment would at least give him the advantage of numbers, and the chance, perhaps, to keep out of Felicity's way. But to have to go there alone. . . . However, the colonel's gaze was stony. Johnny knew it was no use. He saluted and said: "Yes, sir."

Rick Hollister spoke from the corner of his mouth as Johnny rode by. "Give my very best regards to Miss Parmelee, junior. Tell her that the soldiers are coming."

Hollister, tall and dashing, with a jaunty wisp of dark mustache on his long lip had been considerably annoyed when Felicity Parmelee had showed a preference for Johnny's company during the three days the detachment had camped at the ranch before riding into the mountains. Felicity Parmelee had hair the color of ripe corn, shining in the sun, and lively gray-green eyes that had a disconcerting way of looking right through a man when he tried to swagger or strut. As though to compensate for this practical trait, she could use her long eyelashes in a very devastating fashion when she so desired. She certainly had used them on Johnny. After about a day's exposure, he was in love. Two days, and he was walking on clouds. And on the third and last evening, he had given Rick Hollister's watchful eyes the slip long enough to ride for miles with Felicity under the light of a young and wonderful Arizona moon.

Johnny guessed he had made it plain how he felt. He hadn't mentioned love, hadn't even tried to kiss Miss Felicity Parmelee, but he had talked about his hopes and ambitions, and how he would wear stars on his shoulders someday. He didn't believe a girl could listen to that in such dreamy silence unless it meant she was picturing herself as a part of it. He had her kerchief, ridiculously small and fragile, in his tunic, nearest his heart. He had meant to win his battle spurs, so that he would have something to lay before her in addition to his heart.

Now he rode back to Parmelee's contemplating the wreckage of his military career. He had his choice, Johnny grimly reflected, of resigning or being shelved in some musty routine desk assignment where action, and opportunity, would always pass him by. Nearing the ranch, he straightened and drew military preciseness about him like a protective armor, but it was a reprieve when only Jubal Parmelee appeared and came walking to meet him. Otherwise the place looked deserted. Jubal Parmelee was a stocky, assertive man with a mane of coarse graying hair and a weathered neck.

Johnny saluted. "Colonel Burns presents his compliments, and requests permission to bivouac two troops of cavalry at your ranch tonight, sir."

Mr. Parmelee blinked. "I reckon you mean the calvry wants to hang up here at the spread, son," he decided. "Why, sure. Glad to have company. There's only me an' my youngest daughter home. I sent all hands out to drift the horse stock out'n the way of the Chirics."

"Thank you, sir," Johnny said. He dismounted, keeping his eyes carefully away from the house.

Mr. Parmelee peered critically at the approaching detachment. "I don't see any sign of Apache prisoners," he commented. "A dispatch rider passed by about daylight braggin' that you fellers had Natchez corralled somewhere up in the Dragoons."

"The Indians discovered our presence in time to escape," Johnny admitted, wincing.

"They always do," Mr. Parmelee commented. "The Indians always get away from the soldiers. Now, if it had been a bunch of cowboys up there. . . ." He left the rest of it to be imagined. Mr. Parmelee, being a dyed-in-the-blanket cattleman, regarded the efforts of professional soldiers with superior tolerance. He was now eyeing Johnny's red nose. "You've got the sniffles, bub," he diagnosed.

"Must be new to the country. Only pilgrims have colds in Arizona. They bring it with 'em. I'll get Felicity to fix something for you. Both my daughters know more'n most doctors do, anyway." Before Johnny could protest, the rancher bawled: "Hey, F'licity!"

Johnny shuddered. This was going to be worse than he had imagined. Then he stared, shocked, as Felicity Parmelee came hurrying from the door of the ranch house. She was wearing an amazing, dazzling, shimmering gown of white satin. She looked like an angel. Or a queen. She looked like a bride. And that's what it was. A bridal gown. It had a long train which she was holding clear of the dust, thereby revealing very trim, pink-stockinged ankles.

She looked at Johnny, and exclaimed: "Oh, my stars!" She hastily dropped the train.

"Get that thing off," her father commanded. "The calvry's comin'."

"Why didn't you give a person warning, Dad?" she reproved. She smiled at Johnny. "How do you do, Lieutenant. This is a delightful surprise."

Johnny couldn't speak. He couldn't move. He could only stare at that satin affair.

"F'licity's a top hand with a needle," her father boasted. "Both my daughters are. An' their maw can still show 'em a thing or two.

69

F'licity's in a lather to get that dress finished. The weddin' is supposed to take place next Sunday."

"Wedding?" Johnny repeated hollowly.

"Daughter's marryin' George Maxwell," Mr. Parmelee explained. "But George is somewheres in the Dos Cabezos, hidin' out his horse string. Fidelity an' her maw are hung up in Tucson, an' everybody else is layin' low until they see which way Natchez is headin'. Chances are we'll have to put off the ceremony."

Then Mr. Parmelee went to meet Colonel Burns, who was approaching with the troops.

Johnny felt cold and empty. He knew in his heart that he had kept on believing that what had happened to his military career wouldn't make any difference with Felicity. Now he saw that he had again played the part of a greenhorn. He writhed mentally as he remembered those hours in the moonlight and the things he had said. To him, that had been like heaven. To Felicity Parmelee, it had been no more than a flirtation. It jarred him to his heels.

Felicity was saying: "It's a beautiful dress, isn't it? But I'm hoping Mother and my sister will show up today to help me with it. There are still a few things about it that need finishing. But they went to Tucson to shop for the wedding and were marooned there by the Apache trouble."

Then Johnny began to get mad. "I hope," he said, "that you have sixteen children, and all of them have a nice set of buck teeth. I hope this George Maxwell beats hell out of you every time you flutter your lying eyelashes at another man."

Felicity Parmelee's mouth popped open. She seemed dumbfounded for a moment. Then she tilted her head, studying him with her gray-green eyes. She had a temper, also, Johnny perceived. "Why, I actually believe you're jealous," she said, with a toss of her head.

"I ought to beat the tar out of you myself!" Johnny exploded. He turned on his heel and strode stiffly to where the detachment was off saddling.

Rick Hollister was shaving and had his striker busy polishing his boots and furbishing his uniform. Hollister said to Johnny: "I'll take care of things from now on, junior."

Johnny debated whether slugging a superior officer was worth adding to his troubles. He decided against it on the ground that Hollister was in for a jolt, anyway, when he learned the truth about Felicity Parmelee. He made his way to a big, grass-roofed barn which stood at a safe distance from the house.

He wanted only to get out of sight for a while. His eyes were watering, and his head was like a bass drum. Three sleek Morgan horses eyed him from their stalls as he threw himself on a pile of hay. He hadn't slept in nearly forty-eight hours, and he closed his eyes.

The bugle, calling the troopers to horse, aroused him. The setting sun was streaming into the wagon tunnel. Felicity Parmelee stood there in that warm light, looking down at him. "Hiding, just so you won't have to take medicine," she chided. "I've been all afternoon trying to find you."

She was wearing a simple but comely thing of cool lawn material. Johnny got to his feet. She had a small, stone jar and a big, silver spoon. She dipped the spoon in the jar and brought it forth bulging with an evil-looking mixture.

"Now open wide," she demanded.

Johnny backed away, but she cornered him. In self-defense, he was forced to accept the dose. He gagged and looked wan. "Good Lord!" he gasped.

"Sulphur and molasses," she beamed. "A spoonful every hour and that cold will go scat."

"You're very kind," Johnny said icily. "I thought it was only poison."

She was brazen enough to peek up at him through her eyelashes. "I mended the rip in Captain Dudley's breeches," she remarked. "They're almost as good as new. It put him in a better humor."

"Very nice," Johnny said bitingly. "Your father said you were quite handy with a needle. I thought he was only bragging."

She said: "Anybody could get lost up in the Dragoons. I wouldn't let a thing like that worry me."

"You've been talking to Lieutenant Hollister," Johnny remarked grimly.

"I know how bad you feel, too, about having to sneeze when the men were trying to trap the Chiricahuas this morning," she went on. "But you couldn't help it if you had a cold. It could have happened to anybody."

"You and Hollister must have had a dandy long chat," Johnny said. "Did you show him your wedding gown? Or did the matter of your coming marriage slip your mind again?" He bowed. "Now, if you will excuse me. Evidently the detachment is moving out."

"You are so severe, when you get huffy," she said, taking his arm.

She was mocking him now, Johnny thought bitterly, as he strode stiffly toward the house, not looking at her.

All the officers were assembled beneath the

73

grape arbor. The colonel sat in conference with Jubal Parmelee and a weather-beaten, dusty, tired man named Abel Wilkins, who was a civilian scout. Rick Hollister gave Johnny a nasty glare, when he saw who was clinging to his arm.

The colonel looked at his officers and said: "Wilkins picked up the trail of the Apaches this morning. They're heading south, just as we believed they would. Natchez will try to join Geronimo in Mexico. Mister Parmelee knows of a water hole near the south end of the Dragoons. He believes the Apaches will have to head for that tank. It's a thirty-mile ride, but our horses can stand it. We will proceed at once."

"I ain't sure I kin locate that tank, Jubal," the civilian scout said.

"I'll take the soldiers there," the rancher stated. "Shucks! I could find it blindfolded."

"Good!" said the colonel. "I'll leave a detail to guard the ranch. Your daughter will be safe enough."

Felicity had been listening. "You needn't worry about me, Colonel. I'm riding to Tucson tonight."

Her father gave a snort. "It's that cussed dress again, I suppose. Now what's gone wrong?"

"I haven't enough ruching to finish the. . . .

well, I haven't. And I'm short of silk thread. I don't like the way the train hangs, either. I've been hoping all day that mother and Fidelity would show up. I've just got to get help from them on that dress. If the Apaches are heading south, there's no danger meeting them between here and Tucson."

"Ain't she a case?" her father boasted.

The colonel stared. "You're not really thinking of permitting her to ride to Tucson tonight? Why, that's all of seventy miles."

The colonel had said the wrong thing. Mr. Parmelee bristled. " 'Tain't much of a ride . . . for my gals," he smiled.

"At least, I'll give her a troop escort," the colonel said helplessly.

"Your calvry horses would be sulled before that sorrel Morgan of hers even worked up a sweat," the rancher said. "But you might send one man along, if it'll make you feel any better. I've got a spare Morgan he can ride."

A sudden shock of dismay hit Johnny. Before he could make a move, Colonel Burns's grim eyes had singled him out. "You will accompany Miss Parmelee, if she is really foo . . . er . . . is really determined to go, Spring. I might add that it would be very disastrous for you if anything happened to her."

"Yes, sir," Johnny said dully. He knew why he had been selected. The colonel wanted no more bad luck in this latest attempt to round up Natchez.

Mr. Parmelee slapped him on the back. "Don't worry, sonny. F'licity'll get you through right side up."

At his side, Rick Hollister swore angrily. "If you aren't a fool for luck, Spring!" he raged.

"Hollister," Johnny said savagely, "the only reason I don't beat your brains out is that I pity you."

Afterward, Johnny stood alone, watching the detachment ride away into the twilight. The two Morgan horses were rigged and waiting, and the girl now came hurrying from the house.

"I'm ready," she said.

She was wearing a riding habit and a little hat with a wisp of apple-green veil. "Does it look all right?" she asked anxiously, giving the hat another nudge. "I had to hurry so frightfully."

"You'll dazzle every horned toad and coyote on the desert," Johnny said sourly.

He lifted her to the side-saddle, which carried a six-shooter in a pocket holster. Johnny had a carbine in addition to his side arm and saber.

She was clutching a cumbersome package. He knew it was the wedding dress. He had no alternative but to relieve her of that burden.

"Please be careful of it," she admonished.

Returning the salutes of the two grinning troopers who had been left to guard the place, he followed her across the log bridge. They rode through the hot, fading twilight, following the route the detachment had taken.

After four or five miles, the girl turned directly toward the dark bulk of the Dragoons. The Morgans hit a steady canter across the rising bench, and then began bucking the first sharp climb into the *malpais*. They were following a faint pack-trail which the girl said would lead them over a pass some ten miles ahead.

"Your cold evidently is much better," she remarked.

Johnny remembered, grudgingly, that he hadn't sneezed in some time. His head felt better. "Chalk up another victory," he said.

A bright moon cleared the rims, and the Dragoons became a mottled sea of black depths and gray-white pinnacles.

Felicity sighed. "I just adore moonlight."

"Moonlight," Johnny snapped, "is the time when predatory things get in their best licks."

Then Johnny rose in the stirrups in sudden excitement, and abruptly halted, with a whispered word for silence. They were in the shadow of a ledge high on the flank of a rocky slant which dropped away to a dry streambed whose sandbars and alkali flats showed white in the moonlight. Dark figures, tiny at that distance, were outlined against the face of the streambed. The silhouettes moved in a ragged swarm and merged with the shadows on the opposite flank of the cañon.

"Apaches," the girl breathed.

Johnny slid to the ground, standing by the horses. "I'll bet a year's pay it's Natchez's outfit. They've backtracked, guessing the troops would be looking for them south of here. The colonel's riding in the wrong direction."

The Indians had vanished into a draw which led to the opposite ridge. They were heading north. Johnny's guess was that there were nearly a hundred of them. Only a handful had been mounted. He remembered that these Apaches had been on the move since before daybreak.

"They'll be camping soon," he muttered. "I'll have to ask you to ride back to the ranch alone, Miss Parmelee. Send one of the troopers to overtake the detachment. Perhaps you could instruct them how to find this spot."

"I'll do the riding myself," Felicity said positively. "I can cut across the bench and save time. I ought to catch the troopers inside of an hour."

"I forbid. . . ."

"Fiddle-faddle. Don't push your jaw out at

me, Johnny Spring. It'll be easy. But what are you going to do?"

"Trail the Indians, of course."

"And get yourself lost!" she exclaimed.

"I'll blaze my trail," he asserted.

"With what? Your fingernails? Anyway, there's nothing but cactus and greasewood. No timber."

Johnny was almost stumped. Then he solved it. "Something white," he said. "Rags or. . . ." He peered at the girl. "I haven't anything made of white cloth. But perhaps you are wearing . . . er . . . a . . . ?"

"The wedding dress!" Felicity exclaimed. "It's just the thing."

"But. . . ."

She slid to the ground, seized the package from him, and opened it. He watched her begin tearing the dazzling creation into strips.

"There," she said. "Satin will shine out like everything in the moonlight. I'm sure George Maxwell won't object when he hears that it was put to such good use."

"George," said Johnny, "must be a very tolerant man. At least, he'd better be, poor devil."

She handed him the ruins of the bridal gown. "Please be careful," she said, her voice suddenly shaky.

She was standing close to him, and she was

fluttering her eyelashes. Johnny suddenly knew what she was expecting.

"Oh, no, you don't," he snarled. "What kind of a yellow cur do you think I am?" So he kissed her thoroughly. Then he swung her on her horse. "That," he raged, "is what moonlight does to a man! I hope George fills me full of hot lead!"

He slapped the horse. She rode recklessly down the rocky trail, smiling back at him with complete complacency.

Carrying the shreds of satin, Johnny also descended the cañon side at a breakneck pace, sliding through rock and brush. He was wet with sweat, his lungs hammering when he reached the north ridge. Ahead stretched a barren expanse of pinnacles and lava ridges.

He began marking his route as he moved at a jog, hanging gleaming streamers of satin on thorned brush and rocks. Presently he sighted his quarry, crossing a naked rim ahead. They were nearer than he had anticipated, and he dropped flat, fearing he might have betrayed himself.

Reassured, he moved ahead again. His cavalry boots made a fearful racket in this night silence. He pulled them off and left them sitting on a rock. This was a land of knife-edged lava and cactus. Soon he was leaving blood at each step. And his feet were being transformed into a pincushion.

He judged that he had traveled three or four miles when he smelled water, whose presence always carried far in this arid land. His quarry had dropped from sight.

He finally wriggled to a crest and saw below him, in a shallow draw, the stagnant glint of water. The Apaches were camped. He could see them stretched out, asleep already. He scouted the place for an hour, mapping the surroundings and the terrain in his mind until he knew every detail. Then he began his retreat, following his blazed trail of satin streamers. At a safe distance, he tried to get to his feet. But it wouldn't work. His feet were swollen lumps that would not support his weight.

So he crawled. And there were still cactus and lava to take toll. He had traveled for what seemed ages when he heard them coming. He first sighted Jubal Parmelee's flat-crowned hat. Then he glimpsed the advance guard of cavalrymen. They were on foot, following the trail of satin. He called to them.

Colonel Burns arrived, and Johnny saluted from a sitting position. "Sir," he said formally, "Lieutenant Spring reporting. I have located the Apache camp, which is in a position that can be flanked and surrounded."

The colonel looked at Johnny's feet and said: "Damnation!"

"I am prepared to advise on the disposition of the troops for this operation, if you care to listen, sir."

"I'm listening," the colonel said respectfully.

They all listened — even Rick Hollister, who was pulling fiercely at his mustache.

"I am prepared to lead the way, sir," Johnny concluded.

"But . . . ," the colonel began, still looking at Johnny's feet.

"I can assure you I won't sneeze and betray our approach this time, sir."

The colonel cleared his throat. "Damnation! A thing like that could have happened to anybody. Lead the way, Lieutenant."

Two husky troopers supported Johnny as they advanced. It was Johnny who directed the operation. When first dawn came, the Apache camp was surrounded. And when the colonel fired the warning shot, and the fierce, shaggy-haired Indians saw what they were up against, they threw down their arms and stood in sullen acceptance. Natchez was not the man to fight unbeatable odds. There would be another day, when he could again jump the reservation.

Felicity was waiting with the horse guard when they got back on the trail. She took one look at Johnny and began giving orders. "Put him here in the shade. Send a rider to the ranch to fetch a wagon to meet us. Bring me some canteens. Oh, look at those poor feet!"

"I'll see to it that Lieutenant Spring is mentioned for this night's work," the colonel averred.

"It was the weddin' dress that did it," Jubal Parmelee sniffed.

"I'm sorry about your dress," Johnny said to the girl.

She looked at him, wide-eyed, innocent. "Why, that isn't my wedding dress," she protested. "I was making it for my sister. Dad told you that, didn't he?"

Johnny sat slowly up. He didn't say anything until the shock of that wore off.

"It's a nuisance trying to finish a dress when you can't fit the one who's going to wear it," she rattled on breathlessly. "I'm about the same size as Fidelity, but she's smaller through the . . . well, never mind. I was only trying it on, when you arrived yesterday at. . . ."

"Don't burden your immortal soul with any more sins!" Johnny thundered. "You saw me coming and put on that dress deliberately! You figured I'd take the hint! It was a trap to crowd me into marrying you!"

Her voice was meek, but she was using her eyelashes. "Well, you were sort of shy, Johnny."

"Then, when you saw that I had got the wrong idea, you deliberately made a fool out of me."

"Oh, Johnny," she wailed. "I only wanted to see if you really, truly loved me."

"Well," Johnny said. "If there are still any doubts. . . ." He took her in his arms. That kiss was certainly a doubt remover.

"Damnation!" said the colonel admiringly.

Rick Hollister also swore, but not admiringly.

"Hell's fire!" Jubal Parmelee complained. "Now I got to stand the expense of two weddin' dresses."

"That," said Johnny, "is correct, sir."

Fire in Their Stacks

I

The Honorable Phineas Winterbottom was not a man to be taken lightly at any time, and he was extremely emphatic about the matter now at hand. "Mind you, Captain Dill," he repeated, thumping his gold-knobbed cane on the desk. "No racing, understand. It's idiotic. Childish. Dangerous. I prefer my shipments delivered intact at Saint Louis, rather than have them blown to high heaven by some rattle-brained steamboat engineer who doesn't know why boilers are equipped with safety valves." Mr. Winterbottom's weighty watch chain flapped against his important stomach, and his pink muttonchop whiskers bristled as he spoke.

The countenance of Captain Newt Dill, which was about the color of the Mississippi in flood-time, assumed an air of injured surprise. "Racin', Mister Winterbottom?" he protested. "Now, whatever put such an outlandish idea in your noggin?"

"I've heard rumors," Mr. Winterbottom stated darkly, "that your Red Arrow packet line is in the habit of challenging competitors to speed contests on the river. In fact, I regret to say, I am informed that you personally encourage such foolhardy exhibitions."

Captain Dill attempted to laugh lightly, deprecatingly, but thirty years of inhaling channel fogs and of issuing bluntly worded orders to deckhands had rusted his vocal chords somewhat. The sound resembled the grunt of a steamboat whistle off the landing. "You needn't hold no fear on that score, Mister Winterbottom," he hastened to say. "Now maybe I wur a mite reckless in my day, though folks stretch such things in the telling. But a man's blood cools as he grows older. Why, bless you, your cargoes will be as safe as in your own warehouse. Reliability an' security. That's Red Arrow's motto. Speed, yes, but with safety."

Captain Newt Dill arose from his swivel chair, standing so that his knotty, wide shoulders partly concealed a gilded mount of elkhorns which adorned the wall of the packet office. A brass plaque beneath the horns proclaimed that this trophy had been at various times in the possession of such fast river craft as the *Robert E. Lee*, the *A. T. Shotwell*, the *Natchez*, and the *Sultana*. The latest and newest name on the list was that of Captain Dill's prize packet, the *Bluebelle*.

He glanced apprehensively over his shoulder through the office window which overlooked the teeming Natchez levee. A thicket of steamboat stacks cluttered the foreground, but, beyond, Captain Dill had a clear view of the brown coil of the river where it veered around a bend downstream.

A white and gilt steamboat was hovering into sight, closely followed by another. At that distance all packets looked alike to a landsman such as Mr. Winterbottom.

Captain Dill, however, was not a landsman. He noticed the peculiar crimson haze that flickered above the stacks of the two side-wheelers and could see the spurt of foam at their prows. He swiftly emerged from behind the desk. "Safe as a church, Mister Winterbottom," he repeated, snatching up his gold-braided cap. "We'll handle every crate an' cask like it was a settin' of eggs, sir. Let's adjourn now to the Plantation House where I'll offer your good health."

They emerged from the packet office. Mr. Winterbottom paused to eye with approval the activity on the levee. Steamboats were disgorging and receiving cargo. Singing darkies moved in ant-like streams. The rattle and bustle and industry appealed to the practical instincts of a man who had built up a comfortable fortune in trade. It was through just such zeal, aided by solid conservatism that Winterbottom Wholesalers, Inc., had reached its prominent position in the upriver ports. Mr. Winterbottom, whose poise and garb reflected his staid precepts, had just contracted a large consignment of cargo to Captain Dill's packet company, with the promise of more to follow if the service proved satisfactory.

Captain Dill, who had been staying ashore lately to drum up business for his fleet of four packets, needed the Winterbottom cargoes. It was either that or bankruptcy for Captain Dill. Therefore, he was almost forcibly dragging the merchant away from the levee, while at the same time casting furtive glances over his shoulder at the oncoming steamboats.

Mr. Winterbottom paused again, just short of stepping into a horse cab that Captain Dill had beckoned. He frowned. All activity had stopped on the levee. Roustabouts were standing motionless, staring out into the ocean.

Mr. Winterbottom now noticed the arriving packets. Captain Dill swallowed hard.

"Lawdy, it am de *Bluebelle*, an' de *Rivah Jewel*," a darky chanted nearby. "Fum N'O'le'ns, an' dey's got fire in der stacks."

Phineas Winterbottom could see the fire in their stacks, also. It fanned under forced draught from twin chimneys of the packets. He took a startled backward step, as though thinking of taking to his heels as the crafts bore steadily upon the levee, their wheels biting deeply into the river. "The infernal fools!" he exclaimed, aghast. "They're going to pile up on the levee. They must be racing."

They were racing. Just as Mr. Winterbottom was bracing himself to view the wreck of two fine river craft, he heard bells jingle in the engine rooms. The voices of pilots, using the speaking tubes, were also audible on the levee. Their language was of an even higher temperature than the smokestacks whose paint was blistering and scaling away.

The wheels stopped, then reversed madly. A gush of mud and frothy river water rolled up the slanting levee. The three-decked packets towered above Mr. Winterbottom, giving him a startled impression of watching wild-maned chargers rear back at the touch of the check rein. He noticed vaguely that the rails of both boats were jammed with shouting passengers of both sexes, who seemed to be engaged in deriding each other.

One of the steamboats had an advantage of less than half its length. There was a clang as its steel-shod gangplank dropped on the levee. The wild cheering that boomed up from its docks drowned out the thud of the rival craft's plank a few seconds later.

Mr. Winterbottom mopped his forehead.

"Gad!" he muttered weakly. "There ought to be a law."

Captain Newt Dill swallowed again — harder. Mr. Winterbottom then noticed the name painted in ten-foot letters on the wheel-box of the winning packet. *Bluebelle*. His stern eyes jerked upwards and fixed on the insignia between the towering stacks. It was a large, flamboyant red arrow.

Slowly Mr. Winterbottom turned upon Captain Dill. "Your boat?" he asked icily.

Captain Dill could only nod.

"I understood you to say . . . ?" Mr. Winterbottom began in the musing tone of a man who has lost all faith in human nature. He let the question hang there significantly in mid-air.

The cheering was continuing on the decks of the *Bluebelle*, but a desolate silence had closed over the defeated packet. This steamer was equally as handsome, equally as big and resplendent as its rival. Its name was *River Jewel*. It carried the image of a snorting bull as its stackhead insignia. This identified it as the property of Captain Sim Turnbull.

In fact, Captain Sim Turnbull could be seen on the hurricane deck, exchanging remarks with persons aboard the *Bluebelle*. It was plain that Captain Turnbull was not taking his defeat graciously. He was a wide, thick-set man with truculent jaw and a mop of hair the hue of a rusty boiler. "You lucky, splay-footed turtles," Captain Turnbull was saying, among other things, in a voice that carried far, "I'll beat you so fur into Saint Loo you'll sell that tub for a snag boat."

On the levee Captain Dill stood, shifting from one foot to another, chilled by his proximity to Mr. Winterbottom. Captain Dill was already counting that freighting contract with Winterbottom Wholesalers, Inc., as lost.

Mr. Winterbottom intimated as much. "Do you think for one instant," he remarked, "that I'd entrust my consignments to a bunch of blithering boiler-bursters such as you seem to represent?"

The *Bluebelle* was now disgorging its triumphant voyagers. "Seventeen hours, ten minutes," someone with deep lungs was announcing. "From 'O'leans to Natchez. A new reco'd, gentlemen."

Mr. Winterbottom's commanding figure straightened. With disbelief, he watched an oil-smudged, tow-haired six-footer in engine-room blue who came down the gangplank, escorting a fashionably clad young lady in taffeta hoopskirts and an apple-green poke bonnet.

The girl came with a flurry of crinoline and dutifully kissed Mr. Winterbottom on the cheek. "Dad!" she exclaimed. "Did you see it? We beat them, and they used every unfair trick they could think of." Her deep brown eyes were dancing. She drew the overalled stranger into view. "Dad, this is Johnny Riskin, who handled the engines during that race. He tied two kegs of nails on the safety valve, and. . . ."

Miss Sally Winterbottom, who had been delayed a day at New Orleans by shopping duties, noticed that her father was ignoring the introduction. Johnny Riskin didn't know what to do with the hand he had extended. He finally hid it in a jumper pocket. He had a strong-chinned face, somewhat reddened by boiler-room heat.

He shot a quick, inquiring glance at Captain Newt Dill and stepped back a pace to stand shoulder to shoulder with two more executives who had stepped ashore from the *Bluebelle*. One of these was lank and perfumed, wearing a plantation coat and polished boots. His black mustache was rigidly waxed and a large diamond scintillated in his stock. Paducah Jim Peels had never been known to boast that he was the best racing pilot on the Mississippi. He merely let his record stand for itself. The other man, Catfish Kern, bulged the rusty uniform of a packet captain. Catfish was the inventor of a method for delivering small cargo consignments on the fly at unimportant landings. This system, which eliminated the need of reducing speed, had been generally adopted by all fast river craft.

Mr. Winterbottom had a firm grasp on his daughter's arm and was turning away. Captain Dill saw bankruptcy staring him in the face. He refused to meet the gaze of his three executives. "Hold on, Mister Winterbottom!" he exclaimed. "I'll see that this won't happen ag'in. I'm dischargin' these three men."

"Discharging us?" Johnny Riskin echoed.

Catfish Kern opened his large mouth, closed it, opened it again. "Hell's red bells," he said blankly.

Captain Dill assumed a righteous attitude. "Ain't I warned you men about steamboat racin'? Ain't I? It's childish! Rattle-brained! I've had enough of it. You're fired!"

"But . . . ," Johnny Riskin began. "You always. . . ."

Captain Dill turned away. "I won't stand for any such carrying-on with my packets, Mister Winterbottom," he declared. "No sir-ee-e. You kin see for yourself that I mean what I say. You've got passage on the *Bluebelle* for Saint Louis, I believe. I'll have a new engineer an' pilot aboard at once. Safe, reliable men. I'll personally act as captain for the remainder o' the trip."

Sally Winterbottom's little chin was jutting. "It isn't fair!" she exploded.

But her father silenced her with a glare. "Very well," he conceded, bowing to Captain Dill. "I will give you the opportunity of making good on your promises. But mind you . . . no more racing."

II

Because of Mr. Winterbottom's sizable consignment of cargo, the *Bluebelle* was held two hours at the levee, while the stevedores labored. Rice by the ton went aboard, along with sugar and molasses and bales of leather. Hogsheads of salt beef and salt pork, casks of lard, barrels of turpentine, and kegs of rum crowded the hold and freight deck. The delay gave Captain Newt Dill the chance to round up a new pilot and engineer, and it also afforded the muscular skipper of the rival *River Jewel* time to repack a cylinder which had weakened under the strain of the run from New Orleans. Thus it was that the two packets backed away from the Natchez levee at the same time and pointed their prows upstream.

Captain Sim Turnbull of the *River Jewel*

had enviously noticed the heavy cargo taken aboard the *Bluebelle* to St. Louis and knew it to be a consignment for Winterbottom Wholesalers, Inc., whose business he earnestly wished to acquire for his own packet. Captain Turnbull was a steamboat man, bred and born, and it seemed clear to him that he must not only beat the *Bluebelle* to St. Louis but must humiliate that packet so completely that no self-respecting shipper would ever sign a Red Arrow manifest again.

He recognized Captain Dill on the hurricane deck of the rival boat as the packets squared away upstream, but had never encountered Phineas Winterbottom in person. Therefore the portly, large-stomached passenger, standing at Captain Dill's elbow, meant little or nothing to him. Not until his *River Jewel* began to forge steadily ahead did Captain Sim Turnbull realize that the *Bluebelle* was refusing to continue the race upriver. That aroused his deepest scorn. He seized up his speaking trumpet and addressed Captain Dill.

"Crawfishin', hey? Not man enough to take an honest lickin', you're turnin' belly-up right at the start."

"Ignore the fellow," Mr. Winterbottom counseled.

Captain Dill's knuckles, several of which had been battered out of plumb in the past, tightened on the forerail. He turned a gloomy glance upon the lumpy individual who stood at the wheel of his *Bluebelle*. Mr. Souders had been the only licensed pilot available on such short notice. He was temporarily at liberty from his normal duties on a snag boat. Along the river Mr. Souders was familiarly known as Half-Speed Souders. As chief engineer Captain Dill had employed a certain Mr. Weems, who was thin, and cadaverous. Mr. Weems was noted for lack of confidence in both himself and steam boilers. An extreme pessimist, he was generally referred to as Weepy Weems. With such careful executives in charge of the *Bluebelle*, Captain Dill had no choice other than to ignore the bull-necked first officer of the *River Jewel*.

Mr. Winterbottom complacently watched the *River Jewel* steam ahead. He noticed disapprovingly the taunting gestures on the part of Captain Turnbull and heard the catcalls and jeering that came drifting back from the passengers aboard the leading packet.

With considerable less aplomb he discovered his daughter, sitting in a secluded place on the cabin deck below, talking to Johnny Riskin, whose zeal as a hot engineer had cost him his job at Natchez. Johnny Riskin wore a neat, gray suit, a collar, and tie. With the grime of the engine room removed, he was revealed as a resolute, stalwart young man of twenty-six or seven. He seemed much interested in Miss Sally Winterbottom. Worse, she appeared interested in him.

Mr. Winterbottom discovered during the day that Catfish Kern and Paducah Jim Peels, deposed skipper and pilot of the *Bluebelle*, were also aboard, deadheading it back to St. Louis along with Johnny Riskin. Because there was no point in wasting fuel racing a packet which refused to race, Captain Sim Turnbull of the arrogant *River Jewel* was proceeding at humdrum speed, also. To relieve the monotony he took delight in jockeying his craft into a position only a few rods in advance of the *Bluebelle*, wherever the channel was narrow, in order to give the rival craft the full benefit of the back thrust from his wheels. This caused the *Bluebelle* to quiver and groan somewhat. Frequently passengers on the promenade were sprayed by yellow spume from waves, slapping against the hull.

Captain Turnbull employed another maneuver that wore on the nerves of the *Bluebelle* passengers. Each craft carried small consignments for numerous backwoods landings, whose levees consisted of tiny openings in the brush. Whenever both packets were approaching such a port, Sim Turnbull would drop his craft slightly astern, as though to give the

Bluebelle precedence. At the last moment he would crowd his wheels and come churning in at full speed, forcing the *Bluebelle* to sheer off and lie out in the stream, her wheels idling, until he had cleared.

"He's an annoying fellow, isn't he?" Mr. Winterbottom remarked to a fellow passenger after this affront had been repeated.

Mr. Winterbottom lighted a cigar, which placed him two up for the day on the maximum tobacco allowance his physician had prescribed. He attributed his state of nerves to the manner in which Miss Sally was conducting herself. He had spoken to Aunt Hattie Calvin, who was supposed to act as chaperone, and he had spoken to Miss Sally herself, but she insisted on promenading the deck with Johnny Riskin. She also seemed on good terms with Catfish Kern and Paducah Jim Peels.

Darkness was approaching when the *Bluebelle*, edging into a nasty channel with a towhead island to larboard and a nest of snags to starboard, was forced to the brink of disaster as the *River Jewel* came plowing at full speed across her bow to take precedence. Except for Paducah Jim Peels, who peremptorily took the wheel from the timorous hands of Half-Speed Souders, the *Bluebelle* would have drifted upon the snags. Mr. Winterbottom, on the hurricane deck, drew a heartfelt sigh as the *Bluebelle* fought her way clear. He turned slowly, surveying the offending craft.

Sim Turnbull stood on thick legs, hands on hips, on the deck of his own craft, grinning in an aggravating manner. "Next time take passage on a good packet, instead of a stinkin' oyster boat, fatty," he remarked. "You won't get no sand in your beard aboard the *River Jewel*."

He was addressing Mr. Winterbottom. This time it was Mr. Winterbottom's pink hands which clenched tightly on the forerail.

"This fellow," he muttered audibly, "seems to be fairly spoiling for trouble."

Mr. Winterbottom's slumber was disturbed that night. Lying in his berth during the Memphis landing at midnight, he heard brawling sounds. Members of the *Bluebelle* and *River Jewel* crews were exchanging blows. After much clanging and clattering of patrol wagons, quiet was restored.

He had always been an early riser. Emerging at sunup on the promenade for a constitutional, he saw that the July day promised to be one of those humid ordeals when even the channel catfish are said to perspire freely. He shuddered. There, like Nemesis, was the *River Jewel*, steaming arrogantly a stone's throw ahead. That craft, Mr. Winterbottom admitted, was becoming a nuisance.

Captain Sim Turnbull was also a sunrise awakener. He stepped, yawning, from the *River Jewel*'s texas and noticed Mr. Winterbottom on the deck of the rival craft. "So you're still aboard that clam-boat, potbelly?" he remarked in surprise. "You must have hound in your blood, too."

A quick retort trembled on Mr. Winterbottom's tongue, but he restrained it, remembering the possibility of feminine listeners. *Potbelly!* he ruminated. Walking stiffly into the bar, he broke the custom of years by tossing off a neat bourbon as an eye-opener.

At breakfast, the winsome Miss Sally smiled brightly upon Catfish Kern and Paducah Jim Peels, and particularly upon Johnny Riskin who occupied an adjoining table, but Mr. Winterbottom, in a preoccupied mood, took no notice.

Captain Newt Dill was also morose. Half of his engine room and deck crew were now cooling their heels in the Memphis jail as a result of the midnight altercation. The *Bluebelle* was short-handed below and low-spirited above.

In the wheelhouse Half-Speed Souders was once more on duty, and below in the engine room Weepy Weems kept a careful eye on the steam gauge, popping the valve by hand at intervals to be on the safe side. The *Bluebelle*, under their direction, lumbered carefully, though sluggishly, onward during the day.

The *River Jewel*, in contrast, sported around the *Bluebelle* like a graceful zany, showering the phlegmatic packet with smoke-stack cinders and with human hooting. The blazing heat seemed to be having an effect on Mr. Winterbottom, for his jowls assumed a deeper sanguine tinge as the day advanced. Because Captain Sim Turnbull of the rival craft had a habit of singling him out for scathing attention, whenever he appeared on deck, he remained mainly in the smoking lounge, wrapped in a deep silence.

III

Toward sundown, as the first dinner gong was sounding, Mr. Winterbottom ventured forth for a breath of air. Cairo, and the confluence of the tributary Ohio, were astern now. A breeze had sprung up, blowing directly downriver. Though muggy and humid and laden with steamy boiler-room radiation from the *River Jewel*, whose position ahead placed her exactly in the eye of the wind, it was better than no breeze at all, and the majority of the *Bluebelle* passengers moved to the promenade to take advantage of it.

Ladies in dimity and chiffon fanned themselves damply as Mr. Winterbottom made his way to the forerail where he stood like a plump figurehead, glaring at the offending packet ahead. He arrived at an inopportune moment. Three grimy stokers appeared at the rear rail of the *River Jewel's* towering hurricane deck, bearing large barrels. They removed the tops from the barrels and upended the contents into the down-stream breeze at the precise moment that Mr. Winterbottom's ruddy face appeared a few rods astern.

These barrels had been filled with fine, black pitch-soot, mixed with feathery ashes and coal dust, which had been diligently gleaned and scraped from the *River Jewel's* flues and ash pits. An ominous black murk swept instantly down upon the *Bluebelle*. Her decks were raked by a blinding, noxious fog. Startled screams arose, fading into choking sounds. Gentlemen, fighting their way to sanctuary in the salons, began to swear, and then to splutter.

Mr. Winterbottom, because of his exposed position, received the full benefit of the sooty onslaught. He recoiled, but far too late. He was enveloped in a midnight gloom, too thick to breathe. His wide expanse of white linen shirt front stopped a considerable quantity of fire-room residue. His muttonchop whiskers strained out the coarser particles, leaving an accumulation of the finer elements as a somber festoon. He resembled a chimney Santa Claus. He fancied that he heard Captain Sim Turnbull indulging in deep belly laughter as he clawed at his eyes, awaiting a better moment to resume breathing.

The *Bluebelle* staggered clear of the sulled atmosphere, and Mr. Winterbottom saw that his ears had not deceived him. Captain Turnbull was standing on the deck of his craft, viewing the effect with hearty amusement.

Mr. Winterbottom tossed his head like a buffalo bull to clear his vision. He began speaking. He was addressing Captain Turnbull with depth and fervor. Silence fell over both crafts, for his voice carried far and wide. Deckhands paused to listen attentively. Mates, both first and second, began taking mental notes, grasping this chance to enlarge their vocabulary of vigorous terms. Even Captain Turnbull harked with awe.

". . . and we'll beat your stinking scow to Saint Louis, and then I'll have the pleasure of pushing your ugly head into the mud and stepping on it," Mr. Winterbottom concluded. He turned and plowed through sooty, chiffon-clad ladies and smutty-faced gentlemen, who hurriedly made way for him. His voice was booming thunder throughout the length and breadth of the *Bluebelle*. "Captain Dill," he commanded. "Where in tophet are you?"

Captain Dill appeared, garnished with soot.

"Are you a man or a worm?" Mr. Winterbottom wanted to know without lowering his voice. "Or is there hound in your blood? Put this man Peels at the wheel to relieve that chicken-hearted sand-crawler who calls himself a pilot. Find this Riskin fellow and see if he can keep enough steam in this tub to give us a little headway. Or do you propose to let that insufferable pirate continue to make fools of us all the way to Saint Louis?"

Captain Dill's haunted look vanished. Johnny Riskin appeared. Miss Sally was on his arm. Soot on a pert nose like that was an adornment.

"Did you hear, Johnny?" she demanded.

Johnny Riskin had heard. He vanished below. Paducah Jim Peels climbed to the pilothouse and dismissed Half-Speed Souders.

Black smoke gushed from the *Bluebelle*'s stacks, then faded away as the stokers, under the direction of Catfish Kern, wielded clinker bars and sweeps, leveling their fires, thinning it to the proper spread of clean, white-hot efficiency.

It was twenty minutes later when Captain Turnbull of the swaggering *River Jewel*, attempting to crowd into a chute channel ahead of the *Bluebelle*, discovered that the situation had changed. He was now in a steamboat race.

The *Bluebelle* did not give way. Instead, the *River Jewel*'s pilot was forced to reverse wheels to avoid collision. It was the *River Jewel* that wallowed astern in the run through the chute.

The packets steamed into the open river as though hitched stem to stern. In the early darkness their fire boxes cast red reflections into the sky like the intermittent play of heat lightning. The *River Jewel* forged abeam and slightly ahead for a time, having the initial advantage on her steam gauge. This handicap vanished as the *Bluebelle*'s boilers built up pressure.

Mr. Winterbottom stood at the forerail, watching with satisfaction as the packets foamed through the night upriver. The *Bluebelle* had become a thing of lissome grace and power beneath his feet. She carried fire in her stacks and had a bone of saffron river water in her teeth. Her timbers, sawn half through, gave her pliancy and speed. She needed both. The *River Jewel* had fire in her stacks, as well, and was by no means falling astern.

In fact, there were times when the *River Jewel* forged ahead, only slightly to be sure, but enough to cause Mr. Winterbottom to fume. He hurried below. It was hot on the boiler deck. Stokers, stripped to the waist, were sloshing river water over each other. He was not surprised to find his daughter in the engine room. She didn't seem to mind the heat. She was watching Johnny Riskin. Johnny hadn't bothered to don jumpers. Stripped to the belt, his tailored gray trousers were gradually accumulating a heavy coating of engine oil and coal dust.

"You've got to do better, Mister Riskin," Mr. Winterbottom stated flatly. "That filthy barge is staying with us. Captain Dill tells me that we will be in Saint Louis before daybreak. We can't afford to dally at this stage of the race."

Johnny Riskin sleeved his glistening forehead. He glanced wryly at the arm of the safety valve upon which he had hung a blacksmith's anvil, thereby preventing any wasteful loss of steam through the pops. "We've got our work cut out for us," he admitted. "We're short-handed on the stoking deck. Some of our boys are in the Memphis calaboose. We could use 'em tonight, I want to tell you."

"Short-handed, eh," Mr. Winterbottom snapped, hastening away.

He returned shortly with half a dozen of the huskier male passengers. "Willing volunteers," he explained. Without further ado he stripped off his broadcloth coat, his pleated stock, linen shirt, and striped undershirt. Mr. Winterbottom's torso was pink and rounded, but he could swing a coal scoop. What he lacked in skill, he made up for in vigor. He employed a small darky to sluice river water over his sweating form as he worked. He ate coal dust and sneered at searing heat. He twinkled back and forth before the glaring fire boxes like a rotund, muttonchopped satyr, lashing his compatriots to greater energy with a fluent tongue.

Johnny Riskin hung a keg of nails on the safety valve arm, along with the anvil. The *Bluebelle*'s bucket wheels took a deeper bite into the river.

The *River Jewel* no longer forged ahead. For a time, in fact, she had trouble staying abeam. Apparently her safety valve was also weighed down to prevent any unnecessary waste of power.

Mr. Winterbottom uttered a wild whoop of delight whenever he noticed that the rival craft was losing river to the *Bluebelle*. He stepped to the rail and lifted his voice. "Potbelly, am I?"

But after midnight the hated *River Jewel* be-

gan to creep steadily ahead again, sending
Mr. Winterbottom into the depths of despair.

"They're hotter than we are," Johnny
Riskin explained morosely. "They're burning
resin now and pine knots. Racing fuel. They
stocked up on it at Natchez, but we burned
the last of ours in the run from New Orleans
and didn't stow any more, not expecting to
need it after . . . after. . . ."

". . . after you were fired for winning that
race," the piquant Sally Winterbottom put in,
with a lofty glance at her father.

Mr. Winterbottom winced. He watched the
River Jewel edge steadily ahead. The tang of
resin came from her flaming stacks. He returned to his post and shoveled coal madly.
But coal wasn't enough. The *River Jewel* was
soon a cable's length in the lead. And then an
eighth of a mile.

Johnny Riskin shook his head. "They've got
us, if their pitch fuel holds out," he reluctantly
admitted.

"You'd have beaten them if this was your
boat, Johnny," Sally Winterbottom consoled
him.

"Your boat?" Mr. Winterbottom inquired,
leaning on his scoop for a moment's rest.

Johnny Riskin removed a cloth from a small
model of a steamboat, which stood in a place
of honor in the engine room. "Miss Winter-

bottom means this," he said. "It's a model. I've evolved a new hull design. It should give more speed with less power than anything now on the river, but it takes money to build a steamboat."

"What good is a model here and now?" Mr. Winterbottom said gloomily. Then he added hopefully: "Except maybe as fuel."

"What a selfish suggestion," his daughter reproved.

"I'd jam it in the firebox, if it'd help," Johnny Riskin said darkly. "But what we need is something hot, and lots of it. Pine knots. Better still, some nice fat side meat, or a few barrels of lard."

"Lard!" Mr. Winterbottom shouted in a loud voice. "And soaked in turpentine."

He dragged Johnny Riskin violently forward to the freight deck and pointed to great heaps of casks and hogsheads. "Lard!" he repeated. "Turpentine. And rum!"

The lard and turpentine were meant for the fireboxes. And there, it soon was vanishing in a steady stream.

The rum was put to a different use. No one aboard the *Bluebelle* had thought of retiring for the night. Mr. Winterbottom broached several kegs of good Jamaica, setting them up in the lounges and promenades, with orders to the stewards to see that nobody was slighted. He presided personally over the keg in the boiler room.

Cheers began to rise from the decks of the *Bluebelle*. The *River Jewel*'s flaming stacks were no longer dwindling upriver. They were growing brighter.

Johnny Riskin covered the steam gauges with a greasy cloth so that no timorous passenger might have occasion to worry.

Mr. Winterbottom watched tensely as the *River Jewel*'s advantage narrowed. It was only a cable's length ahead now. And then a mere shouting distance. Stepping to the rail, Mr. Winterbottom lifted a tin cup of rum. "So you've got hound in your veins, Captain Turnbull," he taunted. And guffawed loudly.

The *Bluebelle* surged around a bend, and the lights of the St. Louis levee twinkled ahead against the first gray pallor of dawn. Mr. Winterbottom's enthusiasm grew as the *Bluebelle* drew abeam and then ahead of the rival craft. He was a wild figure, dancing on the prow, as the *Bluebelle* surged to the St. Louis levee on reversed wheels and dropped her plank a full two minutes before the *River Jewel* touched land.

He raced to the levee and hurried to greet the defeated packet. He was met by Captain Sim Turnbull as he stepped on the still vibrating gangplank of the rival craft.

"Now, you insulting plug-ugly," Mr. Winterbottom exulted. "I recall promising you a thrashing."

He swung a blistered fist with mighty intention at Captain Turnbull. That brawny person brushed the blow aside as scornfully as he would swat an annoying mosquito. Something hard and violent struck Mr. Winterbottom on the jaw, causing him to sit down with a jar on the unyielding stone levee. He vaguely realized that he had collided with Captain Turnbull's fist.

Then Johnny Riskin appeared on the scene. He proved to be more of a match for Captain Turnbull. From a sitting position, Mr. Winterbottom watched the fight with envious approval. It was furious while it lasted, but it didn't last long enough to suit him, for it was apparent from the start that the *River Jewel* skipper was doomed to defeat. When, at last, Johnny Riskin delivered the *hors de combat* in the form of a devastating right, Mr. Winterbottom arose. Linking his arm in Johnny's, he marched down the levee.

"This new hull design that you've evolved, Mister Riskin . . . ," he said. "If you really think it will add speed to a craft, I might be interested in financing the construction of. . . ."

Someone else had captured Johnny Riskin's

other arm. It was Mr. Winterbottom's vivacious daughter. She eyed her father frigidly. "Johnny will do no more steamboat racing, Father," she stated emphatically. "It's too dangerous. Isn't it, Johnny?"

Over the top of Miss Winterbottom's head Johnny Riskin shot a glance at Mr. Phineas Winterbottom. "Yes, dear," he said obediently, but a rapidly closing eye could still wink and did so at the rotund father of his future wife. Johnny was one who could cover up a steam gauge in an emergency, you remember.

The Lady Was a Dude

Dan Kerrick was in an aggressive mood as he drove into Buffalo Horn to meet the new schoolteacher. In the first place, it wasn't his responsibility. The married ranchers took turns at transporting the children at the south end of Moccasin Basin to and from the district school. This was the week Dan's brother and sister-in-law were to have taken over the chore, but both of them were down with feverish colds, and Dan had volunteered to act in their stead.

Meeting the new teacher in Buffalo Horn was an added errand. The girl who had begun the fall term as schoolmarm a few weeks earlier had gone the way of most of them. She had got married suddenly on Friday after school and was already setting up housekeeping with a young rancher up in Round Valley. Now another teacher was being brought in on a rush call. She was coming from Cheyenne, but Dan understood that she was an Easterner. Most likely, he reflected, she wouldn't last any longer than the others.

In his opinion, the young ladies, fresh from normal school or college, who came into this

Wyoming range country invariably fell into one of two classifications: they were hoping to find a husband for themselves, or they intended only to spend a term or two in Wyoming for the novelty of it.

Dan first cleaned up the routine errands. He picked up grocery orders for half a dozen ranchers' wives and loaded ten sacks of sheep salt for Jim Sealover into the station wagon as well as the new blade for Sam Denton's snowplow. He got the repaired spider for Ed Ramsey's windmill and lashed it on top. He even remembered the baby oil Pearl Wilton had been so worried he would forget.

It wasn't the errands that had him on edge. These were the normal neighborly duties of anyone making the fifty-mile trip to town. It was the glint he had seen in the eyes of the womenfolk and the knowing grins on the faces of the men that graveled him. They all knew he was to meet the new teacher, and they anticipated romance. Therefore, Dan was ready to run scared as he parked alongside Pop Jensen's restaurant, which also served as bus station.

Dan was twenty-five, black-haired, gray-eyed, and blocky of shoulder and chin. He was master of his own soul. He liked to hunt and fish and ride fast horses and drive fast cars, and to go where he pleased, and to kiss any girl he pleased. He was half owner, with his older brother, Art, in a thriving outfit up in the basin, and he had no intention of getting married — at least, not in the foreseeable future.

The Rock Springs bus had made its stop and was pulling out after discharging a young lady and her baggage. There was no doubt she was the new schoolteacher, and very attractive. As Dan walked closer, he had to concede that she was, in fact, as pretty as a red button. She was of medium height, and slender here and not so slender there. She had clear, young, dark eyes and glossy dark hair and a clear complexion in which the keen wind had brought glowing color. She was as lively as a robin.

Dan tipped his hat. "Miss Mary Jane Meadows?"

She was, indeed, Miss Mary Jane Meadows. And she was overjoyed that someone had come to meet her, for she had felt conspicuous standing there alone in this strange town. Her gaze traveled over him, entranced, taking in his tanned skin, his stiff-brimmed range hat, duck jacket and saddle denims and soft half boots. Then she gazed up and down the three-block street. "Buffalo Horn!" she sighed ecstatically. "I wanted this position the minute I heard that name. It's so Western . . . so outdoorish!"

Dan rounded up her luggage and led her to the station wagon. It was a late, snappy model with a two-tone paint job and had red leather upholstery. She gazed fearfully at the conglomerate cargo that weighed down the springs. The windmill spider on the roof particularly appalled her.

She relaxed a little after they got under way. She gazed around at the high, rolling plains, broken by flat-topped hills. "I'm just utterly fascinated," she assured Dan. "I've never been West before. I'm from Indiana. I just love Wyoming. It's so big, so . . . so . . . well, it's just big. All this country, and, my goodness, not even a tree in sight. So wild! So untouched!"

Dan resented the way she described Wyoming. It was as though she were admiring something that did not exist. But it made him easier in mind, too. For it catalogued her. It was evident she had no intention of identifying herself with this Wyoming she tried to be so keen about. She was viewing it as a tourist. She was here only for a few months.

Dan became a little more tolerant of her, now that he felt there was nothing to fear. "It's big, sure enough," he said. "And high . . . and clean."

Mary Jane Meadows asked him his occupation.

"My brother and I run a ranch up in Moccasin Basin," he explained.

"A cowboy!" she squealed delightedly.

"We run sheep mostly," Dan said.

"Sheep?" She hesitated, then added quickly: "How interesting."

But he knew she was disappointed. They left the paving twenty miles out of Buffalo Horn and bounced over gravel and washboard. Dan pointed out landmarks — Teepee Mountain, Signal Butte, Squaw Ridge, the Wind Rivers peeping over the horizon in the distance.

Mary Jane repeated the names reverently. "It's all so romantic," she breathed.

Presently the road topped a ridge, and Moccasin River and the rolling benches and the rugged basin lay before them.

She stared. "It's beautiful," she said a trifle uneasily. "But it is so vast . . . so lonely."

"It isn't lonely after you get acquainted," Dan said. "But I must admit you're seeing it on its good behavior. This mild weather has been hanging on overlong. There'll be a blizzard come tearing down through here 'most any time."

"A blizzard!" Mary Jane hugged herself and shuddered, enthralled. "I've always wanted to see one of your wild Western blizzards. It must be just terrifying." Before Dan could answer

117

this, she pointed and screamed: "There's a cowboy! A real cowboy!"

"It's only Orv Judson," Dan said disparagingly.

Orv always went in for wide-brimmed, tall hats, double-breasted shirts and foxed breeches and stitched, spurred half boots. He was lean and lanky and good-looking, with a little black mustache and thick sideburns. He was riding his blaze-faced sorrel and was hazing along four empty pack horses. Dan guessed he was on his way home after delivering supplies at one of his father's sheep wagons up on the bench.

Orv stopped them and got himself introduced to the new schoolmarm. Dan surmised that he had been hanging around the road just for that special purpose, in case the schoolteacher turned out to be pretty.

Evidently Orv considered that his time had not been wasted. He kept leaning through the window of the car, turning on the charm for Mary Jane Meadows's benefit, until Dan stepped on the gas and took off, leaving him sitting there on his sorrel with his mouth open.

Mary Jane kept staring back. "My, but he was handsome," she sighed. "And so . . . so polite."

Dan merely grunted and drove faster.

Rounding a bend, he braked to a stop. A whiskered, dusty man carrying a sheep in his arms was standing alongside the road, hailing a ride. It was Zack Duvall, a camp tender who worked for Ed Ramsey. His truck had broken down on the return trip from one of the flocks up in the benches. He had with him a young ewe that he had been taking to the home ranch for doctoring after an encounter with a coyote.

Both Dan and the bearded camp tender waited, gazing expectantly at Mary Jane after this had been explained. Suddenly she comprehended that the only comfortable place for the injured ewe was on the red-leather-cushioned seat she was occupying. She looked startled. The ewe was dusty, its wool long and grimy and matted with thistles and caked mud and dried blood. Then she hastily climbed over the back seat and wedged herself among the salt sacks and the snowplow blade and the groceries.

Dan got rid of both the ewe and the camp tender at Ed Ramsey's place. Also the windmill spider. He washed off the leather cushion, and Mary Jane reoccupied that position.

Ed's wife made a big fuss over Mary Jane. Julia Ramsey was a plump woman with a big, infectious laugh. "I do hope you don't let any of these young bachelors around here talk you into gettin' married . . . at least until the finish of the school year," she said. "I declare, but we have a time keepin' teachers." She poked Dan in the ribs. "Not mentionin' any names, of course," she added coyly.

Dan hurriedly drove away. He delivered the snowplow blade and got rid of most of the grocery orders before arriving at George Wilton's place.

Arrangements had been made to board the new teacher with George and Pearl Wilton. The schoolhouse was still some five miles farther up the basin. By that time Mary Jane was no longer saying anything. None of the other ranch wives had been as open about it as Julia Ramsey, but Mary Jane had correctly interpreted the hints they had put out in regard to how easy it was for a pretty schoolmarm to find a husband in these parts.

It was plain that she considered Dan a party to all this. So, all he could do was to introduce her to Pearl and George and drive hurriedly away.

"I'll come by with the kids about seven in the morning to pick you up," he called back.

After he had turned into the main road, in the rear-vision mirror he saw Orv Judson's red-and-cream convertible heave into view and veer into the Wilton Ranch road. Orv hadn't lost much time galloping to his ranch

120

to get out his car, Dan reflected sourly.

Mary Jane had that same aloof, grim look in her dark eyes when he came by in the morning. He had already picked up eight children, and the station wagon was jumping. She chose to sit far in the rear among the children. And she restored order in a hurry. When he delivered her at the schoolhouse, she thanked him politely and walked away, her back straight as a ramrod. When Dan returned to pick up his charges at sundown, he found Orv Judson's convertible standing before the schoolhouse. Orv lolled in the seat, wearing his big, pearl-colored hat, beaded elkskin vest, and brass-studded leather cuffs. He was strictly dressed for the kill. And Mary Jane rode away with him, gazing in awe at his costume. Dan was left to contend with an ant-like swarm of children as best he could. To make matters worse, a general fight started in the car with bloody noses, howling youngsters, and pandemonium.

"I figure," Dan told Mary Jane, when he picked her up the next morning at the Wilton place, "that you better ride the school car both to and from school. You could help control the brats."

"That," Mary Jane said, "is not a part of my contract. And you should be ashamed to call them brats. After all, two of them are your brother's children, I am told."

"There's nothing in your contract that calls for riding around with a drugstore cowboy, either," Dan said.

She gave him a look down the length of her short nose that was intended to put him in his place. "At least, Mister Judson, to whom I imagine you are referring, wouldn't ask a lady to stand aside for a smelly old sheep," she sniffed.

"Don't ever put that to a test," Dan said. "Sheep come first in this country. Even Orv Judson knows that."

Mary Jane got her second lesson in the importance of sheep two mornings later. The weather changed overnight. It started as a cold rain at daybreak. By the time Dan picked up Mary Jane, it was turning to sleet and snow. Dan had put on the chains, and the station wagon was already caked with yellow mud. Mary Jane wore galoshes and had a transparent rain cape over her garb. She was as pretty as a Christmas package. A suffocating sensation came in Dan's chest.

He drove gently, trying to put her out of his mind. He picked up the last of the children. Instead of continuing on up the main highway to the school, he swung off into a road that wasn't much more than a muddy wheel track. It mounted westward up the bench.

"Where in the world . . . ?" Mary Jane began.

Dan explained that he had promised to deliver an important package to one of Pete Ditmar's herders. "Pete couldn't get his jeep started this morning," he explained. "It's only a little way."

The little way proved to be nearly ten miles. The car almost bogged down several times. Then there was another long delay at a point on the bleak, sleet-swept bench while Dan honked the horn mournfully until a sheepherder came riding from somewhere out of the vacancy. The important package proved to contain tins of smoking tobacco, which the herder seized on with delight.

"Do you mean to say you brought us all this way just to hand that old man some tobacco?" Mary Jane exploded.

"Why, he's been out of smoking for two days, "Dan explained, amazed. "Pete just found out about it today."

Her eyes were flashing. "Do you realize I am going to be late, and that the whole day's school work will be disrupted, all because this man couldn't wait a little longer to smoke a filthy old pipe?"

"But the fellow was going to quit," Dan

protested. "Good herders are hard to find. As for school, you can keep the bra . . . the kids in a little longer this evening."

Mary Jane started to say something scathing. Then she noticed that the children were taking all this calmly. Evidently such goings-on were a part of life in sheep country.

Then the station wagon bogged down so completely that Dan had to hike three miles to the main road and wait for help. The upshot of it was that it was mid-afternoon before they got back on the highway, and too late to go to school at all.

"You can hold an extra session Saturday," Dan said.

Mary Jane almost wept. "I had other plans for Saturday," she gritted. "Do we have to arrange our very existence to accommodate sheep?"

"It kind of gets that way," Dan admitted. "Sheep are mighty helpless creatures. You get to feel obligated to take care of 'em. Then, too, when sheep starve, most folks around here quit eating regularly, too." He added: "I'll drive over Saturday night and take you to a dance at Five Points. They'll have a combo playing."

"Mister Judson is escorting me to the dance," she said.

Orv Judson, Dan reflected, was getting to be quite a pest.

On Saturday night he happened to be driving by Five Points about ten in the evening, so he just decided to drop in. The place was crowded. Sure enough, Mary Jane was there with Orv. Dan cut in on Orv as they danced. And Orv immediately cut in, also. Dan cut in right back. One thing led to another. Dan pushed Orv in the face. Orv took a swing at him. A table got knocked over, and a woman who had a glass of beer spilled on her dress whacked Dan over the head with her purse. Orv also took advantage of that interruption to punch Dan in the eye.

Then a committee of husky men, who were insistent on resuming the dance, escorted both Dan and Orv and Mary Jane outside, with a stern request that they do not return. Mary Jane, crimson with humiliation, drove off with Orv, warning Dan that he was never, never, never to speak to her again.

The next morning Dan had a fine black eye to remind him of the incident. That also finished his week's duty on the school route. The ensuing week was Ed Ramsey's responsibility, but Julia handled the chore, for she was a better driver than Ed.

Dan kept out of sight for a few days whenever the school car was arriving to pick up or deliver his small niece and nephew at the ranch where he lived with his brother and Dot, his sister-in-law. That gave things a chance to cool down a little and also permitted his eye to become respectable again. Besides, there was work to do.

Finally he got up the courage to be puttering around the tool shed when Julia Ramsey came driving up in their light truck, which was fitted with crossboard seats to accommodate the children. Mary Jane was sitting beside Julia. She pointedly ignored Dan's existtence. He tried the experiment a couple of times more, with the same result.

He drove past the schoolhouse several times as the day's sessions were ending. There was no sign of Orv Judson's convertible, and Mary Jane rode away each time in the ranch car that was handling the school route on that particular week. Dan approved of that. Evidently Orv was also on probation as a result of that affair at Five Points.

Dan was in an irritable mood. He was losing his appetite. He made a special trip to Buffalo Horn to buy vitamin pills. One day he and Orv got into an argument about some trivial matter as they were helping salvage pelts from some sheep that Jim Sealover had lost in a pile-up near Signal Butte. Finally Orv took a poke at him. Then they skulked all over the place. It ended up without much damage on either side, as usual, except that it was Orv who had the black eye to take home.

Jim Sealover lost thirty-two head in the pile-up. Something had frightened the flock as the herder was moving it to new graze, and the timid creatures had stampeded toward a coulée, in which the lost animals had smothered.

The next time Dan passed the school car on the road, Mary Jane gave him a freezing glare. He guessed she must have heard about his new tiff with Orv Judson. Woman-like, she took credit for being the cause. Dan had a notion to tell her that her name hadn't even been mentioned.

His appetite continued to shrink. He felt listless. He changed to a new vitamin complex.

A full-scale blizzard came roaring down across the plains, and, when it ended, the country lay white and frozen. Even the swift and rumbling Moccasin River was partly imprisoned in ice, with only the fastest rapids open. Gorges formed, creating pools of backwater. Then the gorges would break, turning the river into chaos, and new ones would form.

On a bitter December day Dan's brother came home, scowling, from a meeting of the district school board. Art was chairman.

"You and Orv Judson played the devil with your fighting over that new schoolmarm," he told Dan sourly. "Now we've got to hunt up another teacher."

Dan felt hollow inside. "You mean this Indiana girl is quitting?"

"As soon as the term ends in January," Art growled. "She gave notice today. Everybody knows she's embarrassed by you two clopheads getting into rows over her."

"She had nothing to do with it," Dan protested. "And, anyway, she only came here in the first place because she had movie ideas about the Wild West. She never had any intention of staying. She wanted to see how the natives lived here in Wyoming."

"One thing's for sure," Art said scathingly. "You and Orv Judson didn't do anything to induce her to stay."

The bitter winter weather held. Dan frosted an ear and the tip of his nose rescuing lambs from a drifted-over gully in which they had taken shelter during a storm.

Then Art's turn to drive the school route came up again. But on Sunday morning a phone call brought word that Dot's mother was ailing in California, where she was spending the winter. So Art and Dot left Rock Springs that afternoon to board a plane. That left Dan to take care of everything, including the school-route chore which began on Monday morning.

Dan was shaking a little inside when he drove up to George Wilton's place in the morning, the chains crackling in the hard-frozen snow.

Mary Jane came out. She hesitated, when she saw him. Then her nose went up. Dan explained why he was driving. He explained at length because he didn't want her to get the impression that he was here of his own choice. She continued to keep her nose tilted. She had on a dark red tam-o'-shanter and a gay scarf and a heavy, fur-trimmed jacket, and wore ski pants and waterproof, heavy shoes. She was so pretty that she seemed to sparkle.

Dan kept on explaining. Then he put his arms around her suddenly and kissed her resoundingly. He released her, shocked by his own action. The children in the car were tittering and nudging one another.

Mary Jane went a vivid crimson. "Why . . . why . . . ," she breathed. "In front of all these children?"

"I must have been thinking of some other girl," Dan said miserably.

"Some other girl? Oh, you . . . !"

She pushed indignantly past him and flounced into the farthest extremity of the station wagon. She silenced the giggling with a glare, but smirking grins remained.

Dan, as he drove, didn't dare glance in the mirror. He guessed he had done it for sure — disgracing her in front of the children. He handled the station wagon gingerly, for the chains wouldn't take a bite in stretches where the snow had packed and frozen. He guessed the temperature must have gone to thirty below during the night and was still well under zero.

Julia Ramsey got aboard, along with her two children, for she was going to help Mary Jane decorate the schoolhouse for the Christmas party. The car skidded from one frozen rut to another on the descent from the river. There the road leveled and followed the stream northward. Frost smoke hung over open rapids a hundred yards to the right across snow-drifted fields. Dan saw that an ice gorge had formed just above the rapids. It had backed up the river somewhat, and this quieted pool of water had frozen in the bitter temperature.

Suddenly he halted the car and leaped out, peering. Julia Ramsey got to her feet, staring also. "Merciful heavens!" she screamed.

Sheep — hundreds of them — were on the ice above the gorge. And the gorge itself looked as if it might let go any minute. Big sections of ice were breaking away at intervals and being swept into the roaring open water below. When the gorge finally let go, the ice on the pool it had formed would break up, too, and the sheep would be carried to death.

"It's one of Jim Sealover's flocks," Julia Ramsey chattered. "As if he hasn't had enough bad luck already."

Dan was already running. "Drive to the Duncan place and get help!" he shouted back.

"You be careful, Dan Kerrick!" Julia screeched. "That gorge is likely to go out any . . . !"

Dan was out of hearing, racing at great, lung-straining strides. He came in sight of the herder's camp wagon, which stood in the lee of a small ridge. Two thin, nervous sheep dogs paced about. Thin smoke drifted from the stovepipe that jutted through the roof of the camp wagon.

A figure lay in the frozen snow near the wagon's steps. It was old Antone, a Basque who had tended flocks in the basin for many years. Evidently he had been stricken as he was cooking breakfast and had made it only into the open before the end had come.

Dan saw that there was nothing that could be done for old Antone. He raced on toward the flock on the frozen river. He saw the carcasses of three ewes and the glint of frozen blood. Evidently coyotes had appeared, once their chance had come. The flock had retreated away from this danger and wandered onto the ice. The opposite shore was blocked by a six-foot clay cutbank. Dan could see that a pile-up had begun there, for the massed bodies of a score of sheep were piled up against the cutbank at one point.

Through some whim of chance the remainder of the flock had turned away from this disaster and had started drifting downriver toward the gorge — moving in a gray-white flood in an aimless, blatting swarm — heading into an even worse danger. There were more than a thousand head in the flock. Dan whistled the dogs, and they joined him as he reached the panicky horde.

He began working carefully, whistling and calling, soothing the sheep out of their panic. Eerie, whirring, ghostly sounds raced through the ice — invisible cracks that were running through its heart under the weight of the flock.

A frightened voice called: "What can I do?"

Mary Jane was on the ice a score of yards out from shore. The station wagon had already vanished in the direction of the Duncan place. Dan had not known until then that Mary Jane had left the car and followed him.

"Get back!" he shouted frantically. "Get off the ice!"

She reluctantly retreated nearer to safety, then stood watching with apprehension as Dan worked with the flock.

Gradually Dan coaxed the woolly mass under control and got it moving toward the shore from which it had come. He could feel a queer tension in the ice beneath his feet. Terror grew in him. He looked downstream where the jagged, upended ice floes marked the head of the gorge above the rapids. The gorge was no more than two hundred yards away.

"Hurry!" Mary Jane shouted desperately. "Oh, hurry!"

The leaders of the flock had reached safety on solid land, but now some of the ewes saw the coyote-killed carcasses. That sent the creatures into a frenzy of milling. Dan and the dogs, by titanic effort, finally turned the flock in the right direction again, and more of the sheep streamed ashore.

Less than a hundred head were still on the ice when it happened. It came like a cannon shot. The gorge suddenly broke. Dan felt the ice beneath him give a great surge. He raced toward shore. Great cracks darted across the surface. Then the frozen pool broke into a tumult of upended floes and of blatting sheep, and all drifting with increasing speed toward the rapids.

Dan leaped from floe to floe, heading for land. Safety was little more than fifty feet away, but the rapids were terrifyingly near. Then he slipped and went into water up to his knees. He pulled himself back on an upending segment of ice. He saw Mary Jane racing along the shore, her eyes big and dark against her pale face. Doomed sheep were all around him in the water or vanishing beneath the crunching ice. The breakup was picking up speed now, as the backwater drained into the rapids.

Dan plucked a struggling ewe from between floes at his feet, yanked her onto a broad sheet of ice, hoping she would make her way to shore. That effort capsized the ice cake on which he had been standing, and he went into water to his waist. The cold was like a numbing shock of electricity. He clawed futilely. He was being carried farther from shore and toward the rapids.

Then hands caught his arms and pulled him up on an ice floe. It was Mary Jane who had come leaping nimbly across the ice. With inspired strength she kept dragging him. Then Dan was able to get to his feet himself. The crash and roar of the rapids was so near that the frost smoke swirled around them.

Fear gave them desperate strength, and they literally skimmed over the grinding floes and made the shore in a dozen leaps. Dan's soaked garb was already beginning to stiffen in the temperature. He kept running and made it to the camp wagon, whose interior was snugly warmed by the still hot stove.

Mary Jane helped him off with his jacket and boots. "Trying to save that poor sheep almost cost you your life," she said. Then she added thoughtfully: "But I understand."

Then she left the wagon, and Dan heard her running back to the river. He hurriedly changed to some of Antone's spare clothes, and then raced to join her.

Mary Jane was working at the river's margin, trying to rescue a dozen or more sheep that were still feebly struggling among the drifting ice in shallow water just out of the swift current. As Dan ran to help, she pulled a ewe to safety. Freezing water soaked her and congealed on her clothes, but she looked at Dan with a shining gladness in her eyes. They got half a dozen more animals out before the remainder vanished. Jim Sealover had lost some eighty head, Dan estimated, but the bulk of his flock had been saved.

Dan and Mary Jane looked at each other, panting. Dan suddenly leaned over and kissed her on her cold-numbed lips. "You were the only girl I was thinking about that other time this morning when I kissed you," he mumbled.

Auto horns sounded. Julia Ramsey was returning with the station wagon and bringing other cars and men. Orv Judson arrived in his convertible.

Orv offered to drive Mary Jane home. She thanked him politely but said she guessed she and Mr. Kerrick should gather up the children again and try to salvage part of the day's school work. She climbed into the station wagon beside Dan, and they headed for the Duncan place, where the children were waiting.

She didn't say anything for a while. Then she remarked with vast satisfaction: "I saved four sheep today. All with my own hands." She looked around at the sweep of frozen country and drew a long breath. "It is so big, so grand . . . so beautiful I . . . I wonder if a person ever really becomes a part of it?"

Dan remembered she had said something like that the first day at Buffalo Horn. But this was different. There was an affection, a real yearning in her voice. "You're not leaving Wyoming," he said. It was a demand and not a question.

Their eyes met. Hers wavered ever so slightly. "No," she murmured shakily. "I changed my mind . . . just this morning. I'm going to stay and keep on teaching."

"You're staying," Dan said, "but not to teach."

He halted the car, for this matter required his undivided attention. He kissed her lustily.

"I'm staying," Mary Jane agreed presently, her voice dreamy, "but not to teach. I made up my mind to that when you first kissed me this morning."

Picture Bride

Cebe Buckman couldn't down the fluttery panic that kept crawling up inside him. Now and then he chanced a furtive glance at what sat beside him in the wagon, but mainly he glued his eyes to the front, pretending the team was needing all his attention. Chancellor's store had sunk into the mesquite behind them before he could muster the courage to utter a word.

"Howdy, Missus Buckman!" He tried to say it offhand, but his voice sort of exploded in his face. His ears felt big and red.

Her eyes, beneath her bonnet, turned toward him, then swiftly away. "It sounds real nice, doesn't it?" Sarah's slender fingers lay still in her lap. The plain gold ring stood out prominently against the demure gray of her gown.

She was, Cebe realized, as scared and fluttery as himself. That emboldened him. He now inspected her with more discernment. He had been too muddled-up back there at the settlement to take note of details. He hadn't known whether he was afoot or flying, from the time she got off the stage until they were standing before the parson. Her hair, where it showed beneath the bonnet, was a glossy chestnut. Her mouth was not small, and her lips pressed together to offset the tendency to tremble.

Her cheeks were a mite thin, but in any event a girl with eyes like hers could never be called plain. They were amber and bigger than they appeared in the tintype she had sent him. Cebe's eyes were well above the level of her bonnet top. Cebe shaded six-feet-two in his socks.

She wasn't a farm girl, according to her letters, and her hands showed it. She had been a bookkeeper in a woolen mill back where she came from. Cebe had found her name and address on a slip of paper pinned inside a shirt he had bought at Chancellor's last winter. One letter had led to another, and now here she was, in October, sitting beside him back of the buckskin team, with the wheels grinding over a Texas trail. Cebe Buckman wasn't the first man who'd got his bride's name out of a purchase at the mercantile.

Cebe saw that she was appraising him, in turn, although not openly. He wondered if he measured up to expectations. He ran a finger around the stiff collar that clamped his neck. He didn't dare take a full breath. The store suit he had bought at Chancellor's was a trifle snug at the seams.

"Like it?" he asked with a sweep of his arm. "Different from up north, I reckon."

Before them the mesquite swells rolled away to a far horizon. The trail the wagon followed was a dim wheel track. The country was a pale gray-green monotone. To the west a thin, purple line broke the horizon. This might be clouds, or might be hills. To the south a thread of deeper green showed the promise of a watercourse.

"It's different," she agreed.

"I figured you'd open your eyes, when you saw it," Cebe chuckled.

She heard the lift in his voice and saw that his lank, blunt-chinned face had lost its taciturn cast. He was looking at the country, too, but not the way she was. She sensed that he was meeting a beloved and whimsical opponent whose vagaries were a source of satisfaction and amusement.

"Texas," Cebe added complacently, "is the biggest state in the Union. You could tuck Ioway in one corner of Texas, an' you'd need a ketch dog to find it."

Her lips tightened. "Iowa," she said, "is somewhere out West. I came from Ohio."

"I'm always gettin' them crossways in my mind," Cebe apologized. "All them states up there run to the same formation anyway."

Then he pulled up the team hard, half

140

rising from the seat. For a moment Sarah couldn't make out what he was staring at. Suddenly she saw movement on the skyline ahead. It looked like a line of human heads, peering at them. The heads vanished.

Cebe had started to reach for the Henry repeater beneath the seat, but now he settled back and gave the buckskins their heads again. "Bunch of young does," he remarked.

"I'll hold the team, if you want a shot at them," Sarah volunteered.

"Plenty close to home. No use totin' meat thirty miles when it comes right to your door."

Sarah didn't exactly understand why he had reached for his rifle in the first place if he hadn't wanted a shot, nor could she see any sense to the way the trail meandered crazily through the broken prairie. There were straggling patches of brush here and there, and cutbanks which offered momentary relief from the glare of the noon sun, but the trail always recoiled from these havens, avoiding them by wide margins.

She saw Cebe watching the thickets and coulées, and she began watching them, also, hoping to sight whatever game he was seeking. No game appeared. They reached the stream at noon. She was disappointed when Cebe chose a naked sandbar out in the sun to water the horses. She looked longingly at the shade of timber a few hundred yards upstream. Cebe had brought a lunch along but didn't seem in the mood to tarry. They ate as the wagon lurched onward.

With a start, Sarah realized they hadn't passed a human habitation in hours. She inched nearer Cebe. She couldn't help remembering how green Ohio had been when she had left it. Green and peaceful, with its creeks and rivers webbed among wooded, gentle hills. Rail fences and farm houses. Every inch owned and cared for by someone.

Her shoulder touched Cebe's. She drew quickly away and sat primly. She watched the sun creep down the sky. The gold band on her finger was suddenly a manacle, chaining her to this shallow green vastness which had no beginning, no end. She wished the sun would stand still and that night would not come. This land was alien to her. Cebe was alien. Iowa! Ohio! He didn't know one from the other.

They topped a divide, and she saw timber and the glare of another stream. Cebe pointed, pride in his eyes. "There's the place."

Sarah looked at the cabin. Built of post-oak logs, it was new, but beginning to weather to the inevitable color of its background. It had a shingle roof and a rock and mud chimney. As

Cebe lifted her down, she realized with faltering heart that there was but a single room.

A mule and two milk cows hung their heads over the rails of a corral. She saw slab-sided hogs rooting in the brush along the stream. A stack of wild hay, an empty slat crib for corn, and a smokehouse stood in the ruddy glow of sundown. A frost-blackened vegetable patch showed beyond the corncrib, and there was a sizable planting of corn ready for harvest.

They were now gripped by a vast embarrassment. Cebe steeled himself to touch this girl who had only been a photograph to him until this day. Picking her up gingerly, he carried her formally across the threshold. He set her down. Over his shoulder she saw there was but a single bed in the room. It had one leg, the walls serving as its main support. A slow flame kindled in Cebe's face. His big hands began to tighten on her arms. She turned away, suddenly, and he reluctantly freed her. He went out to fetch her brass-bound trunk and carpetbag.

The back log smoldered in the fireplace, and an iron pot dangled from a hook swung to the front. Skillets, a Dutch oven, a shotgun, and a cedar noggin stood on the shelf. The tables and benches were homemade, and the floor was hard-packed clay. Beneath her hoops Sarah's knees were weak as water. The cooking she had done had been on a stove.

An unearthly uproar rose outside, and Sarah screamed. Cebe peered from the door.

"The neighbors," — he grinned — "are givin' us a charivari. It's Aunt Polly Twitty and Uncle Newt. They must've been hidin' in the smokehouse."

The visitors marched into the cabin. Aunt Polly, heavy-set and homespun, tolled a cowbell, and Uncle Newt hammered on an iron triangle.

Aunt Polly drew Sarah against her capacious bosom. "Sakes alive! You ain't half as big as a minute, are you, child? Nothin' but skin an' bones. You need fattenin'."

"Corn cracklin' an' hog jowl will put some talla on you in no time, Missus Buckman," Uncle Newt predicted. "It done wonders for Ma. She had to stand twice in the same place to make a shadda when I married her thirty years ago. Look at her now."

"You have to put up with such talk after you're married to 'em," Aunt Polly sniffed. "Fetch in the eatables, Newt. I fetched along some grub. It's hardly fittin' for a bride to have to worry over a cook fire on her weddin' night."

Sarah lacked appetite as she sat at the repast Uncle Newt and Aunt Polly spread. She kept her eyes away from Cebe.

144

"You've got a right smart cabin for sure, Cebe," Uncle Newt said. "It's a sight more snug than the other one."

"It ought to be," Aunt Polly declared. "The way he slaved to finish it before Sary got here." She beamed on Sarah. "You caught a man with get-up to him, child. Cebe's a worker. There wasn't anythin' here in the clearing last spring except a heap of ashes."

Sarah stared at Cebe. "Ashes! Then you had another cabin here before this one?"

It was Uncle Newt who answered. "Injuns burned Cebe out last fall."

"Indians?" Sarah was sitting straight up. She was remembering the way Cebe had reached for the rifle when the deer showed on the skyline, and how the trail had avoided all thickets that might conceal an enemy. She knew now why Cebe had watered the horses on that open sandbar.

"The C'manches come raidin' through now and then." Uncle New nodded, whittling a toothpick. "Stealin' horses. They'll lift a scalp, too, if'n they get a chance. But 'tain't nothin' like it used to be. They'd come every full moon. They're gettin' scarce nowadays, what with the rangers drawin' pay to keep 'em in hand."

"You're scarin' the child, Newt," Aunt Polly warned. "Pay him no attention, Sary.

145

I've lived ten years on Gum Creek, an' never lost my hair. Cebe will take mighty good care o' you. He savvies Injuns."

Sarah got to her feet. "Why in heaven's name do people come to . . . to an awful place like this?"

Cebe's rawboned face was a little gray. "I figured you understood, Sary," he said slowly. "Ain't there any Indians in Ioway?"

"In Ohio? Wild Indians?" Sarah began laughing shrilly.

Aunt Polly put an arm around her. She gave Uncle Newt a glare. He knew what that meant. He headed for the door. Cebe reluctantly followed him out.

Sarah began to shake and sob against Aunt Polly's bosom. "I can't. . . ."

"Wait, honey," Aunt Polly crooned. "Don't say anything you'll regret afterwards."

"But I can't! I can't! It's this land. So big. So lonely. It shrivels me inside."

"It ain't the land, child. The land is nothin'. It's where you find something else that you stay put. You've got to give yourself a chance. An' you got to give Cebe a chance."

Sarah's swimming eyes were uncomprehending.

"If you learn to like Cebe, then the land will be different to you. I know what I'm talkin' about. I was a picture bride once. The words

146

the parson said over you today don't mean anythin'. I hated the land, too . . . at first. But now I'm happy wherever Newt happens to be."

Afterward Aunt Polly and Uncle Newt pulled out in their wagon for their claim eight miles down the creek. As the rattle of wheels died in the night, Sarah felt the weight of the land settle down on her. Eight miles! And they were neighbors. The only neighbors. Cebe came close, and lifted her chin. He remembered having seen that same misery in the eyes of a bogged deer.

He dropped his hand. "I'll sleep in the hay tonight, Sary," he said.

"I'll . . . keep my bargain with you, Cebe."

"I don't figure it as bein' a bargain, Sary." He drew a blanket from the bed and went out the door, and told her to slide the bar into place. Afterward, she crept into the big bed and lay with her knees huddled almost to her chin.

She welcomed daylight after that long night. But the open fire was a sardonic opponent. She singed her eyebrows, blistered a finger and a thumb getting breakfast. The smoke-side was fried to a black crisp, and the corn cakes were tough and soggy. But Cebe told her he'd never eaten tastier grub. He manfully cleaned his plate.

She wore her new calico frock. This was the dress she had planned for this first day, and she donned it — in spite of everything. She was aware that Cebe's eyes followed her as she moved about.

She watched him drive the wagon into the field. He was standing erect, meeting the jostle of the vehicle with unconscious grace. A faded slouch hat was hung on his unruly dark hair, and the wind whipped his cotton shirt against the flat muscles of his back. He was not, Sarah realized, a man meant to wear store clothes.

His big hands moved with practiced speed in the corn. She saw the flush of achievement and pride of possession in his eyes each time he came in to unload at the crib. But he carried his rifle every instant he was in the fields.

Aunt Polly rode over on a mule in the afternoon and initiated Sarah into the mysteries of preparing hog jowl and pot likker.

"An' save your wood ashes, child. There'll be lye hominy to make soon. An' soap. Cebe will build you an ash hopper as soon as the corn's in."

Sarah nodded. But her smile was forced.

Cebe labored with a breaking plow in the afternoon, fighting to turn new land which he had cleared of brush. He was dusty and sweaty, when he came in at sundown. He cared for the stock and milked the cows. He went to the creek, and, when he returned, he was scrubbed and wearing a clean blue butternut shirt and linseys. He shaved in the yellow glow of the oil lamp. The deftness of his big hands held Sarah's interest.

"Your hair, Sary," he said shyly, as he sat across from her at the table, "looks right nice in the lamplight. You'd think it was dipped in gold. Daytime it's more of a chestnut."

Afterward, when it came time to turn in, he looked at her with veiled hope. When she did not speak, he shouldered his blanket and went out. Coyotes howled in the night. Sarah buried her head in the blankets.

The open fire was less hostile the next morning, and she did not feel as guilty when Cebe showered compliments on her breakfast. The smell of the coffee grinder was a pleasant thing in the room.

A freight string, hauling cowhides, passed by at noon, heading for Chancellor's. The jerkline teamsters were rough-handed, unshaven men, but they regarded Sarah with awe and deference as they paused briefly. Sarah watched them crawl on across the prairie into the horizon, and her hands were at her throat. She turned to find Cebe, standing at the cabin corner, a deep gravity in his eyes. He took off his hat, ran his fingers through his thick, damp hair. He looked at the fields which he had broken to the plow and brought to harvest, and at the log house which he had built to endure. The lift was gone from his shoulders, and his square mouth showed defeat.

"I'll rig the wagon in the mornin', Sary," he said heavily, "an' take you back."

Sarah choked up a bit. "I never said I wanted to go back."

"You don't have to say it."

"I'll wait until . . . until you get ready for the mill, Cebe," she managed to say. "And the plowing is done. That's only fair. I don't want to cause you an extra trip."

He thought it over. "Plowing always waits for a man. I'll have the corn cleaned up soon. Tomorrow . . . or next day."

She watched him in the field the next morning. He worked with the same tireless thrust of power, but no longer did he pause occasionally to survey his fields with pride brightening his face. He merely shucked corn. He did not glance at her, when it came time to turn in for the night. He only said good night and went out into the moonlight. Sarah looked at the split log door that closed behind him. She stood before the fire for a long time, her hands clasped tightly at her back. The warmth of the embers repelled the frosty chill of the autumn night. The fragrance of the coffee lingered in the room. She slowly undressed and got into bed.

With breakfast out of the way the next morning, she polished the cookingware and used the turkey feather broom until the cabin was pin-neat. Afterward she wandered to the field where Cebe worked in his tireless manner. She watched him a while. "May I help?" she asked.

Cebe nodded. "Two pair of hands will shorten the job," he remarked.

Sarah's head jerked up. "I didn't mean it that way," she exploded. "I only wanted to help." She ran back to the cabin, holding her skirts high, slim ankles twinkling.

That night, after Cebe had gone to the haystack without giving her a glance, she dug her mirror from her trunk. "Skin and bones," she said bitterly.

The corn was in, and Cebe had a wagonload ready to haul to Chancellor's for grinding. The moon was full, and he had gone to the haystack for the night. Sarah slowly packed her trunk, laid out the dove-gray traveling dress. He was taking her to Chancellor's in the morning. There she would take the stage for Galveston to embark for New Orleans and Ohio. She dabbed at her eyes as she closed the trunk. She got into bed and huddled up.

"Talla on my ribs," she moaned, and began to weep. The back log in the fireplace chuckled, burst into small flame, and fell into dull red drowse again.

How long she lay there, trying not to think, she did not know. Then Cebe whispered her name at the door. She sat up with a jerk. She had not barred the door since that first night, and he entered like a shadow. The faint fire glow touched his face. He carried his rifle.

Vividly she knew! She was at his side, fingers wrapped around his arm. That contact repelled the freezing gust of terror that rose inside her. "It's a big war party," he whispered. "Too many to fight. The mule was nervous, an' that awakened me. I saw some o' them cross the cornfield."

He threw a blanket over her nightdress, as he spoke, and pulled her to the door. He took one last look over his shoulder at the room before leading the way out.

They slid along the wall, keeping to its shadow, avoiding the sharp, white line of moonlight. Cebe pushed her down. On their stomachs they wriggled away from the cabin. Sarah felt the flaky rubble of frost beneath her fingers.

She heard the mule snorting in the corral.

Faint in the night was a taint, like the smell of a wild animal — but different. They were clear of the cabin, when she heard the rush of moccasins. She did not look back, for Cebe was dragging her ahead toward the creek brush.

They reached the brush, crawled deep into its shadow. She hardly felt the icy embrace of the stream as she waded into it at his side, for in her ears was the war whoop — a gusty sound that pierced to the marrow. "They didn't sight us," Cebe murmured. "But they'll look around."

They were in water to their knees, and then to their waists. The brush closed over them as Cebe worked beneath a cutbank. He held his rifle clear. She saw the moonlight filtering through the foliage above and felt her bare feet sinking into the soft mud of the bottom.

Cebe drew her to his side, and they stood to their chins in the water. The sullen glint of fire showed from the direction of the cabin.

"Oh, Cebe," Sarah moaned.

Soon the flames were soaring high. The yelling had stopped.

Cebe forced her head back so that she lay half afloat with only her lips and nose above the surface. He sank low in the water beside her, keeping only his rifle dry.

Vaguely she sensed the death flitting through

the brush. Once she heard the thickets rustle. But Cebe's hand, supporting her shoulders, was steady, reassuring.

The red glare blotted out the moonlight. The crib and wagon were burning now. A burst of brands and sparks gushed into the sky, and she knew the cabin roof had fallen.

She thought of the aroma of fresh-ground coffee and frying smokeside. She remembered the vast pride with which Cebe had once looked upon the house he had built with his own hands. All these things were gone now.

The fury of the fire faded, and it was safe to lift their heads again. Warily Cebe guided her through the icy water clear of the brush. They waded out, and he stood listening for long, motionless minutes.

"I heard ponies pullin' out," he finally murmured. "I figure they've lit a shuck."

He left her, and she waited an eternity. The nightgown was a shroud of clammy ice, and the cold shook her with ruthless violence.

He came back at last. "No sign of 'em."

"The Twittys," Sarah chattered. "Aunt Polly and Uncle Newt. They'll be scalped."

"The braves were headin' the other way," he said. "If anything happened to the Twittys, it happened before the Indians got to our . . . my place."

She didn't miss the way he corrected himself in using the possessive. She kept thinking dismally about it as he led her to the warmth of the glowing heap of logs that had been a cabin. That figure of speech seemed the most important thing that had happened on this night.

Daybreak came. Sarah looked toward the corral, and did not look again. The two cows were down, lanced and dead. The mule lay dead beside them. The buckskin team was gone. The crib and loaded wagon were wind-fanned pyres of smoldering corn. It was all gone. To the last timber in the cabin. All that Cebe had built with sweat and pride. Only the fields remained as they had been before.

A score of armed white men came riding by after sunup. They were rangers and settlers who had been trailing the war party. Uncle Newt and Aunt Polly were with them. The raid had missed the Twitty place.

"I'm headin' for Chancellor's," Aunt Polly said as she took charge of Sarah, "until things simmer down."

"I've got a cash account at Chancellor's store, Aunt Polly," Cebe said. "See that Sary gets the first stage to Austin. There's money enough in my account to buy fare for her to Ioway . . . Ohio, I mean." He took Sarah's hand, held it gently in his big palm. "I'll send more money from time to time, Sary," he promised. "Whenever I can get my hands on some."

Sarah didn't exactly understand that he wasn't going to Chancellor's with her until he mounted one of the spare horses the rangers had brought with them. She tried to run and stop him, but it was too late. They were riding fast, heading up Gum Creek on the trail of the Comanches.

She looked at Aunt Polly and Uncle Newt, and the three saddle-worn men who had remained to act as their bodyguard to Chancellor's. "There'll be a fight," she said, and now her voice was like dry sand in her throat.

"I reckon," Uncle Newt nodded, looking enviously after the departing riders. "Some o' them C'manches won't ever see the Staked Plains ag'in. Mebbe none of 'em. They'll. . . ." Uncle Newt's voice faded.

For Sarah was on her knees, and her lips were moving.

It was four days later when Cebe rode into sight of his claim again. He was mounted on one of his buckskins. The other buckskin would never come back again.

Cebe had a Comanche shield and a bow slung on his back as trophies. A dark, dust-caked beard filmed his jaws. He slid slowly from the horse and looked at the soot-smudged girl who stood where the cabin had burned. The ashes and charred logs had been cleared away, and the area was leveled and ready for new base logs once more.

Sarah wore a pair of men's breeches and a butternut shirt. She had pulled her hair into a tight knot at the back of her head. The piece of braided rawhide she used as a belt served to set off her figure.

"Look, Cebe," she said. "I fetched enough food back from Chancellor's to carry us a while until we can jerk some venison. I've salvaged the kettle and Dutch oven and the pothook. And I piled up the ashes. I'll run the ashes through the hopper after you get time to build one. Aunt Polly promised to teach me how to make lye hominy and soap. We can get the cabin up before winter sets in, with me giving you a hand with the work and doing the cooking and. . . ."

Afterward, when she got a chance to talk again, she cuddled closer in his arms. "It's so pretty here on the creek," she whispered. "I don't ever want to leave it, Cebe, unless . . . unless you do. And I never did bar the door against you after . . . after that first night."

The Day the Outlaws Came

Hay shaking was something new to Dan Beals. There was, he admitted, an art to it that a man had to acquire. It was a matter of craftsmanship, like heeling a calf or handling a branding iron. Dan Beals had never seen a job he couldn't lick, if he put his mind to it. He swung the scythe energetically, trying to discipline himself to the pendulum-like precision he had absently noticed in other men while riding past harvest fields on his cow horse in the past. Swing and recover — swing and recover — swing and. . . .

He regretted that he hadn't paid more attention to the hay hands at ranches where he had punched cattle. He might have picked up some pointers that would have lightened his task now. He hadn't been told, when he hired out as tender at Brandy Flat stage station, that putting up fodder was part of the job. That knowledge likely wouldn't have made any difference, anyway, for a man with a wife and two sprouts to support couldn't be choosy, with all the outfits laying off riders.

The voice of Pal, his ten-year-old son, sounded from the black willows along the torpid creek: "Dad, I durned near got one. Knocked the fuzz off'n him. Come an' see where I barked the tree."

"Can't right now," Dan replied absently. "I'm busy."

Pal was working with his slingshot on the jays and gophers around the station. Thus far his score was a blank. Sistie's sun-bleached yellow hair bobbed up from the shadow of the sod stage station where she was patting mud pies.

"Make him stop killing the birdies, Daddy," she demanded. "Make him come an' play with me."

"He ain't . . . hasn't killed anything yet," Dan assured his daughter. He lifted his voice to the boy. "Pal, you play with Sistie a while."

Dan swung the scythe. Stubborn tenacity was in his weathered, rawboned face. At times he would be led to hope that he was mastering the art. Then again he would flounder. The scythe would haul and teeter him around. He was cutting hay, but it was by brute force rather than skill. The stubble he left was fluted and crocky. It looked like the haircut he had given Pal the day he had mistakenly decided that he could do a better barbering job than his wife.

The sun baked the back of his neck and burned through his blue cotton shirt where it stretched tight against the flat of his lean back. Pollen and dust mingled with his sweat. His back muscles were feeling it now, and that made him remember that he was nearing forty. The thought aroused a chain of dismal thoughts that had grown all too familiar lately. Forty years old, and here he was working as a hostler and flunky at a branch-line stage station, with the world rolling by, with the kids going barefoot all summer to save shoe leather, and with Nettie still forced to string out every penny to the limit of its value.

Dan recalled the ranch venture he had started and the mining prospects he had pursued with the same zeal with which he tackled the mowing job. More than once he had seemed on his way to a solid future, only to have it cut from under his feet. He and Nettie had seen their droughts and blizzards and had had their share of doctor bills and debts. They owed no debts now. To Dan, a debt was something to worry about. Freedom had been his most cherished possession as a rider of the open range, and it was his creed to be beholden to no man. Nettie felt the same way about it, and they had cleaned up the doctor bills before planning anything else.

Pal came out of the brush, stuffing the slingshot in his hip pocket. Enviously he watched Dan swing the shining blade, and then demanded a chance to try his hand at it.

Dan grinned and refused. "You ain't . . . aren't . . . big enough yet, button. You got to eat a few more barrels of flour. You'd likely chop off a leg. Some day, though."

"How soon you quittin' this job?" Pal demanded. "When are we movin' up to the ranch?"

"Pretty soon, I hope," Dan muttered.

Dan had done a lot of talking and daydreaming about a little range claim up in the Rubies that could be picked up cheap. The deal could be swung for a thousand dollars.

"There's plenty of room for a cow man to spraddle out in the Rubies, if he keeps his saddle polished," Dan had said.

The kids, listening to Dan and Nettie talk about it, considered the thing assured. They talked about that ranch as though it were their own. They didn't know how slowly the dollars were accumulating in the sock that Nettie kept cached out somewhere in the soddy. The forty a month which the Wagon Mountain Stage Lines paid its tenders didn't leave much margin. It would take time, Dan was thinking. Too long, perhaps.

The rattle of wheels and a shout jerked him out of his reverie. He whirled. With a snort of dismay, he dropped the scythe and began hot-footing it.

161

The upbound stage from Doble was already swinging out of the creek ford upon the station. Dan was in the habit of depending on Nettie to keep him apprised of stage time, but, occupied with his task, he had forgotten that she had gone to Doble in the carry-all, on a store and post office trip.

Pal, who had learned the importance of split-minute mail schedules, raced along at Dan's heels, his sun-browned face taut with consternation. "Good gawsh, Dad," he panted. "We pulled a batter, didn't we?"

They raced into the barn. Dan slung collars and worked headstalls while his son darted around the horses, taking care of breeching and belly bands. Even amid that flurry of haste, Pal kept an eye on Dan, attempting to copy his father's mannerisms and stern-set expressions.

The stage ground to a stop in the yard as Dan fumbled with the pole chains. He glanced out and braced himself for trouble. It had to be his luck, he thought, that Kirby Leach, the division super, would be riding this stage out from Doble today.

Leach hit the ground running and descended with weighty fury on the barn. He was a sandy-haired, blustering man, with a wide expanse of white shirt front. "So!" he stormed. "Asleep on the job. Or are you drunk?"

"Time slipped up on me," Dan said.

"Your job will slip away from you the same way, Beals. You're delaying a mail stage. Only a week ago I got a report that you were late with the team on this same run."

Ben Lemon, the driver, descended and put in a word. "That wasn't Dan's fault last week, Mister Leach. It was a green swing horse thet lamed himself after Dan had. . . ."

"I'll take care of this, Lemon," the stage boss fumed, and turned to worry Dan. "Step lively, Beals. Can't you move faster than a crawl, you . . . you lunkhead?"

Dan turned, rose to his lank height. He measured the point on Leach's big jowls where a fist would do the most damage. Then he saw Sistie, standing in the background among her mud pies, a frightened look on her thin, sensitive face. Her bare legs were long and reedy, for she was growing right out of her dresses this summer. And there was Pal, in his patched jeans that Nettie had made over from Dan's cast-offs, staring with shocked resentment.

Dan let his muscles go slack. He hooked up the whipples and led the team out to the waiting stage. He cleared the sweating roans which had made the run out from Doble, and hooked the fresh band of bays to the Concord. The bays were solid-bottomed, heavyhaunched animals, built for power rather than speed. From Brandy Creek station the trail quit the sage flats and scaled Brandy Ridge on a series of switchbacks that looked like the track of a sidewinder. Beyond the ridge the route pitched higher up the timbered cheek of Wagon Mountain to Clum City where stamp mills thundered and hard-rock men burrowed pay ore from deep formation.

Dan noticed that J. C. Clum was riding inside. Along with him were two husky, slant-hatted men whose faces fitted the cigar stubs that jutted from the hard corners of their mouths. Dan knew these two by sight. They were express company trouble-shooters, employed to ride treasure guard.

J. C. Clum, who was an old-timer, nodded placidly to Dan. "Howdy," he said. "Them two kids of yours have growed a foot this summer."

Dan, busy lining the team for the driver, only jerked his head in acknowledgment. J. C. Clum continued to eye the freckled boy and the leggy girl. His puckered eyes were wise with age. He had spent the biggest part of a lifetime prospecting, or as he put it: " 'Bout a year prospectin' an' the rest o' the forty huntin' my burros." Then J.C. had hit the Hattie C strike which was the genesis of Clum City on the mountain. J.C. was shading seventy now, and the wealth was rolling in, for the Hattie C was a bonanza. He had named the mine after an only daughter who had died thirty years in the past.

Kirby Leach was pecking at Dan's heels. "Hustle, man," he goaded. "Blazes. Are you all thumbs?"

Dan turned to him. "Mister . . . ," he began. Then he let it ride. He passed the reins to Ben Lemon and stepped back. Leach scrambled inside, tucked his coattails beneath him.

"You'll hear from me later about this delay," Leach assured Dan. "See that you have the stock out when we come down the grade. We'll need the duns. I intend to make connections with the Limited at Winnemucca tonight. We're bringing out the Hattie C clean-up today. If we miss that train through any more blundering on your part, I'll skin you alive."

Ben Lemon kicked off the brake, and the bays snatched the Concord out of the yard.

Leach leaned from a window, shouting back. "That doesn't mean you can shirk the job on the hay," he bawled at Dan. "We won't be back till sundown. You can put in three good hours on the fodder before getting out the duns. I want a showing made on that field. I want. . . ."

The stage carried his querulous voice out of

range. Sistie blinked, and her brown eyes were wet as she stared after the stage. Pal moved a little closer to Dan, watched the vehicle veer out of sight into the talus rubble and presently emerge higher up on the open trail. The bays were down to a walk now, shoving hard into the collars.

Kirby Leach was looking down. From that elevation he had a bird's eye view of the hayfield in the flat and could estimate the progress Dan had made.

"You ain't skeered of him, are you, Dad?" Pal demanded hopefully.

"You mustn't say 'ain't,' " his sister admonished. "Remember what Mamma told you. You ought to have said 'aren't.' Ain't that right, Dad?"

Pal ignored this interruption. "You could handle him if you was of a mind, couldn't you, Dad?" he persisted.

Dan was standing hip-shot, with his thumbs hooked in his belt. The boy started to copy that posture, then changed his mind. He shifted his bare feet and scrubbed his sunburned hair with a nervous hand.

Dan felt something akin to desolation enter his mind. He felt that he had lost caste with his son. "Let's rustle some dinner," he said gruffly. "I'm hungry."

As he turned toward the door, a man,

wearing a faded, checked shirt, saddle-worn breeches, and a sweat-stained range hat stepped around the corner of the sod building, leading a saddle horse.

"Howdy," the stranger said. "Mind if I water up?"

Dan indicated the horse trough and its bubbling stream of piped water. The stranger filled his canteen, put his mouth to the pipe, and drank noisily. He was in need of a shave and had quick, sun-faded eyes that missed no details around the place.

"You the boss here?" he asked. "Are them your two kids?"

Dan nodded. The stranger inquired the distance to Doble, and rode on his way, merging into the sun glare on the flats to the east.

"Where'd that fella come from?" Dan frowned. "Did you kids know he was hangin' around the station?"

They shook their heads. Dan walked around the building. The hoof marks showed that the rider had come up from the creek brush on the blind side of the sod building. The way Dan read the sign the man had been standing back there out of sight for some minutes.

Dan shrugged. The unshaven man might be a 'puncher who had come in from of the outfits in the Conejo Hills. Then again, he might be wanted somewhere and had elected to stay out of sight of the express-company specials aboard the stage. At any rate he was gone now.

Dan went into the soddy, fired the cook-stove, and heated the leftover from the previous evening's beef stew, as per Nettie's departing instructions. Pal and Sistie ate in a hurry and raced back to their play. Dan chewed moodily. He was remembering the way Pal had, for once, refused to imitate his mannerisms. That hurt.

He felt the desolation grow inside of him. He pushed back his plate finally, put on his hat, and fortified his mind for the ordeal of three hours in the hayfield. He turned, hearing a step. Two men stood in the open rear door, which looked out across the hay flat. They had six-shooters in their hands.

One of them said: "Take it easy. You won't get hurt 'less you ask for it."

He was the unshaven stranger in the faded, checked shirt who had ridden east thirty minutes earlier. The other was taller, dryer, harder. His nose was thin, with the skin drawn purple-tight across the bridge. Above his blue bandanna neckerchief rose a wedge-shaped head, mounted on a lean neck. A dewlap of loose skin hung under his chin. It was that dewlap more than anything else that caused Dan to recall the descriptions he had heard of Yermo Zett.

They advanced on Dan and ran hands over him to make sure he was unarmed. He was prodded into a corner.

"Bring in the kids," Yermo Zett ordered. Then he moved a swift pace back as he saw Dan's expression change, and added narrowly: "Stand hitched, you."

Dan's stomach pulled into a knot as he heard Sistie cry out in terror. Two more hard-visaged men appeared then, one carrying the girl, the other hustling Pal along by the arm. Pal's eyes were bugged out from a face that was ashen with fear.

"Daddy!" Sistie wailed.

"Make them kids shut up," Yermo Zett ordered.

Dan took Sistie in his arms, and nodded Pal to stand by his side. "It's all right," he soothed them. "Don't be scared."

The girl clung to him, hiding her face. Pal swallowed noisily, and squeezed close against Dan's leg.

"What time'll the down stage pull in from Clum City?" Yermo Zett demanded of Dan.

The unshaven man spoke up. "I told you I heard that blaze-faced stage boss say it'd be aroun' sundo. . . ."

"Shut up, Cal," Zett snapped. "I want this peeler to answer."

Dan saw the layout now. He recalled that Kirby Leach had blurted out the information that the Hattie C bullion would be on the down stage. And Cal, which seemed to be the name by which the unshaven one was known, had been standing back of the station, listening.

Dan hesitated. "I couldn't say," he finally answered.

Yermo Zett laughed. "I just wanted to see if you thought you was tough. We'll take that out of you. We know what's on the stage. Might as well make yourselves to home, boys. We've got three, four hours to kill."

Pal's hand was trembling in Dan's palm. "What'll they do, Dad?" he whispered.

"Don't worry, Son," he counseled. "They're only foolin'."

"They ain't," the boy choked. "They're robbers."

"Sure," Zett boasted. "We're outlaws, kid. How'd you like to have me slice off your ears an' wear 'em as a watch charm?"

"Lay off the boy," Dan said, his lips gray.

Yermo Zett hit Dan across the mouth with the muzzle of his gun. The sight tore a gash in Dan's cheek, and blood trickled from a split lip. Sistie wailed again, while Pal began to sob.

"Muzzle them damned kids," the outlaw raged.

Dan stroked Sistie's hair, whispering in her ear until her terror faded. She kept her face buried against him so that she couldn't see the outlaws. Pal hid back of Dan.

"Keep them kids in hand," Zett snapped. "An' follow orders. We're all stayin' here until the stage comes back. Then you'll get the dun team out an' have it ready as usual, when they roll up, so they won't be suspicious that anything is wrong. We'll step out as you're changin' teams. They won't be expectin' anything here at the station. We'll get the drop on 'em. They won't be able to put up much of a fight. Do you savvy?"

Dan nodded. "I savvy."

They let him move to a bench. Pal huddled close to him, and Sistie cried softly in his arms.

Cal spoke up suddenly. "The stage boss was givin' this jigger hell about gettin' the hay cut," he said. "Told him to make a showin' this afternoon or get canned. They can see the hay flat as they come down the grade. Do you reckon they might notice there's been no work done an' maybe begin to wonder why?"

Yermo Zett studied it over a moment. "Maybe so," he said. "Then again, maybe not. No use overlookin' a bet, though." He jerked a thumb at Dan. "Drag out there and chop hay," he commanded. "We want this to look good from every angle." Sistie clung tighter to Dan's neck, and the outlaw flew into a rage. "Do what I tell you, mister. The kids stay here in the shack with us. You wouldn't want to do anything to make me real mad, would you? You stay in plain sight in that hayfield every minute. Do that an' nothin' will happen to anybody. You get what I mean, I reckon."

Dan felt fear crawling all through him now. He had never believed half the stories that were told about the Zett gang of desperadoes. But he did now. They were vicious, depraved, lacking in any quality of mercy or compassion. He spoke to Pal. "I'm going out and cut hay, Son," he said quietly. "You stay with Sistie. Don't be afraid. Do what these men tell you. I'll be out there within hearing all the time." Dan could see the sick terror that throbbed in the boy. "Show 'em that you're game and tough, Son," he added gently.

The boy braced up. He put his arms around Sistie as Dan placed her beside him on the bench. "Don't cry, Sistie," Pal said shakily. "See! I ain't cryin'."

Dan stood, looking down at them with fierce pride. He looked at the outlaw. "Zett," he said slowly, "if either of these kids get hurt. . . ." He turned and walked out into the hay flat. He picked up the scythe and began swinging.

The afternoon heat weighed upon the field with drugging force, but Dan no longer felt it. Dust and pollen rose, filming his face, gathering in the creases of his shirt. He swung the blade, working his way across the face of the stand away from the sod buildings.

Silence settled over the stage station, but each time he glanced that way he could see the outlaws, watching from the kitchen door. An hour snailed by. An L Bar K rider, dragging the sage for strays, came off the range, pulled up a moment to talk to Dan about the heat and the weather, then rode on southward after watering at the trough. The rider merged with the roll of the flat land in the direction of Sheep Springs, and Dan continued to cut hay.

A mule haul lumbered up the trail, bound for Clum City. The freighter lifted his whip in salute to Dan, but did not stop. The outfit bucked Brandy Ridge grade, and for an hour it was in sight off and on, creeping back and forth up the zigzag trail until it finally tipped the rim and shoved into the deeper mountain.

Dan kept the scythe going and watched the sun wheel down the sky toward Wagon Peak. He worked his way again across the east face of the field to the creek brush, then started his cut westward up the flat. This carried him farther from the stage station and left an intervening square of waist-high hay two hundred yards wide between him and the buildings.

The armed men kept watch on him across that eye-level lake of standing fodder. Dan's head and shoulders were visible above it, and they could see his scythe flash in the sun as he worked. He was careful never to stoop down. He remained always in sight of the men in the door as he labored. But now a harsh tension was upon him, and his breath was fast and dry and rasping in his throat. He kept glancing eastward, praying that Nettie, who usually made a day of it in town, would not come back ahead of time. His prayers in that respect were answered, for the trail in the sage flats remained vacant.

The sun rimmed the mountain. Long shadows marched across the hayfield and on into the distance on the flats. Dan, looking up, saw the stage swing into sight high on the Brandy Ridge grade and begin whipping dust around the switchbacks in its descent. He dropped the scythe and hurried to the station. A savage excitement held the outlaws now, for they were also peering from windows, watching the distant stage.

"Snake out your fresh team," Zett hoarsely

ordered Dan. "Act jest like everythin' was peaceful here."

Dan looked at Pal and Sistie. They were wan, but dry-eyed. In fact, Dan had a hunch that Pal was beginning to enjoy his experience. This bout with outlaws would be something for a kid to yarn about at school in the fall.

Dan hurried to the barn and harnessed the duns. He kept glancing at the ridge trail, watching the coach thread its way nearer, vanishing and reappearing around the curves, growing larger. He brought the six-horse team around to the yard with the whipple-trees dragging dust and the pole chains jingling. He spotted them before the door of the little waiting room and heard the outlaws hunker themselves out of sight inside the open door a few yards away.

The stage passed down the last leg of the open trail above and dipped out of sight into the scrub cedar and boulder jumble on the talus foot. That was a five-minute trail through the talus, but the five minutes passed and lengthened into ten while Dan stood there, thinking of Pal and Sistie who were inside with the hidden outlaws.

At last the coach came rattling out of the dry coulée, and the team stretched out as they felt the flat country beneath their hoofs. Ben

Lemon was alone on the box, and, as the coach came up, Dan glimpsed Kirby Leach's white shirt bosom and J. C. Clum's gray slouch hat in the shadowy interior. Ben Lemon looked at Dan as he tooled the team into the stage yard and set the brake. Their eyes locked for an instant.

J. C. Clum clambered stiffly from the step, flexing his muscles. Dan saw that there was only one of the shotgun guards inside with Kirby Leach. Leach made his presence known. "Shake a leg, Beals," he yelled. "Lively now."

Dan moved to free the jaded team from the rig. Behind him he heard the rush of boots as the outlaws came stampeding through the door into the open.

"Lift your hands," Yermo Zett bawled. "Up with. . . ."

A gun exploded inside the stage. The bullet cut Yermo Zett down in mid-stride. He dived forward, firing a useless shot as he went down.

Many things were happening as that first shot roared. Ben Lemon tumbled from the box to the offside of the coach and came up with a six-shooter in his hand. J. C. Clum had shaken a pistol out of his coat and was rabbiting for cover back of the water trough. He reached it and crouched there, spotted in a flanking position.

Dan ducked around the dun team at the same time, using the animals as a momentary protection. He could hear the gun inside the stage roaring again, and he caught a glimpse of the unshaven outlaw reeling around with a spurt of dust drifting lazily from the front of his faded shirt where a bullet had whacked home. The express-company trouble-shooter inside the coach was doing the shooting, going about it with business-like speed. It had all been done with prearranged precision. The remaining two outlaws dug in their boots, halting their rush, while terror burned in their faces as they understood that they were in a deadfall.

"Stand your hand," J. C. Clum yelled. "Hold your fire, Jerry. We've got 'em."

The two tried to turn and dive back into the stage station, but someone inside slammed the door in their faces before they reached it. They were caught in the open, flanked two ways. They crouched a second and heard J. C. Clum's repeated order to surrender. The fight went out of them with a rush, and they dropped their guns, shouting hoarsely for mercy.

Dan raced to the back and entered the kitchen. Pal and Sistie were crouching there, and they came rushing into his arms. The second express-company guard was inside with them, grinning. It was he who had slammed the door upon the surviving desperadoes. He lowered the hammer of his gun and slapped Dan on the back.

"J.C. guessed they was holdin' the kids in the house," he said. "He sent me hustlin' through the talus and around to the back. They held the stage in the talus a few minutes to give me time to circle."

Dan lifted Sistie, took Pal's hand, and walked out. The unshaven outlaw was lying stretched out, breathing hard.

J. C. Clum straightened from an inspection of Yermo Zett. "Gone under," he said. "An' good riddance."

Kirby Leach was barging excitedly around. He rushed toward Dan. "My congratulations, Beals," he said magnanimously. "A smart stunt, I must admit. I didn't think you had it in you. We'll forget about that reprimand I promised you. The company avoided a heavy loss through this piece of work."

Dan released Pal's hand. He reached out, snagged Kirby Leach's florid nose between the crook of his fingers. Then he pressed down with his thumb. Leach emitted a roar of pain and went to his knees. Dan released him and stepped back.

J. C. Clum looked at the stage boss whose eyes were streaming. "You ought to have known better'n to insult a man thataway," he remarked. "Beals wasn't thinkin' about the bullion, when he pulled this stunt. He did it to save our lives. The Zett gang would have shot some of us. They like to see blood spilled. It's the way they're built, I reckon." J.C. eyed Dan sternly. "But you was a cussed fool at that, Beals," he criticized. "Risking the kids thataway. It'd gone hard with 'em, if Zett had guessed what you was up to out in the hay."

One of the captured outlaws lifted his head sullenly. "What'd this feller do?" he asked. "How'd he tip you that we was bushed up here in the station?"

J.C. chuckled. "He done a little printin' with his scythe. He carved Yermo Zett's initials in letters twenty feet long on the fur side o' the field where he was working. He carved an arrow pointing to the stage house. We read the message as we come down the grade. That was all we needed to know. Y. Z. are purty well-known initials in this country."

Kirby Leach got to his feet, holding his throbbing beak. "I'll discharge you for this, Beals," he raged. "I'll. . . ."

"Shut up," J. C. Clum said sourly. "Beals has already quit. A man with five thousand dollars in his poke don't need any job hustling stock for a stage jerk. There're plenty of good cow spreads in this country that can be took over for less."

"Five thousand?" Dan gasped.

J.C. indicated the stage. "I ain't a piker," he stated. "Neither is the express company. There's near onto seventy thousand dollars' worth of bullion in the boot. I'll see that you get the usual reward. Pay it out'n my own pocket if necessary. I got more money than a man needs, anyway." He grinned at Pal and Sistie. "Maybe you'd let me call around at your outfit once in a while," he added wistfully. "I had a girl once. Wanted a boy, too. But now I haven't got even a girl. Her name was Harriet. I called her Hattie."

Wheels rattled, and Nettie, driving the carry-all, appeared out of the creek ford. She rose, staring at the scene in the stage yard, and her quiet brown eyes were wide with sudden fear. Dan strode to meet her, taking Pal and Sistie. He lifted her from the rig, marveling as he always did at the way she seemed always so cool and neat and fresh and young.

"The kids are all right," he said.

"We sure are," Pal chimed in. "Me 'n' Dad took care of Sistie, Mom. We trapped a gang of outlaws that tried to stick up the stage. Dad took a fall out of that big-mouthed stage boss, too. Twisted his nose for him an' made him holler uncle. Ain't that right, Dad?" Pal was trying to deepen his voice to the same pitch as Dan's as he spoke.

"Don't say 'ain't,' Brother," his sister said reprovingly. "He should have said 'isn't.' Ain't that right, Mamma?"

Pal ignored her. He lengthened his stride to walk in step with Dan as they moved toward the stage station. He watched Dan closely, copying Dan's mannerisms to the letter. And in his eyes shown a mighty pride in his father.

Five Aces West

I

"CARAVAN OF DESPAIR"

The caravan surged through the bleak, driving rain and hub-deep mud of the Laramie plains with arrogant, resistless power, spurning the elements and spurning the evidences of disaster which lay on every hand: for this trail was strewn with the bones of animals and the junked wagons of so many thousands who had failed in the past. Seven hundred miles astern was Leavenworth and the Missouri settlements. A few miles ahead stood Fort Emigrant on the Platte River. Nightfall would find them camped there. Beyond were the Rockies and the Idaho country where some of them were bound with trade to be bartered for furs. Still farther — much farther — were the destinations of the remainder: Oregon, California, or the busy silver camps of the Washoe in Nevada.

The travelers were well equipped to wind their way through to their various objectives. There were thirty canvas-hooded wagons in the line, each built of oak and hickory and bowwood. Even the lightest of them had eight corn-fed, cat-hammed oxen in span. The bigger Pittsburgh freighters, loaded to their hoops, were each powered by fourteen plodding beasts which were the pick of the Missouri bullyards.

The caravan made a picture of primitive force and even of grandeur against the drab background of the rain-swept plains, and a regret touched Duke Cool, as he rode nearer, that it was not within his skill to preserve such a vital scene in canvas and color. Duke Cool was regarded as an artist in his particular vocation, but he had never used a palette or painter's brush in his life. Still, he had an eye for beauty of this kind, as well as an appreciation of the allure of a pretty feminine face or a glance from a flirtatious eye. However, it was the more practical matter of finance and ethics that had caused him to look up this particular wagon train as he headed westward, bound for the Washoe. As he rode among the lurching wagons, his dark eyes scanned the faces of the bullwhackers and swampers and overseers in search of the man he sought.

His passage aroused a faint antagonism among the muddy, leather-booted men who had not had opportunity to shave or furbish themselves recently. But it also kindled a flutter of animated interest among the petti-coated members of the company, who peered from beneath lifted wagon flaps or from the shelter of the towering bows.

To all of them, even the middle-aged and motherly, Duke Cool accorded a courtly bow, lifting his fine beaver hat. But to the youngest, and especially the comeliest, he swept his hat elegantly low, and his white teeth showed in the warmest of smiles against his olive-tan, handsome features. He singled out one girl in particular, and his flashy palomino single-footed grandly at a touch of his knee. The girl was fair-haired and sat like a queen beneath the forward bow of a big Springfield freighter. Slim-throated, with proud features framed in a fashionable poke bonnet, she wore a gold thimble on her slender finger as she toyed with her needlework.

"A thousand pardons, miss," Duke Cool said, leaning from the saddle as if fearing to miss the music of her voice. "This, I trust, is the caravan captained by Nathanial Standish?"

There was perhaps a trace of cool calcula-tion in her violet eyes. Duke Cool excused this on the grounds that she was, no doubt, much sought after and, therefore, experi-enced in classifying her suitors. What she saw seemed to meet approval. Beneath his ulster Duke Cool wore a fawn-gray broadcloth afternoon coat and bell-bottomed checked trousers which were obviously the product of a fashionable St. Louis tailor. His pleated shirt was immaculate in spite of the weather. A pigeon's blood ruby smoldered against the background of his jade green stock. His tooled-leather saddle was pointed with horn silver. Even the sleek, mouse-colored pack mule which carried his belongings sported a red tassel on its hackamore.

"This is the Standish company," she acknowledged.

Duke Cool's delighted expression indicated that he was her devoted slave for being the bearer of such glad tidings. The fact was that he had known since leaving Julesburg that this was the caravan he sought. He knew, from descriptions given him, that this girl was the daughter of Nathanial Standish.

"Ah!" he smiled. "I trust then that we shall be fellow travelers on the remainder of this tedious journey. I, too, am bound overland. One more favor, I beg of you. Is a certain gentleman named Gan Keeler a member of this company?"

"You should find Keeler among the bull-whackers, I imagine," she shrugged. "He is wagon boss for Mister Brady Bledsoe. You will find him riding ahead with my father, Nathanial Standish."

A chiding voice spoke from the depths of the wagon, and she withdrew at once. Duke was favored by a haughty glance from the girl's mother, who was petulant-faced and tired of travel.

Duke replaced his hat and rode jauntily ahead. Brady Bledsoe, riding pilot with Nathanial Standish, twisted in the saddle and identified Cool without pleasure. The name of the overland trading company Brady Bledsoe owned was painted on the tilts of eight of the heavily laden wagons. Bledsoe's manner indicated that he was not overjoyed by Duke Cool's appearance on the scene. They had met on a certain occasion in the past.

Duke singled out a bull-necked, black-jowled man, riding a saddle mule as he oversaw the efforts of Bledsoe's 'whackers.

"Greetings, Keeler," Duke said, as he pulled up alongside the man. "I learned in Julesburg that you were accompanying this train. It is a raw, blustery day on which to transact business. I trust I am not inconveniencing you."

Gan Keeler's small, cloudy eyes went sullen and hostile. "What's eatin' you, Cool?" he demanded.

Duke produced a small leather pocket case, opened it, and brought out several slips of paper. "These," he said, "are IOUs signed by you, which I held as obligations after a poker game in Saint Louis last spring. You neglected to take care of the matter before leaving town, my friend. The total is seven hundred and fifty dollars."

Gan Keeler was slab-muscled, deep-chested. His tough, thick features bore the scars of more than one barroom and wagon-camp combat. His big, bruising fists and the wicked belt-knife and six-shooter he carried represented the only authority his hardcased bullwhackers respected. A man who bossed a wagon train in the Indian country had to be tougher than the men he commanded. Gan Keeler filled the requirements.

He looked at the papers with vast scorn. "If you rode acrost the plains to dun me fer thet money, Cool," he said, grinning, "you've wasted yore time." Then he added sanctimoniously: "I always figgered there was somethin' queer about thet poker game, anyway."

"Meaning that you think the game was crooked?" Duke questioned politely.

"Yo're damned hootin' I do, mister."

Duke sighed regretfully. "When a gambler loses money in a poker game," he mused, "then the gambler is regarded as a square-shooting, honest person. But when the gambler wins, he is classified as a crook. It's all so inconsistent. Well . . . I regret this, Keeler, but it seems that I must insist on payment."

Duke's hands shot out, closed on Gan Keeler's slicker. He leaped from the saddle, dragging the man down into the mud with him. Keeler, taken by surprise, uttered a grunt of anger, braced himself, and swung a devastating punch. He missed. He did not get another chance to swing. A right hook caught him on the jaw, rocking his shaggy head. A left straightened him, and another right sent him spraddle-legged, his knees suddenly rubbery. He reeled. Duke measured him methodically and knocked him cold with a final smash. Gan Keeler hit the mud full length and lay there, his eyes rolling whitely.

"That," Duke remarked, "was worth seven fifty. I figure I'm paid off now."

Brady Bledsoe put spurs to his horse and came storming to the scene, followed by Nathanial Standish.

"What in damnation?" Bledsoe snapped.

"Only a rival business misunderstanding," Duke said. "Our mutual friend Keeler left a financial matter unsettled when he left Saint Louis. I was merely calling the error to his attention."

"A poker debt, hey?" Bledsoe snapped.

"A poker debt," Duke nodded.

"Who is this fellow?" Nathanial Standish demanded. "It seems to me I've seen his face somewhere."

"No doubt," said Bledsoe. "He shows up here and there. He's a gambler. They call him Dandy Duke Cool."

"Gambler?" Nathanial Standish looked shocked. He was a sparse-fleshed man with a long neck and a dewlap of wrinkled skin beneath his chin. He was somberly garbed, and his voice had the rolling quality of one much in the habit of preaching, or of quoting the Scriptures. His ascetic, lined features and his fierce, cold, blue eyes were uncompromising. His pursed mouth was intolerant of all vices. He eyed Duke condemningly. "Do you mean that you had the impudence to start a brawl over a gambling debt here in the presence of respectable men and women?"

Duke straightened his cuffs. "Some men buy corn or hogs, or merchandise, hoping to sell them at a profit," he said reflectively. "They're gambling, in other words. When they sell, they expect to be paid. It happens that I am a buyer of poker hands, hoping they will prove profitable. When I lose, I pay my losses cheerfully. When I win, I expect to be compensated."

Nathanial Standish glowered. The comparison had hit home. The two wagons he owned were loaded with flour and hardware which he expected to sell at a handsome profit in the Nevada silver camps. "Bah!" he snapped. "A

189

dose of tar and feathers would be proper payment for sharpers of your stripe. Mister Bledsoe, we are wasting valuable time here. This brazen fellow is holding up the entire company. The wagons are stopping. We must make haste at once, if we are to camp at the fort tonight."

"Stretch out!" Bledsoe bawled. "Keep 'em rolling."

Whips popped, and the halted freighters lumbered into motion again. Men placed Gan Keeler's stunned body in one of the wagons. Nathanial Standish wheeled his horse and rode back to his place as pilot.

Brady Bledsoe lingered a moment, eyeing Duke sourly. "You asked for grief when you slugged my wagon boss," he said. "Gan Keeler will be looking for you, when he wakes up."

"May I depend on that?" Duke said, brightening. "I'm beginning to doubt that I got my money's worth, after all."

"Maybe I'll tell Gan to hold off . . . for a while, at least," Bledsoe said ironically. "You took me for more than a thousand dollars in that game in Saint Louis last fall. You were covered with luck that night, Cool. I've been waiting a chance to lock horns with you again . . . before anything violent happens to you. I rather pride myself on my stud game."

"Let us both hope, in that case, that nothing violent happens to me," Duke stated.

He watched Bledsoe ride away. The man wore the garb of a prosperous trader. He was big and brawny with sandy red sideburns and florid features. Some day he would become fat and gross. Now he acted the part of a gentleman. He had earned a reputation as a successful Indian trader and owned a chain of trading posts beyond the Platte. He was said to have the confidence of both the Army and the tribes.

Duke saw the trader pause beside the Standish wagon and lift his hat to the fair-haired girl. Marcia Standish smiled at him and fell into gay conversation. Her glance lifted once, and she looked icily through Duke as if he did not exist. She had heard the news that he was a gambler.

Duke now became aware of a stir of interest along the line of wagons. 'Whackers were peering ahead, craning their necks.

"It's a pack o' them cussed Saints," a voice guffawed. "Look at 'em, wallerin' in the mud like hawgs."

Hoots and catcalls arose from Bledsoe's tough wagon men. Through the slatting rain Duke saw a forlorn swarm of activity off the trail ahead. A long line of grotesque two-wheeled vehicles was drawn up in the rain. There was one prairie wagon in sight with four yoke of gaunt, exhausted oxen in span.

The wagon had slid off the trail into a buffalo wallow and was bogged down to its bed in the gumbo. Weary, rain-soaked men in ragged homespun were laboring to free the vehicle, but their efforts were futile. Duke saw skirted figures in shawls and capes, working in the mud along with the men.

It was a Mormon handcart party, bound for Salt Lake to join Brigham Young's Deseret colony. Duke estimated there were nearly a hundred and fifty men and women in the company. Many small children stood forlornly huddled in the cold rain, watching their parents. On foot, accompanied only by one ox-drawn supply wagon, these people had dragged their cumbersome carts by hand over the plains from Leavenworth.

The Mormons sighted the oncoming bull train, and a swirl of hopeful excitement arose. A delegation of three men, headed by a gaunt, patriarchal leader, came hurrying to meet the caravan. Duke rode to within earshot as the Mormons accosted Nathanial Standish and Brady Bledsoe.

"Praise the Lord," the patriarch said, his bearded face marked by fatigue and the evidence of short rations. "Help has arrived at last. Ye see our plight, brothers. Our oxen are unequal to the task of freeing the wagon from the bog. The loan of one of your teams to assist us to Fort Emigrant would earn our eternal gratitude."

Nathanial Standish's austere face was like stone. He did not rein down his horse but kept moving ahead. The aged Mormon was forced to stand aside or be trampled. Standish passed him by as if he did not exist.

"Forward," Standish bawled. "No dallying. Forward."

"Wait, in the name of mercy," the Mormon implored. "We have sick men and women in that wagon. We have money to pay for your trouble. Not much, I admit, but. . . ."

Nathanial Standish rode on, paying no more heed than if the man had been one of the mounds of bunch grass.

"Why don't you send for Brigham and his apostles?" Brady Bledsoe jibed at the Mormons. "Maybe they could preach you out of the mud."

The Mormons stood by helplessly as the caravan plowed past. A wailing sound of despair arose as the handcart people realized the Gentiles were not intending to stop.

II

"A GAMBLER SHEDS HIS COAT"

Bledsoe's tough 'whackers hurled taunts at

the Mormons as they swung their whips and urged the teams to greater speed ahead, but other travelers, belonging to Standish's party, remained silent. They were frowning and dubious. It was evident they sympathized with the Mormons but were reluctant to oppose the domineering man who acted as their spokesman.

"Assistance to such people would be an affront to the true Word," Standish said scathingly as he rode on. "Truly they have earned the wrath. Did they not learn their lesson at Nauvoo?"

"Fanatics like that never learn anything," Brady Bledsoe answered. "Look at 'em. Down on their knees in the mud. Prayin' for a revelation, I reckon."

Duke watched the Mormons, kneeling in the deep mud around the stalled wagon, and heard the pathetic wailing of the dispirited children. Touching the palomino, he rode among them. Their thin, ragged attire was pitifully inadequate for this weather. The handcarts also were showing the stress of the journey. Rudely built, the majority of them were held together by ropes and plaited thongs of rawhide, or strips torn from blankets or clothing. Duke's palomino disdained the deep mud, but he forced it to the bogged wagon and peered inside. The interior was jammed to suffocating capacity with sick men and women and children who had succumbed to the rigors of the trail.

Duke returned to where Brady Bledsoe and Nathanial Standish were leading their caravan relentlessly ahead. "What price do you ask, Bledsoe," he inquired, "for one of your Pittsburghs and about five yoke of your best stock?"

Bledsoe stared. "What's that? Price?"

"I'm in the market for a bull wagon. It's just a whim of mine. Name your figure for a wagon and ten oxen. I don't want the contents, of course. You can transfer the merchandise to your other wagons. You will still have seven, and they can handle a little extra weight on to the fort. It's less than three miles ahead, I believe."

Nathanial Standish had turned, listening. His head reared challengingly. "I believe I understand," he said caustically. "Your gambler friend sees a chance to turn a profit by hiring or selling a wagon to those sacrilegious scum back there."

Even Brady Bledsoe found something grotesquely amusing in that. The thought of making a profit from the forlorn handcart people was ludicrous. The poverty of the Mormons was all too apparent to an unbiased eye, but Brady's commercial instincts were aroused. He scented a chance to turn a profit. He cleared his throat judiciously. "I don't see how I can spare a wagon," he began. "I. . . ."

"We'll skip the usual trading methods," Duke said curtly. "I detest haggling. You not only can spare a wagon, Bledsoe, but will be happy to dispose of it. Part of your trade is intended for your post at the fort ahead. I'm giving you the chance to get rid of an outfit you won't need any longer. Name your price."

Bledsoe hemmed and hawed. He pointed out one of his wagons, the most battered of the eight. "I could let you have that one, Cool. Along with five yoke for . . . say, five thousand dollars in cash."

"Christianity," — Duke sighed — "thy name is sometimes greed. Five thousand! That outfit probably set you back around fifteen hundred at Leavenworth. A neat profit in six weeks' time, Bledsoe."

"Take it or leave it," Bledsoe snapped, following the accepted procedure of horse trading. He plainly expected haggling and was prepared to slash the price.

But Duke pulled a heavy money belt from around his waist and began counting out gold coin. "Sold," he said. "Write out a bill of sale."

Nathanial Standish, standing by, was flabbergasted. "Wait!" he exclaimed, stunned disappointment in his eyes. "Why, sir, I have a wagon I will sell you for four thousand. . . ."

"Too late," Duke said. "You had a chance to speak up. I've closed the deal with Brother Bledsoe. And I'm a man of my word as well as a fool with my money."

"And it ain't exactly friendly to try to whip-saw me," Bledsoe snarled at his companion, forgetting for once his gentlemanly diction, "Keep your sharp snoot out o' this."

Duke paid over the money. He carefully read the bill of sale, nodded, and pocketed it.

The wagon train halted. Bledsoe organized his crew for the task of distributing the contents of the vehicle among his seven remaining wagons. "Lively," Bledsoe ordered. "Handle those bags with care. I'll flay the hide off any fool that fumbles."

Duke saw that all of Bledsoe's wagons were loaded with flour in strong cotton sacks of the hundred-pound weight. His brows lifted a trifle. Bledsoe had a reputation as an Indian trader, but flour was a commodity scorned and despised among the meat-eating plains tribes who knew nothing of its use. He decided that the flour was destined for the Army forts and outfitting stations along the trail which catered to white men.

With a score of husky men moving at a trot, the work of transferring the load proceeded swiftly. Duke waited in the rain, chewing a cheroot, ignoring the covert gibes of Bledsoe and his hardcase employees. The news of the price he had paid for the wagon had gone around, and he was looked on as a fool and a sucker. He saw even Marcia Standish and her mother tittering scornfully as they talked it over with other women in the company. Duke lifted his hat and bowed cheerfully in the girl's direction, but she turned her back on him instantly.

The last of the bags of flour were being moved, when a little stump-legged swamper slipped in the mud and went sprawling. The bag he carried hit a rock almost at Duke's feet. Brady Bledsoe came running to the scene, white with rage. He kicked the fallen man to his feet, then sent a fist crashing into his face, hurling him into the mud again.

Bledsoe snatched up the fallen sack. The cloth covering had burst, and flour spilled down the trader's clothes. He acted like a man demented as he turned and sent the ruined sack hurtling into a rain-filled gully off the trail where it sank out of sight.

His fury subsided then. His quick, shrewd eyes rested briefly, searchingly, on Duke. It seemed to Duke that Gan Keeler and many more of Bledsoe's unsavory wagon men were also watching him with keen alertness. He had an eerie impression of an electric tension in the air, a feeling as if he were the vortex of an unseen, inexplicable storm of violence that needed only a word or a spark to touch it off.

Bledsoe's burst of fury had seemed unreasonable and childish to Duke. The destruction of one sack of flour was petty in comparison to the profit the man was making on the wagon, but Duke caught the faint tang of whiskey in the air. That, apparently, was the explanation. Bledsoe was doing some secret tippling. His explosion was due to whiskey nerves.

Duke shrugged and turned away. The more he saw of Brady Bledsoe the more he despised the man. He wondered what a girl like Marcia Standish could see in him. The wagon was cleared of the last of the flour.

"It's all yours, Cool," Bledsoe said, patting his money belt with satisfaction.

"Stretch out," Nathanial Standish bawled, still disgruntled. He gave Duke a scathing glance. "A fool and his money," he sniffed.

"Keno," Duke agreed cheerfully.

The 'whackers hurrahed Duke for his gullibility as they plodded past. Gan Keeler rode by on his mule but offered no verbal taunts. However, his pale eyes were flat, dangerous. Gan Keeler's jaw was swollen and bruised. He had not forgotten.

Duke looked at the Mormons who were still struggling desperately to free their bogged wagon. He threw away his rain-soaked cheroot and dismounted into the mud. Picking up a goad, he plowed through the gumbo and unhooked the five oxen he had purchased; then, prodding them around, he headed them toward the stalled wagon. The Mormons stood, watching. When they realized that help was actually coming, a shout of joy went up.

"Praise be. The Lord has answered us. Praise be!"

"The Lord will feel more kindly toward you, if you'll give me room to handle these mud crawlers," Duke said.

A small, muddy figure which had been laboring in deep mire around the stalled wagon came wading eagerly to his side. "Give the gentleman room! Make way! Give him a hand! Step lively!"

Duke grinned in amazement. The muddy Mormon was a girl, although he had to look twice to make sure, for although she wore skirts, they were plastered by rain and mud to her figure so that at first glance she might have been mistaken for a boy. But no boy was this Mormon girl; and neither was she a child. She was trim-waisted, shapely, and with a rich share of vital beauty. A sunbonnet, so sodden it was only a rag, framed a vibrant face. Gray eyes, big and with depths of womanly perception, regarded him. Small freckles dusted her forcefully tilted nose. Her cheeks showed the pallor of overwork and short rations.

Duke picked her up bodily, carried her clear of the ooze. "A bath and a square meal would make a raving beauty of you," he predicted. "Which wife are you? Number five? Or maybe number seven? And who's the lucky man?"

She drew herself up. For the first time in his life Duke Cool felt suddenly abashed in the presence of a girl.

"My father is in that wagon . . . ill," she said simply. "I want to be near him. I want to help."

She left him and went wading through the mud back to the wagon.

Duke tooled the oxen into position. He sank to his waist in water and gumbo. Because his soggy ulster and undercoat were an impediment to his activity, he stripped them off and cast them impatiently away. His fine linen shirt became a mass of mud as the oxen floundered about in the ooze. He threw his hat away, also, because it interfered with his movements.

The handcart people swarmed around, proving more of a hindrance than a help as he hooked his team in ahead of the exhausted beasts which had given up the effort. He took a bullwhip from the hand of a Mormon. The lash crackled with a report that sent the long string of oxen surging forward against the yokes as if they had heard the voice of final authority. The bogged wagon moved. With a sucking sound the mud heaved, and the running gear labored clear. Slowly the vehicle rose from the buffalo wallow and lurched to firmer ground above. Duke scraped mud from his face and grinned.

"Bless ye, brother," the leader said fervently, and the words were echoed by a hundred voices. "I am Jethro Sloan, elder in the church. And ye . . . ?"

"Duke Cool is the name."

"Ye are a trader, perhaps?"

Duke looked ruefully at his mud-filled boots and scraped more mud from his face. "Nope," he said. "Gambler. I prefer stud to draw poker. More action."

"Gambler?" Jethro Sloan tugged at his beard. He was a rawboned man with craggy features and kindly eyes. He turned to his followers. "Let us pray for the salvation of Brother Cool's soul," he boomed. "Let us lift our supplication that he be led into the paths of righteousness."

"Hogwash," Duke snapped. "My soul can wait a while longer. There's work to be done.

Transfer some of those sick people to my wagon. I'll split up my team and whack you ahead to the fort. Shake a leg. It'll be dark before long, and making a wet camp after sundown never was my idea of good solid fun."

In spite of himself, his glance wandered to the Mormon girl. It angered him to find that her lips were moving in prayer and that her gray eyes showed pity and sympathy — for him. Duke impatiently busied himself, preparing the two wagons. The gusty rain chilled him to the bone as he labored with the heavy trace chains and yokes.

A clear voice spoke at his side. "This will help." A blanket was thrown over his shoulders. It was the gray-eyed girl. Her lips were blue with the cold. Except for a sodden shawl around her shoulders she had no protection.

With explosive wrath Duke jerked the blanket from his shoulders and wrapped it around her. "And save your prayers for those who need it," he snapped.

She bit her lip in humility, and hurried away. But soon she was back, carrying the hat and coat and ulster he had abandoned. "At least take these," she pleaded. "They're wet and muddy but will be some protection. I had intended to . . . to dry and clean them in camp tonight before returning them."

Duke accepted them with sudden meekness. But as soon as she was out of sight, he wrapped the fine broadcloth coat around two shivering children, and forced the ulster on a woman who was shaking with the ague.

III

"HUNCH-PLAYER"

Duke piloted the two wagons the three miles to Fort Emigrant. Bleak, rainy dusk was setting in when they sighted the stockaded military post which stood on a bluff overlooking the muddy Platte. Below the bluff a mongrel settlement had sprung up with Brady Bledsoe's trading post as its nucleus. Half a dozen bars and gambling houses catered to the soldiers of the garrison and travelers on the trail. Lights gleamed invitingly from these places, and the music of a hurdy-gurdy drifted through the rain as Duke led the weary Mormon handcart train nearer.

The caravan captained by Nathanial Standish had usurped all of the flat adjoining the settlement. Their wagons were spread out so that the highest, driest ground was occupied. The tired Mormons were forced to make out as best they could in a brushy mud flat near the sullen river.

Firewood was wet and stubborn, and it was

an hour before the place began to resemble a camp at all. Duke frowned as he watched Jethro Sloan deal out the rations. It was plain that the provisions were at the vanishing point.

"You've got seven hundred tough miles ahead of you," he said to the elder. "And you're about out of grub. How do you aim to make it through?"

"We must buy provisions here," the elder explained. "We had hoped the Lord would provide us with buffalo on the plains, but none was to be found. We have a little money set aside for such emergency. I will go to the trading post and buy what we can. Help from Deseret will be awaiting us when we reach Fort Bridger."

The elder and two of his lieutenants walked to the settlement to dicker for provisions. But they returned soon, with despair and defeat in their faces.

"No grub to be had?" Duke questioned.

"There are provisions at the post," the elder said sadly. "But for Mormons the price is one dollar a pound for flour and salt and smoke meat. Beans are the same. Blankets and clothing are priced at their weight in gold. And our funds are limited . . . very limited."

Duke squatted by a fire, drying out. He watched the gray-eyed Mormon girl — Zoan

Jessup — who had a group of the smaller children gathered around a fire where she was cooking and telling them gay stories, keeping their minds occupied, doing what she could to cheer them. Yet — as Duke had already learned — her mother had died two weeks ago on the plains, and her father was a patient in the sick wagon.

Duke listened to the faint hurdy-gurdy music from the settlement. He hefted his money belt and smiled wryly. The belt was empty. The money he had paid for Bledsoe's wagon had taken his entire capital down to the last gold piece. He fingered the ruby stickpin in his bedraggled stock. That stone was worth two thousand dollars. His ivory-handled six-shooter could probably be sold for cash in the settlement. And there was his palomino and the pack mule.

He arose and moved casually to where Zoan Jessup was busy with the children. "Wish me luck," he said. "I'm superstitious about gals with pretty red lips."

She straightened, studying him gravely, and the compliment he had passed actually did bring the natural color back to her shapely lips for a moment. "I was watching you," she admitted. "I believe I know what's in your mind. Elder Sloan learned in the settlement that you bought that wagon and oxen with your own funds in order to help us. It took all your money, didn't it? Now you're thinking of risking that beautiful ruby in a . . . a gambling game."

"It wouldn't be the first time," Duke said lightly. "That's the way it came to me . . . in a poker game."

"It's sinful," she said meditatively. "But . . . but . . . wait!"

She hurried away among the handcarts in the darkness. In a few moments she was back. She drew Duke away into the shadows. She was excited. She thrust something into his hand.

"It's . . . it's all I have," she breathed. "You're welcome to it."

Duke looked at the two five-dollar gold pieces that lay in his palm.

"I . . . I do wish you luck," the girl whispered.

Duke was silent a moment. He had his full share of gambling superstition. He recognized a true hunch when it touched him. Suddenly he pocketed the money and nodded. "You've bought a partnership in a stud game tonight, Mormon gal," he said. "I reckon the Lord will overlook this sin . . . at least as far as you are concerned."

"And you will be forgiven, also," she said positively.

Somehow during the exertion of setting up camp she had found time to change from her rain-soaked garb to a dark skirt and tight-bodiced waist whose severe lines gave her a poise and dignity. She met his gaze levelly, without false humility. She knew she was comely, desirable.

Duke kept remembering that as he rode out of camp on the palomino. His garb was bedraggled, but his bearing was jaunty as he jogged into the rough settlement. His course had carried him past the Standish camp on the flat, and he had glimpsed Brady Bledsoe paying court to Marcia Standish, who sat in comfort beneath a wagon-sheet shelter near the warmth of a roaring fire.

Bledsoe's trading post was the biggest structure in the settlement, and Duke glimpsed wagon folk and buckskin-clad buffalo hunters in the mercantile room, dickering with clerks for supplies. With practiced eye he appraised the half-dozen gambling houses. The majority were shoddy establishments, some with canvas roofs and clay floors and plank bars set on whiskey barrels. The biggest and most pretentious was named the Platte Northern. It was frame-built of milled lumber that had been hauled across the plains. It sported stained-glass swing doors.

Duke chose a smaller place for his first

foray. With the two gold pieces as his stake he sat in a faro game for an hour. When he cashed in, he had three hundred dollars in his pocket.

He had seen Brady Bledsoe return to town from the Standish camp, accompanied by Gan Keeler. They had entered the Platte Northern. Duke now made his way to the bigger gambling house. Its gambling layouts were ornate, and its bar and back buffet would have done credit to a St. Louis establishment. Play at all tables was high. One poker table, covered with blue velvet, bore the sign of no-limit action, but this table had no patronage at the time. A silk-hatted, cadaverous man with the flat stare of a professional sat at this table, waiting for trade.

Bledsoe and Gan Keeler were tossing off a drink at the bar. Bledsoe looked up as Duke entered, his florid face breaking into one of his supercilious grins. It was plain the man had been expecting Duke to appear.

"Where's your halo, Cool?" he jibed. "Didn't the Saints convert you?"

"I hung the halo on my saddle horn before I came in," Duke said. "I didn't want to get it tarnished."

Gan Keeler said nothing, but bystanders who had heard of the fight at the wagon train edged gingerly away, ready to duck for cover.

Duke approached the blue table. "Greetings, Whitey," he said casually. "I haven't seen you since that game in Fort Smith two years ago, if I remember right."

The gambler, Whitey Jack, nodded. There was no friendship in him. Whitey Jack was a human machine, who knew every crooked trick in the deck.

Duke took a chair. "It's nice weather to stay indoors and enjoy a sociable game," he remarked. "Any chance of scaring up opposition? Four-handed stud would agree with my mood tonight."

Brady Bledsoe moved up eagerly. "I haven't forgotten that night in Saint Joe, Cool," he challenged. "I'd enjoy a chance to even the score. Come on, Gan, if you feel lucky."

Duke's dark eyes were suddenly cold, hard. He looked at Gan Keeler. "Not you, Keeler," he said. "Welchers never sit at the same table with me a second time."

The black blood eddied in Gan Keeler's surly face. He might have drawn then and shot it out, but a hasty word from Brady Bledsoe halted him: "No shooting in here, Gan. It's hard on the glassware. Besides, I want a chance at Cool first. You two can settle your differences another time."

Bledsoe beckoned a sallow, slit-mouthed man who was also patently a house player.

"Sit in, Missoula," he ordered.

Duke knew then that he would be playing against the three of them. The signs indicated that Brady Bledsoe, in addition to owning the trading post, was owner of this place, also. Whitey Jack and Missoula were his employees.

Duke placed his three hundred dollars in gold before him and gave the impression that it was a beginning. They had no way of knowing this was his entire stake. They took it for granted he was well-heeled. Otherwise, they could have stripped him in a few hands.

Duke bet the first hand that was dealt him. He caught black aces and eights. It was the winning hand, and he raked in a small pot.

Brady Bledsoe was the bludgeoning type of player. He liked to use the power of his bankroll to bluff his way through tough hands. Duke played methodically, tuning himself to the run of the cards, feeling out his opponents, testing his luck. He lost an indifferent pot, dropped out of the next two. Then he won. And won again. And again. But that was the run of the cards. He was catching winning hands on fifth card, raking in money without final opposition.

His stake grew to a thousand in half an hour, hung steady for a time, then began to climb again. At the end of two hours' play he was more than three thousand dollars ahead of the game. The cards were running his way.

Brady Bledsoe was drinking hard now, and all his mask of geniality had faded, leaving him surly and dangerous. If Brady had expected help through crooked dealing on the part of his two housemen, he was disappointed. Whitey Jack and Missoula knew their man too well for that; the game was being played on a strictly honest basis.

Two sizable pots came up. Bledsoe won both of them by slam-bang tactics. He would raise five hundred dollars at a clip, and raise again if the bet was tilted. On both occasions Duke abandoned his hands after seeing three cards, rather than pay heavily to buy his last cards.

Bledsoe tried it again a third time, with two aces showing against Duke's pair of fours. This time Duke met his raise, jumped the bet a thousand dollars. Bledsoe studied him, decided he was bluffing, and called. Duke had a four in the hole, giving him three of a kind against Bledsoe's aces.

It was on the heels of this defeat which shook Bledsoe's confidence that Duke sensed the big break in the game.

IV

"BULLETS ARE ACES"

Whitey Jack was dealing. Duke's hole card was the deuce of clubs. His first up card was a queen — the queen of hearts. That red queen reminded him of Zoan Jessup.

Bledsoe's up card was a black ace. The two house men caught lesser cards. Bledsoe bet three hundred dollars on his ace. The house men stayed. Duke raised it five hundred.

Bledsoe blinked, studied his cards, then examined Duke with shrewd eyes. "Up another thousand," he said.

The house man dropped out. Duke met the raise.

Duke caught the seven of hearts, Bledsoe the ten of diamonds. His ace was still high, and he bet five hundred. Duke met the bet.

Duke's third up card was also a heart — the ten. Bledsoe's was another black ace, giving him a pair of aces showing.

Bledsoe bet a thousand dollars. Duke met the bet. He now had thirty-three hundred dollars in the pot. That left him busted, although Bledsoe was not yet aware of it. Every gold piece Duke had won was now on the table.

All other play had stopped in the room while men watched. Soldiers from the fort, buckskin-clad buffalo hunters, and wagon men in hide boots waited in silence.

Duke had three hearts showing above his hole card. His play indicated that he had another heart in the hole and that he was trying for a flush. As a matter of fact, having a club in the hole, he had no chance of topping even the pair of aces Bledsoe had showing.

Whitey Jack flipped the fifth card to Duke. The onlookers sighed. It was a heart, also — a king. He had four hearts showing.

Brady Bledsoe caught another ten, giving him two pairs in sight — aces and tens. Bledsoe hesitated for the barest space, and the little blue veins on his florid cheeks stood out a trifle more prominently. That told Duke all he wanted to know. The two pairs were all that Bledsoe had. A ten or an ace in the hole would have given him a full house, which would have beaten a flush. But the hole card was worthless. And two pairs were worthless against a flush. That was what Bledsoe was thinking.

Bledsoe tried to bluff it out, tried to appear that he was holding a full. He beckoned a bartender. "Fetch me some money," he ordered.

He shoved fifteen hundred dollars in gold into the pot.

Duke reached up, removed his ruby stick-pin. "This is worth two thousand," he said. "Whitey Jack will verify that. I won it from Whitey a couple years ago. I'll drop it in against your fifteen hundred. And. . . ." He produced a slip of paper. "Here's a bill of sale for a wagon and bull team I bought today, worth five thousand dollars," he added suavely. "I'll shove that in at face value as a little sweetening."

Bledsoe slapped a fist on the table. "What the hell?" he jeered. "Five thousand dollars fer that . . . !"

"Surely it didn't deteriorate in value in only a few hours," Duke said quietly. "You set the price yourself today when human beings were in need of help out there. You don't mean to go back on your own word, do you? This is only a poker game. There are no children wailing in the rain, or sick people waiting for help, Bledsoe. Surely you won't haggle now."

The score of bystanders lifted a brittle murmur of approval. They had heard the story of the wagon sale but hadn't heard it the way Duke was telling it. Up to now they hadn't given much thought to the wailing children or suffering Mormons. They were thinking of them now.

Brady Bledsoe realized he was in an ugly situation. His sharp dealing had boomeranged. As a face-saving gesture he was forced to acknowledge that slip of paper he had signed.

He looked down at the bill of sale. To meet Duke's bet meant shoving five thousand dollars in cash into the pot. "You're bluffin'," Bledsoe said. He was pulling his breath in and out with an effort. "You're tryin' to run a sandy."

"So?" Duke said, his brows arching.

Bledsoe glanced at his house players, hoping for some helpful sign. But neither could help him, for they had no way of knowing whether Duke was bluffing.

Bledsoe began to sweat. He studied the cards, studied Duke's face. Suddenly, with a curse, he picked up his hand, hurled it petulantly against the wall.

"You've got it," he raged. "A flush. Tryin' to draw me into bettin' against an unbeatable hand."

Duke turned his cards face down, shoved them toward Whitey Jack. Before the man could pick them up, Bledsoe snatched them from the table and looked at Duke's hole card. The action was contrary to the rules of the game. Bledsoe's refusal to call Duke's bet did not entitle him to see the hole card.

Brady Bledsoe looked at the black deuce and realized he had been bluffed from the very start by a man with greater poker savvy and steel nerve. "Why, you four-flushing . . . !" He propelled his bulk across the table, his fingers reaching savagely for Duke's throat.

Duke shoved his chair back. Sitting there, he smashed a fist solidly into Bledsoe's face, sending the man toppling to the floor. He whirled out of the chair, crouching, for he had never forgotten for an instant that Gan Keeler was in this room, nursing his grudge.

Keeler had seen his chance to square accounts. He stood at the corner of the back bar, and his six-shooter was already clear of leather and rising. Duke fell aside, drawing, as Keeler's six-shooter exploded. Duke fired as he moved, his shot coming as an overlapping reverberation to the blast of the wagonmaster's gun. Gan Keeler's head rocked gruesomely, and a hole appeared above his flat nose. He took a blind step, and he was dead before his slumping body hit the floor.

Duke backed against a wall, his eyes flickering over the room. Brady Bledsoe was on his hands and knees, blinking incredulously at Gan Keeler's body which lay crumpled before him. The two gamblers had ducked to cover but were making no move to take up the fight. Tough bouncers and bartenders had guns in their hands, but they were hesitating.

"Stand your hand," a knotty-jawed Army

sergeant barked at the house crew. "That was self-defense. I'm backin' Duke Cool's play. Keeler asked for that . . . an' got it."

A dozen voices chimed in. Bledsoe and his followers were none too popular with the soldiers and plainsmen in the place.

Bledsoe got to his feet. He looked at Duke and at his dead wagonmaster. "All right," he croaked. "All right, Cool. But you can't always be that lucky." He walked groggily down the room and out of the Platte Northern.

"*Gracias*, gentlemen," Duke said to the bystanders.

He took an apron from a barkeep, raked the gold pieces into it, formed a bundle and threw it over his arm. He followed Brady Bledsoe across the muddy street into the trading post. Bledsoe was heading for his private office at the rear of the room, but he paused, glowering, as Duke entered. Brady Bledsoe's face was ashen with fury. "Do you think I'd sell you an' them damned Mormons grub, an' be paid off with my own money?" he said thickly.

"I reckon," Duke said suavely, "that would be more pleasant than being treated to a new suit of tar and feathers and being toted out of town on a wagon pole. What do you think, Bledsoe? You don't seem to be any too popular with the citizens or the cavalry in this place."

Many of the patrons of the Platte Northern had straggled into the trading post at Duke's heels. "Better sell," the tough Army sergeant advised judiciously. "You named your price, Bledsoe. Stick to it."

Bledsoe was helpless. There was murder in his eyes, but he nodded to his clerks. "Sell him what he wants."

Zoan Jessup came hurrying into the store. White-faced she rushed to Duke. "I heard about the . . . the shooting. Are you all right?"

"Still foot-loose and fancy free, little one. We'll go back to camp and fetch Brother Sloan and the wagons. I've made a deal for provisions that will feed your Mormons to Fort Bridger."

"Food?" she said incredulously. "You mean . . . ?"

"Grub," Duke nodded. "Enough to fill plenty of craws. It's your share of the poker game."

She stood, looking at him. Once again he felt his stature diminish, felt humbleness come upon him. "Why do you have to be so hard?" she asked.

Duke pointed through a rain-blurred window at men who were carrying a blanket-covered stretcher out of the Platte Northern. "Some men can do things like that and sing psalms afterwards," he said, and his voice was a harsh discord. "But I can't."

Her eyes remained gentle. "That, too, will be forgiven," she said with conviction.

Duke scowled. "No converting," he warned angrily. "And none of your praying for my immortal soul. It's too late for that." But she had her arm linked in his, and she was smiling mistily as she led him out of the store.

The clank of a cavalry sword sounded. An Army lieutenant and a squad of troopers in heavy capes emerged from the darkness. Nathanial Standish's angular form loomed among them.

"There he is, officer," Standish boomed, leveling a damning finger at Duke. "He killed a man in a gambling row a few minutes ago."

"I'll handle this," the cavalry officer said brusquely. He looked Duke over. "A dozen witnesses say it was self-defense, Cool. We'll let it ride that way. But you're out of bounds in Fort Emigrant after tonight. Gun fights breed gun fights. It's damned nasty digging graves in this weather. You'll be on the trail tomorrow, I take it."

"Since you put it so adroitly, Lieutenant," — Duke bowed — "I shall take the hint."

"The fellow should be behind bars," Standish fumed.

The Army man ignored him. He walked with Duke and the girl down the street. "Sorry, old man," he said sincerely, "that I had to exile you. Our turkey-necked friend just had a session with the colonel. Standish swings a political club back yonder. He seems to have it in for you."

"My sin was offering help to some insufferable Mormons," Duke sighed. "Also refusing to give Mister Standish a chance to profit by their predicament."

"I know. I heard all the dirty details. I'd enjoy a poker session with you, but I'd probably be a babe in arms. I've heard of you. However, it will be for your own good if you shake the mud of this place from those bench-made boots of yours. Gan Keeler should have been hung years ago. You deserve the thanks of Congress for that little chore. But the fellow has a certain type of friends here who aren't particular which rib they slide a knife under, as long as it's in the back. You . . . ah!"

A gun had bellowed from the shadows a hundred yards away. The bullet passed between Duke and the Army man, missing Duke's cheek by a hair. Duke whirled the girl around a building corner and crouched there, his gun poised, seeking vainly for a target. But the rainy darkness was impenetrable.

"You get my point, I presume," said the lieutenant from the prone position he had immediately assumed nearby.

"I do," Duke agreed. "Fact is I was 'way ahead of you. I rather expected a calling card, though not quite so soon. It isn't hard to guess whose name was written on it."

The officer and his troops made a search of the vicinity, but the bushwhacker had made good his retreat.

"Good luck, gambling man," the lieutenant said as they parted. "And if that Mormon gal has a pretty sister, let me know. I've never been to Zion, but it would be worth the trip."

Zoan Jessup clung tightly to Duke's arm as he located his palomino. He lifted her back of the saddle, and they headed for the Mormon camp. She was shaking, but not from the cold. "The cowards," she said between set teeth. "Demanding your arrest. Shooting at you from the dark. Exiling you."

"Life," Duke said, "has its hazards. Also its compensations."

She understood. She laughed softly, pleased.

V

"RED MAN'S RIOT"

The Mormons crossed the river next day, using the cable ferry, and Duke accompanied them. "I'm in no hurry," he explained to Jethro Sloan as the party organized on the north shore to resume the march. "And you people need looking after. Use my wagon as long as you need it. Oxen fare better pulling against a load. They walk on their toes. They get sore-footed flatting along ahead of an empty freighter. I'll dally along with you."

Jethro Sloan's wise eyes twinkled. He glanced toward Zoan Jessup, who was rearranging the load on a shambling handcart. "And Sister Jessup, no doubt, could use another shoulder at the wheel." He nodded.

Duke had the grace to grin weakly. The call to stretch out was sounding along the line. Men and women — and children, too — were applying themselves to the cumbersome carts.

Duke approached the girl, who was struggling with her vehicle. "I'll handle this go-devil," he said casually, as he ducked beneath the shafts and put his shoulder to the bar. "You better trail with the hospital wagon and look after your father."

"Dad is better today," she said. She was smiling. He had not seen her really smile before. It was worth watching. "The fever has gone. He'll be on his feet in a day or two."

"Then ride the palomino," Duke commanded. "He's gentle with pretty girls and kids. He gets that from me. He can carry some young ones. So can that lazy mule. I've told the elder to use both of them in giving a lift to the carts whenever needed."

Ahead, the Mormon band of four pieces of brass struck up industriously, giving forth the stirring, rhythmic beat of the handcart marching song. Every voice in the long line took up the refrain, sending the challenge loud and clear over the Platte:

> **For some must push, and some**
> **must pull,**
> **As we go marching up the hill;**
> **As merrily on the way we go,**
> **Until we reach the valley — o!**

Zoan Jessup's head was up, her tawny hair blowing in the wind. She faced the west, her eyes shining as she sang the words. The wobbling wheels of the handcart train began turning, heaving through the mud. The two wagons lurched ahead as the bullwhips popped, their canvas tilts slatting in the breeze. The rain had ended. The sun was peering out now through breaking clouds.

Duke leaned against the shoulder bar, dug his fine boots deep, and wrenched the cart from the mud. He sent it forward.

With the weather relenting, and with food enough to stave off the immediate danger of starvation, the Mormons' spirits rose. The handcart party crawled westward, pushing the long miles behind them. With the days, Independence Rock and Devil's Gate fell astern.

Nathanial Standish's company, which had lingered three days at the fort, overtook them on the Sweetwater. Standish's party had dwindled to ten wagons, for some of his company had withdrawn from his leadership at the fort and had elected to wait for some westbound caravan. Brady Bledsoe and five of his big, heavily laden freighters accompanied the caravan. Marcia Standish was riding a paint horse alongside the trader as the bull wagons overtook and crawled past the slower-moving handcart train. She singled out Duke in the line of march.

He was no longer the resplendent figure of that first day on the plains. His boots had succumbed to the rigors of the trail. He now wore moccasins, which he had won from a squawman at Independence Rock in a Spanish monte game. His fine pantaloons were ragged and rolled half to his knees. He was bare to the waist, for the weather had turned hot and dry. Alkali dust had mingled with the sweat on his back, outlining his flat muscles. His skin beneath the dust was tanned a golden bronze.

The passing bullwagons set their course to

windward and gave the handcart toilers the benefit of more choking clouds of dust as they surged powerfully past and ahead. Brady Bledsoe looked at Duke and rode on without change of expression. Duke had been carrying his six-shooter on the handcart, but from that time on he always had it strapped around his waist, or within reach of his hand. And he was careful not to outline himself against the cook fires after dark.

Split Rock and Three Crossings offered their tedious opposition and were conquered. They crawled up the Sweetwater, mounting the imperceptible sweep of the Continental Divide toward South Pass. Zoan's father had recovered now and was able to spell Duke at the pushing bar in the easier going. Heber Jessup was a mild-mannered, steadfast man with an abiding faith in the future.

At such times Duke mounted the palomino, with a borrowed Sharps rifle, and hunted buffalo and antelope to reinforce the supplies. The sign of Indian hunting parties was plentiful in the region, and on one occasion Duke sighted riders in the distance, attempting to cut him off from return to the handcart party. He staged a swift retreat in time. This was the hunting ground of half a dozen tribes, none of whom was adverse to lifting a white scalp, if the sign was right.

They were two camps west of the Crossings, and Duke was a dozen miles north of the trail, pushing through a *malpais* of yellow buttes, moving in on antelope whose white rumps had flashed distantly in the sun, when he twisted around and watched an overtaking figure. It was Zoan, riding the grulla mule. She wore masculine breeches instead of a skirt — a garb that was more practical on the trail but which had brought shocked criticism from the majority of the Mormons. Her face, beneath the sunbonnet, was excited as she rode up. "I was beginning to think I'd never catch up with you," she said. "A band of Gros Ventres threw a scare into the party not long after you pulled out on your hunting trip this morning. I was afraid you might run into the Indians and have trouble."

"Gro'vaunts." Duke frowned. "How many?"

"Only a dozen or so. But they were drunk and ugly. They first demanded whiskey. When we told them we had none, they retreated to a distance and fired a few shots that did no damage. They whooped and rode around for a while. They went away, when the men armed themselves and got ready to go after them. We were too many for them."

"Drunk?" Duke questioned. "They demanded whiskey?"

"Several of them had stone jugs of rum.

227

And they were all smeared with something white. It looked like flour. Even their ponies were covered with it. And . . . and Duke . . . the men are sure that some of those Indians were carrying those new repeating rifles we've heard about. Henry rifles. That party of Gentiles who passed us yesterday carried a few Henrys, according to some of our men. The Standish company. Elder Sloan fears the Gentiles have met trouble. The wagons of Bledsoe the trader were loaded with flour, you remember. There may have been a massacre."

Duke's dark eyes had thinned. "Flour?" he said slowly. "You say they were smeared with flour. And they had jugs of whiskey. And Henry rifles."

Flour and whiskey. The mention of that combination brought flashing into Duke's mind a scene that was almost forgotten. He was remembering that day in the rain on the Laramie plains, and the burst sack of flour one of Bledsoe's men had dropped. And Bledsoe's volcanic outburst, and the way he had so hastily hurled the broken sack into concealment in a mud hole. And that taint of whiskey that had lingered in the air. Whiskey was contraband in the Indian country. All passing wagons were subject to search at Fort Emigrant for liquor. Trading in guns and ammunition among the Indians was also prohibited.

"Hell's blue flames," Duke breathed. "A whiskey trader. There was a busted jug in that sack the 'whacker dropped. And likely a Henry rifle. That's how Bledsoe has got rich as a trader."

He believed he knew now why Bledsoe and his men had eyed him so tensely at the time. They were wondering if he had detected the broken whiskey jug buried in the sack of flour. It explained why Bledsoe had so quickly disposed of the incriminating evidence. It was a prison offense to smuggle whiskey into Indian country.

The girl was startled by the wild look in his eyes.

"Which way did those Gro'vaunts head, when they pulled out?"

"Back up the trail. Later on some of the men scouted around and saw another party of Indians, off in the distance, riding in that same direction. They were too far away to make much out of."

Duke glared at her. "With the country full of drunken Indians, you came out here alone to warn me. Are you loco? Are your father and Jethro Sloan crazy, too, to let a girl do that?"

His voice was rough, angry. But she did not quail. "They didn't know I was leaving until it was too late to stop me," she admitted. "I'll get a jawing for it, I suppose."

"You ought to be spanked. Hell's fire. You might . . . !"

"Don't swear, Joseph. It is unseemly."

Duke glared helplessly. "How did you catch on that my front name is Joseph?" he demanded.

"I noticed it written on the tailor's tag that day when you threw away your coat on the plains. It is a good Christian name, Joseph."

"Blast my name. You're heading back to the outfit now as fast as . . . no, confound it. I can't send you back alone. You might bump into some more drunken Gro'vaunts."

"But you're coming with me!" she exclaimed in dismay. "Do you hear me? The Indians are on the warpath. There's likely been a massacre already, and. . . ."

"Quit screaming at me while I think," Duke said. "I've got a hunch there's been no massacre . . . yet. But there probably will be one unless somebody stops a certain whiskey-peddling hypocrite." He looked at the girl, and suddenly all the harshness drained out of him. "You've got to go with me," he said reluctantly. "I can't let you wander alone out here. If anything happens to you. . . ."

He left it unfinished. There was a mischievous twinkle in her eyes. "The way you said that makes me feel that I really count, even if I am a Mormon girl," she murmured with false meekness.

Duke looked sardonically down at his tattered garb. "How well you know that," he stated. "You made a dray horse out of me, didn't you? I've wallowed in muck, eaten dust, fought barroom brawls, scratched flea bites, blew in all my money, and have been run out of an Army post as an undesirable. You and your prayers. You and your psalm-singing Saints."

She was still meek. "You will be rewarded in heaven, Joseph."

"Bah! That's a long time to wait. Well, come on. We're riding to overtake the Standish company. They can't be more than a dozen miles ahead. They only passed us two days ago. It's time they learned they are traveling with a rum peddler . . . if it isn't too late." He told her the story of the broken flour sack. "It all ties together," he said. "I wondered why an Indian trader would be packing flour. Indians have no use for flour, except to daub themselves and their horses. But Henry rifles . . . the devil ought to be strung up."

The Henry was a new gun that was just beginning to make its appearance in the West. Firing eighteen shots, it was a tricky but devastating weapon in comparison to the usual percussion guns and muzzle-loaders.

"All of Bledsoe's wagons are loaded with flour," he said. "Which means that there probably are rifles and whiskey in every sack. He fooled the Army by saying he was bound for Virginia City, I imagine. Instead, he was aiming for the Snake River to trade rotgut and arms to the Indians for furs. He's likely met the tribes moving toward Fort Emigrant with their pelts to trade and has grabbed a chance to make a quick and early profit. I've seen samples of what whiskey has done to the Indians. It's like grabbing a bear by the tail. Once you start feeding them whiskey, they won't let you quit."

She nodded, her eyes wide.

He led the way westward. Following the shelter of bluffs and breaks in the plains, staying off the skyline, they pushed ahead as the westering sun crawled down the sky ahead of them. Twice Duke halted, and they remained under cover while distant streamers of dust that might have been stirred by antelope or Indians vanished into the horizon. Duke finally pointed, and the girl saw a tiny line of white dots far to the west. It was the Standish caravan, following the brushy course of a stream more than half a dozen miles away.

"They'll be camping soon," Duke said. "We'll overtake them by dark."

They were crossing a small stream, when Duke again halted suddenly. The girl's breath caught in her throat as they listened to a faint, disturbing uproar in the distance.

Duke slid from the saddle, tossed her the reins. "Wait here," he said.

He pushed through the brush upstream, and the uproar grew louder in his ears. Working his way through thickets, he at last lay flat, peering out at an Indian camp on a sand flat.

It was a temporary hunting camp of only three lodges, but there were twenty or thirty warriors in sight, drunk and daubed with paint. The place was a bedlam. Coated with flour, the warriors were reeling around in an alcoholic frenzy. The squaws and children had withdrawn into the background in fear. Duke saw two or three dead or wounded Indians lying about, victims of crazed camp fights that had broken out. Even as he watched, a tomahawk battle was staged to its bloody conclusion by two frenzied Gros Ventres.

In the background loomed one of Brady Bledsoe's big trade wagons. Bledsoe himself was not present. Four of his hard-faced men were working frantically, loading bales of beaver plews and bundles of winter-trapped marten and wolverine pelts into the wagon. Empty bags and the white flour scattered over the camp showed the method of trading. Duke saw a dozen broken whiskey jugs. Many of the Indians were brandishing Henry rifles.

Bledsoe's traders kept glancing apprehensively at the howling Indians as they worked feverishly to pull out. The Gros Ventres suddenly became aware that the whites intended to depart. Their mood changed, and they surrounded the wagon, brandishing weapons. Duke knew nothing of the language, but that was hardly necessary. The Indians were demanding more whiskey.

The wagon men argued, pleaded, and then became desperate. A warrior tried to climb into the wagon, which still contained a half load of flour bags. One of the men felled the inquisitive brave with the butt end of a bull-whip. That was a fatal mistake. With a scream the crazed Indians fell upon the four. It was over almost before Duke realized it was happening. The four whiskey traders died swiftly in the midst of the howling horde that fell upon them.

VI

"THE GUNS ARE EMPTY"

Duke was white-faced. Nausea crawled in the pit of his stomach as he silently began to retreat from that scene. As he crept away, he sighted another bigger party of Gros Ventres, hurrying to the scene. The word of the whiskey trading evidently was spreading over the hunting ground, attracting every thirsty warrior within reach.

Duke returned to the girl, and they retreated from that place. Dusk was coming now, offering welcome concealment as they pushed ahead. They soon sighted the far beacon of wagon fires marking the Standish camp, which was still some two miles away.

They had not covered half of that distance when Duke halted, and they peered at the movement of light near at hand in the creek brush ahead. The deep voices of white men drifted faintly to them. And they heard the thud of tools.

Scouting ahead, Duke discovered another of Brady Bledsoe's wagons drawn up amid the brush alongside the wagon trail, with the idle oxen chewing their cuds as they waited. The big Pittsburgh, which was loaded to the tilt with flour bags, was canted drunkenly on a broken axle. Four disgruntled men were laboring by candlelight, lightening the load and jacking up the wagon in preparation for repairs. It was evident the remainder of the caravan had pushed ahead to a better campsite for the night, leaving the crew to take care of the disabled freighter.

Duke stepped out of the brush. "Forget about the wagon . . . tonight at least," he said tersely. "That bunch of Gro's that Bledsoe tried to trade out of their furs have tasted blood. And they're still thirsty for both blood and rum. They've wiped out your pals, and they may be hunting more scalps tonight."

They stared, recognizing him. "Air you tryin' to say that Moosejaw an' them other boys air . . . ?"

"Dead," Duke nodded. "They stayed too long in that Indian camp. I happened to be watching, when it happened. Those Gro's are on the warpath for fair. And more are joining them. Whiskey draws Indians. Better make fast tracks to the main camp. If any trouble starts there, every man who can fire a gun will be needed. Better hide this wagon. I reckon it's filled with whiskey, too. And rifles. Let's hope the Gro's don't stumble onto it."

He helped them drag the crippled wagon into deeper brush where it was fairly well concealed. They freed the oxen, and Duke rode ahead with the girl while the bullwhackers hurried along on foot at their heels.

Full darkness had settled, when they rode into the Standish camp. It was pitched on a grass flat that sloped gently toward the stream. The stock herd lolled in deep, rich graze. The wagons were thrown into a loose half circle that fronted on a swift, deep mountain stream of icy trout water that swept smoothly in a narrow channel thickly overhung by black willow and aspen. The aromas of frying trout arose from the cook fires as they rode past the wagons. The circle was ragged and open, for Indian trouble along this section of the trail had been infrequent and minor since the unmolested days of the 'Forty-Niners. This was only the dawn of the twenty-year war in which the Sioux and their allies were to contest bitterly every inch of a losing battlefield. Men were not yet disciplined to forming the tight frontier phalanx which was to be the bulwark of wagon camps in the future.

Duke rode to the central fire, singling out Nathanial Standish's ascetic figure. Brady Bledsoe was present there, along with Marcia Standish and her mother.

Standish rose to his domineering height as he recognized his visitors. He glowered at Duke and gave the girl an intolerant stare, scorning the masculine breeches she wore as they dismounted.

"Standish," Duke said, "I'd keep my stock caught up tonight and a double guard out. I'd pouch this wagon circle tighter and see to it that every man keeps his guns loaded, and handy. A big bunch of Gro's are gathering less than ten miles away, and they're painting for war." He looked at Brady Bledsoe. "Those furs your trade wagon bought weren't such a bargain," he said. "Moosejaw and the three other men you sent to that Indian camp aren't coming back . . . ever."

Brady Bledsoe went white.

"What's the fellow talking about?" Standish snapped.

"I don't know," Bledsoe said hollowly. "Are you loco, Cool?"

Duke said: "I ought to put a slug in your rotten heart, Bledsoe. But I might need the bullet later on."

"You dare come here and insult my friend?" Nathanial Standish roared. "What . . . ?"

Zoan caught Duke's arm. "Listen," she breathed.

They all heard it now: a deep, sullen murmur in the distance. The sound resolved into the oncoming drone of many unshod hoofs. Now the gusty, explosive outburst of savage lungs came through the darkness.

"Indians!" Duke snapped at the gaping wagon people. "They've come faster than I figured. Guns! Guns, you fools! Arm yourselves! Are you deaf as well as dumb? Can't you hear?"

They broke into bewildered, horrified confusion. Women scattered, screaming for their children. Men blundered dazedly around, fumbling in the wagons for stored weapons.

Duke turned, snatched up Zoan, tossed her aboard the palomino. "Clear out of here," he commanded. "Ride for it. You can make it across the creek. They're coming from the other direction." He slapped the horse into motion.

A deep sigh arose from the wagon folk. A rising moon had topped the bluffs to the east, and its light picked out the shadowy wave which moved out from the deeper shadows of the brush into the open flat north of the wagon camp.

Men lifted their rifles to their shoulders, but Duke shouted a command. "Hold your fire. They're not attacking yet. They wouldn't come like that if they were ready to fight."

The Indians came on, whooping and milling about, but it was still only an aimless display. Duke judged there were now nearly two hundred Gros Ventres in the party.

"Wait," he ordered again. "Don't open fire. Does anybody speak their lingo?"

A French 'breed bullwhacker nodded.

"Order them to halt where they are," Duke said. "Tell them to come no closer. Keep them at a distance. If they try to move in, I'll give the order to fire. They've got us outnumbered eight to one, or better. Your only chance is to keep them away until we can fort up."

The bullwhacker lifted his voice, rattling the Indian jargon. The Gros Ventres came to a halt and sounded derisive, angry yells. Then one, who evidently was a chief, brought silence long enough to make himself heard. He rode in advance of the main body, swinging a lance and speaking at length.

"He say, *m'sieu,* he want to trade de furs for de whiskee, *oui?*" the 'breed reported.

"Whiskey?" Nathanial Standish exclaimed in disgust. "Tell them we have no whiskey."

"He won't believe it," Duke said dryly. "He knows it's here. Stall him off, Frenchy. Be long-winded about it. Play him along, so as to give us time to shove these wagons together and barricade."

Standish caught Duke's arm belligerently. "I resent your implication that we are carrying whiskey," he thundered. "I. . . ."

Duke turned to one of Brady Bledsoe's wagons nearby. He reached up, dragged a bag from the load, let it thud on the ground. Taking a knife from his belt, he slashed the cloth with a swift stroke and kicked into view a wicker demijohn, and the disassembled parts of a Henry rifle.

"All right," he said. "Now you see what

brought the red ants to the picnic. Wake up, you lard bellies. Jam those wagons together. The Gro's know what these Bledsoe wagons are carrying. They've had a taste of it already. Get your kids and women in the clear. Barricade beneath the wagons. Bust open more of these sacks and set up all these Henrys you can find. Dig up ammunition."

Bledsoe was retreating toward the shadows of the creek brush, but Duke overtook him with long strides.

"No welching," he commanded. "You're not sifting out of camp now, leaving your friends to pay the piper. They'll need every trigger finger soon." He slapped the man in the face so hard Bledsoe hit the ground on the seat of his breeches. Duke's mock jauntiness left him then. "I'll kill you in your tracks, if you make another move to escape," he said.

The French 'breed was making a lengthy reply to the Indians. Under cover of that delay, the wagon men swarmed frantically about, rolling the vehicles together. A measure of calmness returned, and they worked with desperate speed, heaving out barrels and casks of supplies and personal effects to form a hasty barricade for defense. Other men were frantically breaking out rifles from the flour sacks stored in the three Bledsoe wagons in camp.

A roar of fury arose as the Indians realized what was going on. The French 'breed broke off his rambling speech and dove hastily to cover. "Queek, *m'sieurs*," he screeched. "Dey are coming, *oui!*"

"Wait, in God's name!" Nathanial Standish screeched, addressing the Indians, forgetting the difference in languages. "We'll give you another whiskey, if that's all you want." He appealed to the interpreter. "Talk to them. Tell them they are welcome to the vile stuff, if they will only let us alone."

"No!" Duke snarled. He caught Standish by the shoulder, sent him violently spinning away. "Tell them if they come nearer, they'll go to the happy hunting grounds in a hand basket. All they need is a little more brave maker and nothing on earth would stop 'em. Whiskey makes 'em think they're bulletproof. Whatever you do, don't offer rotgut. Talk big to them. Tell them we have many, many guns that shoot all day and all night without reloading. And that we're all dead shots. Tell them every man here has counted coup fifty times on greater warriors than any brown-skinned, dog-eating Gros Ventre that ever lived. A hundred coups. That's the only talk they'll heed now. The rest of you get ready to shoot and shoot straight. Don't miss. Pile 'em up. You men with the Henrys. Don't waste powder at long range. Those repeaters don't carry enough kick to kill a rabbit except at close quarters. Then they really talk."

The interpreter began a grandiose speech, but it was drowned out by a new roar from the Gros Ventres. The sound was different. It was deeper, purposeful, suddenly filled with racial hatred. And then the Indians were coming.

"Wait!" Duke kept chanting. "Save it for closer range. Then pile 'em up. Don't miss. Shoot to kill. Don't let them reach the wagons. They've got us outnumbered . . . *now* . . . give them holy hell!"

There were some thirty guns in the hands of the defenders; but only three had Henrys which were effective, for it had been impossible to put any of the guns from Bledsoe's wagons into operation in the short space of time. A ripple of powder flame whipped from the line of wagons. Sharps, Spencers, and Springfields were in action. The Indians were massed, and the storm of lead tore a gap through their ranks, piling up ponies, sending wounded warriors toppling beneath milling hoofs.

Duke had fired a single-shot Sharps which he snatched from a woman. Then someone pushed a loaded muzzle-loader in his hands, taking away the empty Sharps. It was Zoan.

Duke couldn't believe it. He had taken it for granted that she had escaped across the stream minutes ago and was by now safely on her way back to the Mormon camp fifteen miles east. There was no time to talk. The Indians had reeled but recovered, and were charging closer. In spite of the speech of contempt he had put in the interpreter's mouth, Duke knew that the Gros Ventres were a fighting tribe.

For hectic seconds it looked as if they would carry the wagon circle and come to knife grips with the outnumbered whites. But thanks to the three Henrys the Indians broke at the last moment, stricken by their losses. Their chief had gone down. The attack had been unplanned and hurriedly launched, and they were at a disadvantage. The confused mass of warriors recoiled, then turned, racing away to cover of the timber.

"Saved!" Nathanial Standish croaked. "We were too much for the bloodthirsty rascals. They've learned their lesson."

Duke watched the vague movement of the Indians in the moonlight. "You're crowing too soon, mister," he said. "This was only the first skirmish. They're spreading out to circle us. Hear 'em crossing the stream above and below us? Get busy. Move some of those wagons around to close this circle, or they'll be cross-firing us from across the crick in a minute."

Subdued, the defenders hurried to obey. Duke ran through the camp, kicking the cook fires apart, stamping out the embers. Rifles opened up as the Indians found positions across the creek with the moon at their backs and the deep brush for cover. The firelight was blotted out, but the moon was bright enough for fairly accurate shooting.

Slugs snapped around Duke. Henry rifles were in action in the hands of the Gros Ventres. A bullwhacker was killed in his tracks, and another wounded. That reduced the fighting strength of the party to a scant score, for four men had been slain in the first Indian onslaught, and three more were seriously wounded. Several others were nursing minor gunshot wounds.

"Stay under cover," Duke ordered. "Here you . . . and you . . . and you. Do you know anything about rifles? Get those Henrys from the Bledsoe wagons cleaned of flour and loaded. Get busy. Break out every gun and set it up. You'll find a rifle and a jug of whiskey in every bag of flour. We're outnumbered, but with that many repeaters we ought to be able to hold all the Indians this side of kingdom come. Where's Brady Bledsoe?"

"Layin' here bleatin' like a bogged sheep,"

said a whiskery wagon man named Jake Sevier. "I spotted him, tryin' to sneak away across the crick, so I thunked him on the head with my shootin' airn an' hogtied him. Want me to put a slug in him, sir?"

He said it with such evident eagerness that Duke Cool grinned. Then he was moving away, saying over his shoulder: "Use your own judgment, though it's a waste of powder. The Army will hang or send him to the calaboose for life for this little stunt he pulled. And never mind the 'sir.' I wouldn't know who you were referring to. Save it for the first gentleman that comes along."

Duke was roaming about, peering for someone. At last he located his quarry.

"So there you are," he said scathingly, towering over Zoan Jessup. She was with the women, working on the wounded and dying men who had been moved into shelter back of a barricade of wagon boxes. "Where's my palomino?" Duke demanded. "By the blue flames, didn't I send you high-tailing out of this mess?"

"I'm sorry." She sniffed plaintively.

"Don't you be a-talkin' to this lady thetaway," a spunky wounded man bristled at Duke. "I seed her give the hoss an' mule to thet high-toned Standish gal an' her maw so they could light a shuck out o' camp ahead o' the Injuns. An' this leetle lady done some fast gun loadin' fer us when the red devils was comin' at us. You got no right to bulldoze her around."

Duke looked about and saw that Marcia Standish and her mother were gone from the wagon camp. "Oh, hell," he said helplessly. "Do unto others . . . and all that, eh?"

He picked the Mormon girl up in his arms, lifting her clear of the ground. He kissed her resoundingly on the lips. Kissed her again.

"Oh, Joseph!"

"Wal, thet's better," the wounded man approved.

For a moment she stayed close to Duke, with her face against his shoulder, and he was quite unaware of the sound of the Indians' guns.

An excited man came racing up, disregarding the searching bullets of the Indians who had sighted his shadow in the moonlight. It was one of the three Duke had assigned to the arms detail.

"We're out of luck," the man groaned. "We've got rifles enough to patch hell a mile, but there ain't a handful of ammunition for the Henrys to be had. Brady Bledsoe says the ca'tridges air in the wagon thet broke down before we camped. It's settin' back down the crick more'n a mile away. It might as well be on the moon with all these Injuns around."

VII

"DOWNSTREAM TO DESTRUCTION"

Duke raced to where Brady Bledsoe lay tied hand and foot, guarded by the grim-lipped Jake Sevier. "Is it true, Bledsoe," he asked tersely, "that all the ammunition is in the crippled wagon down the crick?"

Brady Bledsoe looked shrunken and old. He had a purple welt on his head where Jake Sevier had felled him with a gun muzzle. He winced each time a bullet passed near, and cringed whenever a war cry sounded. "It's in that wagon, packed away in sacks of flour," he mumbled. "About seventy rifles are on that wagon, too."

Frowning, Duke snapped: "How many Henrys were in that first wagon that Moose-jaw took to the Indian camp?"

"Forty-odd," Bledsoe admitted.

"How many cartridges?"

"About four thousand rounds."

Duke was silent a moment. The Indians, in addition to outnumbering the defenders, held a staggering advantage in guns and ammunition.

"Stay near me, Cool," Bledsoe said hoarsely. "These fellows are threatening to hang me."

Duke thought of the shot that had been fired at him that night in Fort Emigrant. Bledsoe must have guessed what was passing in his mind for he uttered a moan of despair, and fell silent.

Nathanial Standish bent over the bound man. "You fiend!" he raved. "You brought this on us. We'll burn you at the stake . . . rend you limb from limb!"

Duke turned away, leaving Standish to his futile denunciation. He moved around the wagon circle, taking an inventory of the company's armament. The result was none too encouraging. The supply of shells for the Henry rifles had been nearly exhausted in repelling the first attack. Less than thirty shells remained for the repeating guns.

There were more than a score of Sharpses, Springfields, and Spencers in camp, but they were single-shot guns, and many of them were muzzle-loaders as were the four shotguns he counted. The defenders assayed only five cap and ball six-shooters.

"If the red brothers really come at us for a finish fight, we won't last long," he told Jake Sevier, who was showing a quality of leadership that ranked him as a man to depend on. "Right now they're a little wary of us, for they suspect we may all have Henrys and are ready to give them a warm welcome. But they'll learn after daybreak that we aren't so tough."

The Gros Ventres made a sortie at that moment. A skirmish line charged in from upstream. They came on foot and used the dark brush as cover. The attack was repelled with small loss to the Indians, but the last of the shells for the Henrys was exhausted.

"It was only a feint to feel us out," Duke shrugged. "They didn't really mean it that time."

But another of the whites had been killed in the skirmish, and a child had been wounded. The Indians now settled down to a harassing sniping duel. Another wagon man was killed, and a woman was hit, before the defenders learned it was death to expose themselves above the barricades.

Duke wriggled to a vantage point and lay peering at the creek that rushed swiftly past in its deep, brush-shaded channel in the moonlight only a rope's length away. He spoke to Nathanial Standish. "The Mormon handcart party is only about fifteen miles away. There are seventy or eighty men in that outfit able to fight. And downstream is a wagonload of Henrys with plenty of ammunition. I doubt if the Indians know about that abandoned wagon."

Wild hope tore at the man. "We must get word to those Mormons!" he exclaimed. "They must come to our assistance."

"Must?" Duke chided caustically.

"Surely even a Mormon would not stand by and let savages massacre us? They couldn't be that inhuman."

"Aren't you the same lard belly who refused to give a helping hand to these same Saints back on the Laramie plains, or have I got things twisted?" Duke remarked.

Zoan Jessup, who had been within earshot, busy with the wounded, came crawling nearer. "Stop it, Joseph," she said reprovingly to Duke. And then to Nathanial Standish: "My people will send help, of course. It will take time for them to get here, but they will come. I'm sure of that. Your wife and daughter should be nearly to our camp by this time. I told them to follow the stream. They can't miss the camp."

"Sure," Duke said grimly. "The Mormons likely will be fools enough to try it. All they've got to fight with are a few old muzzle-loaders and their bare hands. They'll walk into two hundred Indians who're packing guns that never stop shooting. It'll be great sport . . . for the Indians."

Standish protested wildly. "But the Mormons can arm themselves from. . . ."

"From Bledsoe's wagon down the crick? Use your head, man. Even if your daughter knew about that wagon, do you think she's the kind of a person to be the first to tell the world she has been flirting with a whiskey peddler? That's one subject that won't be mentioned to the Mormons. Anyway, your womenfolk don't know the truth about Bledsoe or about the rifles in that wagon. They pulled out of camp before the story came out."

"We must get word to those people somehow," Standish chattered. "If they are properly armed, they can scatter these savages easily."

There was a silence. Jake Sevier spoke heavily. "How in tophet is anybody goin' to get out of this trap? Them Injuns has got us sewed up."

"There's the stream," Duke observed quietly.

"Gawd Almighty! Them Injuns will be watchin' the crick aplenty. They're smart enough to know it's the way we might try to slip somebody through. An' in this moonlight. . . ."

"It's the crick or nothing," Duke said. "There's no other hope. Too much open ground in all other directions."

Again there was a silence.

"A man who keeps his head," Duke added, "might drift through underwater. He could weight himself down so he would stay well under the surface. That stream is swift and deep along here. And overhung with brush. A man could push himself to the top now and then under cover of brush to get a fresh lungful of air."

"How would you know you wasn't comin' up jest where some brave was squattin' with a tommyhawk in his paw?"

"That," Duke said dryly, "is what will make it interesting."

The silence fell again.

"Who'll go?" Nathanial Standish demanded insistently.

"I'll make a try at it," Jake Sevier growled.

Three or four other men muttered a willingness to volunteer. But Standish remained silent.

"Can you swim?" Duke asked Jake Sevier. "Do you know how to handle yourself underwater?"

Reluctantly Sevier shook his head. Of the other volunteers, only one had confidence in his ability, and this man, although he tried to make light of it, had a bullet wound in his right arm.

Duke signed dolefully. "A man who can't swim would only be committing suicide. It'll be tough enough even for anyone who knows how to take care of himself in deep water. I was hoping there would be at least two of us. Even if one hit bad luck, the other might wiggle through."

"You?" Standish questioned eagerly.

"Unfortunately I know how to swim," Duke remarked. "As a kid I spent half my time diving for coins at the Saint Louis steamboat levee."

The Mormon girl suddenly bust into tears. "You can't do this alone, Joseph. I. . . ." She stood on tiptoe and kissed him.

Duke held her in his arms a moment. "The moon's getting higher," he said huskily. "I better step lively. It'll be a long walk to that Mormon camp. I'll likely catch cold traveling in wet clothes. I aim to be back by daybreak."

He released her, tried to occupy his mind with the business of preparing for his attempt. From the blacksmith stores he selected a three-foot length of strap iron. The object had weight enough, he decided, to offset the buoyancy of his body without serving as an actual anchor. It would also come in handy as a weapon.

Wearing only breeches and moccasins, and with a skinning knife in his belt, he made a swift survey of the terrain. Buffalo and alder brush offered cover the few rods to the stream. Men whispered encouragement, patted him on the back as he wriggled through the barricade and out of the wagon circle.

Only an occasional shot was being fired by the Indians. Gunflame darted twice from the thickets beyond the creek as Duke wriggled ahead, but the bullets were aimed at the wagons. They had not sighted him. Willows and aspen overhung the stream as he drew himself to the margin. A filter of moonlight laid a ragged silvery pattern on the black surface.

Duke lowered himself over a four-foot cutbank into the water and was scarcely aware of its icy chill in the tension of the moment. It was deep water against the brushy cutbank, and his feet did not find bottom. He clung to a protruding root for a moment to get his bearings. Faint movement in the brush above his head startled him. Then a shadowy figure slid over the cutbank into the water beside him.

It was Zoan. She, also, carried a length of iron rod as a weight. She had tied a cloth around her hair to keep it in place. She clung there beside him, only her head showing above water. "I, too, can swim," she murmured.

"Go back," Duke groaned. "You can't try this."

She shook her head. "You said there would be a better chance, if two of us went. I can

255

handle myself underwater. I've known how to swim and dive since I was big enough to walk."

Duke saw that it would have to be this way. There was no turning back now. It was impossible to climb back over that overhanging, brushy cutbank without making a commotion that would certainly attract the attention of the Indians. Protest was futile; regrets were vain. "I'd hate to play poker with you in a freeze-out," he murmured, and his lips brushed her cheek. "You've got too much sand. I'll lead the way. Give me a minute's start. Two minutes. And pray that the stream doesn't shallow below this point."

He kissed her again. Filling his lungs he sank beneath the surface, and sent his body gliding downstream with a powerful shove.

VIII

"UNTIL WE REACH THE VALLEY"

Duke let his body go limp, conserving his energy and letting the current do the work. He used the iron rod to fend himself away from bottom and from the bank. His body touched obstacles now and then, or collided with cutbanks, as the stream rushed him along in its meandering course. But it was deep clay channel through the flat, with no boulders.

He could see the deep shadows of the brush and the glow of moonlight on the surface above. At intervals he pushed himself beneath those black shadows and came to the surface in silence among water-trailing foliage to replenish his lungs. Then he would sink again and let himself drift onward.

Time and again he rose. He judged that he was now nearly clear of the flat. Suddenly the current sharpened, and he was carried with a rush through a small rapids between big boulders. He collided with a boulder with breathtaking impact and went chuting down a five-foot cascade into the boiling plunge of a sizable pool.

He drifted clear of the troubled water beneath the cascade and was carried toward the downstream outlet of the pool. He thought of the girl who likely was drifting downstream to plunge into this same danger. The rapids had taken him by surprise. His lungs were compressing with the need for air. Full moonlight played on the lower end of the pool. He tried to stay submerged, but the stream widened and shallowed, gathering momentum as it left the pool. A cross current drove his drifting body to the surface in spite of his efforts. The water was less than waist deep at this point, and he lifted his head, gasping for air.

As he did so, he heard a startled whoop. He glimpsed three or four warriors leaping into the water ahead and around him. He had been discovered by sentinels stationed at this point. He braced himself against the current and came to his feet in the water. He swung the length of iron and landed a glancing blow that sent the first Indian sprawling beneath the surface.

A gun exploded in the hands of a warrior on shore, but the shot missed. There was no more shooting, for Duke was surrounded by Indians in the next instant. He was thinking of Zoan, who was no doubt drifting toward this same trap into which he had fallen. Clawing hands were grabbing at him, seeking to pull him down. He sensed they wanted to take him alive. The length of iron was jerked from his hands. He had no time to get out his knife, and he tried to fight them off with his fists, but they were too many. He reeled, fell, rose again, and fought his way through the shallowing water toward a dry gravel bar, carrying the battle away from the spillway of the pool.

An Indian got a hand grip on his hair, and the flat of a tomahawk glanced from his temple. His senses reeled. He managed to flounder ahead, carrying a screeching opponent on his back. In that instant he believed that he saw a vague shadow, and a floating sheen of tawny hair drift by in the rush of water out of the pool and vanish downstream, but the Indians were too busy with their captive to notice.

The tomahawk struck again then, and Duke fell on his face in ankle-deep water. That was all he remembered for many minutes.

He came slowly to a painful realization that he was still alive. A pole had been passed between his bound hands and feet, and he was being carried by two Indians in the manner of a deer carcass. Half a dozen more Indians trotted along ahead and back of the burden bearers and took turns shouldering the pole. His swinging body collided roughly with boulders and crashed through the brush as they labored with him up the ascent from the stream.

He played 'possum, although at times this was not entirely pretense. Blood dripped from a gash on his head. Now and then cold nausea overcame him completely, and he lost track of events for minutes at a time. He aroused to find himself being carried into the midst of a score or more of excited Indians. A small campfire burned in a swale. He could hear the occasional report of a gun nearby, and he realized he had been brought back to the vicinity of the besieged wagon circle.

He continued to pretend unconsciousness but was prodded out of his pose when a knife point was pushed against his ribs. He winced, and a howl of delight arose. He opened his eyes. He was jerked to his feet and slapped and prodded around by ungentle hands. A painted Indian came dancing at him, twirling a steel hatchet, whose whetted blade looked razor-sharp. The brave made a great show of his dexterity as he whooped and leaped, keeping the hatchet whirling in a dazzling arc around Duke's head, grazing his hair many times.

Other Indians arrived to slap and upbraid him and dance around, pounding their chests while they shouted in boastful dialect the story of their prowess as warriors. Duke understood they were counting coup on him. In other circumstances he might have felt flattered, for in the Indian scheme of things to have so many braves count coup on a single captive was proof that they regarded the victim as a man of ability. But Duke knew this was only a preliminary to something else. They had let him live this long for some purpose. He refused to speculate on what that might be.

The coup counting went on hour after hour. Midnight passed. From the number of warriors who visited the camp in relays for the ceremony Duke guessed that more Gros Ventres had arrived to join the siege of the wagon train. Vigilance over the embattled wagons was not allowed to lapse. Duke heard scattered firing continue.

He fixed his thoughts on one objective, and that helped fortify him. He kept Zoan's face pictured in his mind. One thing was certain: at least, she had not fallen into the hands of the Indians. There might have been other rapids below the one where he had been captured, and her body might now be. . . . He refused to consider that, also. At least, it would be better than being a prisoner of the Gros Ventres.

The coup counting dwindled. A paunchy, flat-nosed chief at last gave an order, and Duke was freed from the sapling to which he had been tied all night. The thongs were removed from his ankles. He was kicked and prodded into walking. They marched him through the brush. He soon saw the creek flat ahead and the besieged wagons.

The moon was sinking behind fleecy clouds to the west. The morning star was kindling in the east. From the signs, Duke saw that the Indians were organizing for a general attack to storm the wagons. He lifted a shout, yelling — "Get set, men!" — his voice carrying sharply over the flat. "There're coming at you soon."

An Indian smashed him in the face with his hand, silencing him, half stunning him, but he had sent his warning. They tied him to a tree on the edge of the clearing. Warriors went scurrying about, hunting dry brush. They heaped the brush around him until he was submerged to his shoulders. They were going to burn him alive there under the eyes of the wagon folk. It was a plan calculated to horrify the defenders and destroy their courage.

An Indian was sprinkling gunpowder over a twisted wisp of dry grass. Another stood ready with flint and steel to ignite the torch. Gray daylight was beginning to etch out the timber as formless shapes.

"Jake!" Duke called. "Jake Sevier! Can you hear me?"

"I hear yuh, sir," the bullwhacker's voice came faintly from the wagons. "But cain't see you. Too dark. Whar are yuh? Has them devils got yuh?"

"They've got me. But there's still a chance. The girl may have got through alive. Fight to a finish. But your first bullet is for me, Sevier. You'll be able to see me in a moment. Do you understand? They're making ready to burn me. Shoot straight. Don't miss. I'll thank you for it."

262

There was a moment of silence.

"I'll do it, sir," Jake Sevier responded. His voice was heavy, weary.

Sparks were flying from the flint. In the timber the Indians were moving forward, setting themselves for the charge. The powder had not yet ignited. The flint was stubborn. Duke's head lifted. He listened to a deep, vibrant murmur that rolled through the dawn. It erupted into the crackle of gunfire from the downstream end of the clearing. He heard Indians screeching.

The skirmish welled into a strident, booming uproar of rushing, oncoming men. The gunfire spread, ran through the brush until the flashes formed a long, arcing line that surged nearer at the pace of running men. The Indians were breaking. The warrior with the flint and steel came to his feet, staring for an instant. Then he, too, was running.

Bullets were raking the thickets. Duke saw warriors falling, sprawling in full stride. The gunfire was now a sustained roar, proving that many repeating rifles were in operation. The oncoming line swept through the timber, rolling up the Indian formation in a flanking attack that left a heavy toll of dead and dying underfoot as it surged onward.

Bullets snapped around Duke. Then the oncoming line of Mormons reached him. He made out Elder Jethro Sloan's gaunt, angular form in the thin light of daybreak. The elder paused only long enough to kick away the pile of brush and slash the bonds that held him.

"Sister Jessup is back there, brother," the elder roared, jerking a thumb over his shoulder. "Praying for your soul. She believes you are dead. She found us as we were making forced march to the assistance of the Gentiles. A Gentile girl and her mother had arrived at our camp earlier, riding your horse and mule. They told us of the Indian trouble. Sister Jessup led us to an abandoned wagon, and we armed ourselves with these fine weapons. We smashed many whiskey jugs and proceeded at forced march."

Duke walked like a man in a dream back through the ranks of the Mormon fighting line. He located the rear guard and saw the small, wan-faced figure among them.

She came toward him slowly, her lips moving in prayer. "Joseph," she said. She fainted dead away into his arms then.

She was still in his arms when the Mormons and the rescued wagon folk came streaming back after abandoning further pursuit of the fleeing Indians.

South Pass was now astern. Ahead lay the forks of the great trail. To the left was the

264

route that led by Bridger's and through Echo
Cañon to Salt Lake. The trail to the right followed the Fort Hall route to the Humboldt.
The handcart people were pushing eagerly
ahead, inspired by this milestone, knowing
now that their journey was well on its way to
success.

Duke and the girl halted, standing in the
bars of the Jessup handcart.

"Which way is it to be?" he asked.

She smiled remotely, as if it were an imma-
terial question. "It is for you to say, Joseph.
Wherever you go, I will go."

"We'll toss a coin at the fork," Duke said.
"Right?"

"Right," the Mormon girl agreed. "Though
it will be frowned upon by Elder Jethro."

Duke lifted his voice in song, and the girl
joined in. The entire company took up the refrain:

> **For some must push, and some**
> **must pull,**
> **As we go marching up the hill;**
> **As merrily on the way we go,**
> **Until we reach the valley — o!**

Together they put their shoulders to the
bar. They sent the handcart surging forward.

Hung Up at Parley's Store

A north wind had stripped the last of the leaves from the row of poplars Mrs. Knight had planted around the ranch yard, and the range was taking on the pinched-out, bone-picked look that means the end of another season. Out on the flats the tumbleweeds were hurrying south, and Swanee was about to follow them. He finished lashing his warsack on the horse Charlie Knight was loaning him to ride to town and then walked to the house to say good bye to Charlie and the missus.

"Think over what I told you yesterday, Swanee," Charlie urged, regretfully shaking hands. "If you change your mind, the offer still stands."

"I sure will," Swanee promised. And he meant it. He always meant it. Charlie Knight wasn't the first rancher who had tried to talk him out of quitting when his summer's wages were burning his pocket. Charlie had kept him on after the roundup crew had been laid off. He wanted Swanee to stay now as range boss and put his money into cattle, with the idea of becoming a partner in Stone Corral

Ranch later on. Swanee avoided the missus' eyes. Women always acted queerly when a man quit a job and headed for town. "I'll show up for calf brandin' in the spring, at least," he told her.

"What you need, Swanee," she said, "is a wife to settle you down."

"Trouble is," Swanee said solemnly, "Charlie saw you first, Missus Knight. Looks like I'll just naturally have to die in single harness now."

That softened her a trifle. The missus had been married to Charlie nearly twenty years and was the mother of three children, but Swanee knew all women like to be flattered. "Hold on a minute," she ordered as he reached for a stirrup. "As long as you're set on going, I'd be obliged if you'd ride by Parley's and leave a bundle. I've got a winter coat and a few other things that've got too small for me. Missus Parley can make 'em over for herself." She went hurrying into the house.

Her husband grinned. "Watch out for Maw," he warned. "She's settin' a deadfall for you. There's a gal over at Parley's of marryin' age."

"I can handle things," Swanee stated complacently and studied his shadow. He was lank and tall and twenty-five, and he was wearing his double-breasted flannel shirt with pearl buttons, his buckskin jacket, foxed saddle pants, and his Sunday hat and yellow-stitched boots. "That redhead Parley girl is kinda thin," he added. "Got pipestem legs, most likely. I rode past Parley's a couple weeks ago and took at look at her. It wasn't worth the trip."

"Between you and me," Charlie confided, "she was wearin' men's britches the other day. I was over that way and saw her with my own eyes."

"No?" Swanee was incredulous. "Men's britches, huh? That I've got to see. It must have been a sight."

"Don't ever let on I told you," Charlie warned hastily. "They say she's got a hair-trigger temper."

The missus appeared and handed Swanee a parcel. "Tell Missus Parley I'll drive over and visit this Saturday, weather permitting," she instructed. "Give my best to Miss Joncie. It's a blessing having white women only thirty miles away. I hope Ancil Parley can make a go of it with his store."

"He won't," her husband said. "He's a knothead. Don't savvy the Indians. Some day he's goin' to get into bad trouble with some old buck."

Swanee shook hands all around again and hit the saddle. He was aware of a deep sense of parting. This mood, he reflected, would fade with the passing miles. It always had. But, as he rode through the wan sunlight, he kept recalling the cheery glint of the log fire that had been burning in the living room back of the missus as she stood in the open door, watching him leave.

Charlie and the missus had come into Montana after the Indians had accepted reservation. They had seen some lean pickings in their previous years but seemed to have hit the right combination now. Their brand was prospering. Their new log house was big and solid and meant for permanency. Barring a possible flare-up by the Indians, which was still the biggest gamble in this range, Charlie and the missus seemed set for life.

Fording Muddy Creek, Swanee headed across country. Descending from the Kinni-kinick Divide, two more hours of steady riding brought him onto the reservation road which was used by freighters and Army supply outfits. This detour to Parley's was adding fifteen miles to the trip to town, but time held no urgency for Swanee now. A month from now, or two months, he likely would be jingling his spur chains in the Silver Dollar Bar in Denver. Or maybe he'd take a notion to swing south by way of Salt Lake and take a look at the Mormon gals. After that, Arizona or Texas, or perhaps a *pasear* into Mexico.

Parley's Store lifted out of the loneliness of the land ahead. Its tar-paper roof reflected the waning daylight. Two south windows looked blankly from its plank and bat walls. A rickety wagon shed and a frost-seared garden and corn patch flanked the building. An ancient harness mare was staked out on the flat. Two Indian ponies stood at the tie rail before the store, their rumps hip-shot against the chill wind.

Swanee spotted the Parley girl hanging up clothes back of the house. He peered, hoping to view the britches, but, when she heard his horse and moved out into the open, he was disappointed. She was wearing a heavy dark winter skirt and a gingham apron. She appraised him with eyes that were of the gray-green shade. She looked cold and wind-blown, but there was a tilt to her nose. She drew herself up a little. "There they are," she spoke tartly, "if you want to take a look at 'em."

She pointed to a pair of jeans that were hanging on the clothesline. Swanee flushed. He was not, he surmised, the first cowboy who had come riding by Parley's in the hope of seeing a female in britches.

"Howdy, ma'am," was all he could think to say, right at that moment. He racked his horse and went into the store, carrying the bundle

Mrs. Knight had given him.

A gaunt, mahogany-faced Cheyenne stood at the plank counter, gloomily studying the few jars of candy on the back shelf. Swanee knew this Indian. He was Yellow Jacket, a sub-chief who lived with his lodge of relatives and in-laws a dozen miles west. The Cheyenne wore a black felt hat that was several sizes too small, a blue cotton shirt turned inside out, and blue jeans out of which he had cut the seat, exposing a red flannel breech clout. His fat, middle-aged squaw sat cross-legged beside the door, earnestly working on a lollipop.

A meager line of canned goods, soda pop, tobacco, and drygoods was on display. Beyond the partition that separated the tiny store from the living quarters Swanee could hear Mrs. Parley busy at a washboard. Ancil Parley stood back of the counter, glowering at the Indian. He was an underslung, head-strong man with bushy, graying hair. Years of slow ferment had soured him against life. He had drifted into the country the past summer and traded a wagon for this enterprise, at which two former owners had failed.

"Make up your mind," Ancil Parley was saying impatiently to the Indian. "I ain't got all day to dally here while you spend a nickel."

The Cheyenne debated weightily. He lifted

271

a finger to point, changed his mind, and fell into profound thought again. Finally he took the plunge. "Some!" he exploded, indicating a jar of peppermints. He thrust a finger into his mouth, fished around among the coins he had deposited there, then triumphantly expectorated a nickel on the counter.

Parley snorted and filled the order. "Now, git!" he commanded. "Vamoose!" He turned to Swanee. "These damned Injuns," he said. "He's been here all day, an' he's only spit out three nickels. Now what can I do for you, mister?"

"Missus Knight at Stone Corral asked me to deliver these to your wife," Swanee said, handing over the bundle.

"Second-hands!" Ancil Parley bristled. "I ain't in need of charity, friend. Just take 'em back and. . . ."

"It isn't charity," the redheaded girl spoke up, coming into the store, "and, even if it was, we could still use them." She took the bundle.

"I'll thank you to mind your own blasted business, Joncie," her father said, and stamped out.

She spoke to Swanee but didn't look directly at him, for her nose was still up a little. "Thanks for bringing them. Would you care for a bottle of pop?"

Swanee caught on. She was trying to take

272

him down a peg or two by treating him like a kid. She was sassy, all right.

"Reckon I'd rather have one of those Lily o' the Valleys," he said, pointing to some violently scented fancy soap on the shelf alongside the candy jars.

Joncie Parley looked surprised. There had been no demand in the past for that ornately wrapped soap that some former owner had stocked, but she handed a bar over to him. She refused payment.

Yellow Jacket was still standing there, pretending not to be interested. Swanee chuckled to himself, as an idea struck him. The redheaded girl eyed him suspiciously. However, when he innocently pocketed the soap, she picked up the bundle and went into the back room.

Swanee got out the soap, stripped back the wrapper. Turning, so neither Yellow Jacket nor the squaw could see, and keeping the bar concealed in his hand, he deluded the Indians into believing he had taken a generous bite. He smacked his lips and looked pleased. Yellow Jacket sniffed that lily fragrance. It had come from the candy shelf. It smelled fine. He rapped on the counter just as he had seen white men do. Ancil Parley appeared.

"Some!" Yellow Jack croaked, pointing to the soap.

Parley was astonished. "Well, you could well use some of that," he decided. "A dime." He spread his open hand twice.

A wet dime hit the counter. Yellow Jacket picked up his purchase, tore off the wrapper, and helped himself to a man-size sample.

The redheaded girl came back into the store and halted, staring in dismay. Yellow Jacket's jaws moved once, then became motionless. A pained disbelief spread over his features. "Some damn!" he said, and expelled the offending morsel. He tossed the remainder of the bar of soap on the floor, eyeing it morosely. He gazed at Swanee with considerable respect.

Joncie Parley guessed the answer. She gave Swanee a look. "I'll bet you pull the wings off grasshoppers, too," she remarked.

"Yeah," said Swanee, "an' push old ladies in the mud . . . 'specially if they wear men's pants."

Her father walked out from back of the counter, glaring. "I ought to have run 'em out hours ago," he fumed. "Look at that floor!" Before Swanee could interfere, he grasped the Cheyenne by the breech clout and shirt collar, hustled him to the door, and sent him sprawling on the half-frozen ground. "Git!" he raged.

He turned on the squaw. Swanee grabbed

him before he could touch the Indian woman. "Take it easy, man," he protested, alarmed by this turn of affairs.

Through the window he watched Yellow Jacket get to his feet. There was nothing ludicrous or meek about the Cheyenne now. He stood, looking at the store with infuriated eyes. Then he and the squaw mounted and rode away, pounding their ponies with moccasin heels.

"You ought not lay hands on a Cheyenne," Swanee told Ancil Parley. "They're proud."

"Proud? The copper pots?"

"That was Yellow Jacket," Swanee said uneasily. "He helped wipe out Custer on the Little Bighorn. That was only a few years ago. He was a war chief. Still is, I suppose."

The girl watched the departing Indians, standing at his side at the window. It occurred to Swanee that he had been wrong about her being skinny. She wasn't plump, either. Viewed at close range she was just about right. Straight and supple. Her hair was thick, shining, and more of the rich buckskin shade in this light.

"You think . . . ?" she began and didn't finish it.

Swanee looked at Mrs. Parley, who had come in from the kitchen. She was a small, faded woman. "Maybe we better take the

275

womenfolks over to Stone Corral tonight, Mister Parley," he said dubiously.

"What? Travel thirty miles just because you've got Injuns on the brain? Hogwash!"

Swanee was between the devil and the deep. Ancil Parley didn't understand these plains Indians. They were still wild, unpredictable. Yellow Jacket might cool down and forget the indignity he had suffered. Then again, he was a warrior to whom an affront was a serious matter.

"I'll hang up here tonight," Swanee decided.

He saw Joncie Parley draw a deep breath and knew that she, at least, was glad he was staying.

Her father gave him a tolerant grin. "The only Injuns you'll see will be in your dreams. It was that blasted, high-toned soap that started the fuss. Whatever made that Cheyenne think it was candy?"

Swanee didn't say anything. Neither did the girl. For that he was grateful.

He ate supper with the Parleys. Afterward he slipped out, tied his roan pony and the Parleys' harness mare close by the kitchen door. Turning, he found Joncie, standing in the chill darkness, wrapped in a heavy coat. "Mom and I want to start for Stone Corral," she confessed. "But Dad's too stubborn. I'm scared."

"I'm steady as a rock," Swanee sighed. "It's just the wind rattlin' my pants legs that makes 'em look like that."

Her mother called fretfully from the house: "Janice!"

"All right, Mom," the girl answered.

"Janice, huh," Swanee commented. "That's where they get that Joncie business."

She nodded. "What's your name?" she asked casually.

"Jim Orcutt. But they call me Swanee."

She eyed the pistol he had thrust in his belt. It was a battered gun, the cedar handle scarred from pounding coffee beans on rocks in endless trailside camps. He had been carrying the six-shooter in his bedroll. Evidently the sight of the gun comforted her. Swanee didn't tell her he had only one live shell in the chamber. He had used the rest of his ammunition long since on rattlers and prairie dogs.

When he got a chance to question Ancil Parley before bedtime, he learned that Parley had no .44 shells in stock. Furthermore, the man's only weapon was a rusty bird gun. Ancil Parley had no shells for that gun, either. "An' I wouldn't lose any sleep loadin' shells tonight, even if I had any powder, which I ain't," he stated.

Swanee spread his tarp and blankets on the floor of the store. He didn't expect anything until toward daybreak, for it would take Yellow Jacket that long to return with his bucks — if he meant to come back looking for trouble.

Nevertheless, he stayed awake. After a while Joncie came stealing back into the store. She couldn't sleep, she whispered. She was dressed and had brought a quilt from her bed to wrap up in.

They sat there in the darkness while the stove warmth died out of the place and the cold crept in. They didn't have much to say. Swanee rolled a cigarette, and in the flare of the match he got a shock. She was wearing 'em now! Joncie Parley had on men's jeans!

She knew he had seen. "Skirts," she said argumentatively, "are a nuisance, if you have to ride or do much footwork."

"I reckon," Swanee said.

He, at least, had her on the defensive. She fell into a sulky silence. Time dragged, and they listened to the occasional shuffle of the horses outside, and the snoring of Ancil Parley and his wife in the back room.

Midnight passed. Joncie began to doze. She finally fell asleep, sitting there against the wall, and gradually sagged against him. Swanee pulled her head to rest on his shoulder. He didn't mind sitting there motionless so as not to disturb her.

She started awake, realized where she was, and sat up rigidly.

"I was afeared you'd crack your neck," Swanee was moved to explain.

"I didn't mean to bother you, Mister Orcutt."

"It wasn't any bother."

They again sat in silence for a long time. Swanee finally moved to the window. He was there half an hour, and the first pale promise of daylight was in the sky, when he spoke suddenly: "Wake your paw and maw, Joncie."

She was at his side instantly.

"They're out there," Swanee said reluctantly.

He heard her quit breathing for a moment. Then she sped silently into the back room.

Ancil Parley came stumbling through the darkness. "It ain't possible," he mumbled.

"Help me get the horses into the kitchen," Swanee ordered. "They'll be killed out in the open."

Parley seemed too bewildered to understand. It was Joncie who helped prod the two animals through the door into the dirt-floored kitchen. These sounds were heard, and the Cheyennes knew their presence had been discovered. For the first time in his life Swanee heard a real, honest-to-God war whoop. It did things to a man. He had heard folks say it

279

turned blood to thin water, and he could believe that now.

Rifles exploded at a distance. Bullets shook the plank walls. Window glass began to fall. Swanee pushed Joncie down on the floor, called to her parents to lie flat. He crouched at a window with his pistol but could see nothing except the flash of guns. Then the shooting died down. Presently the wagon shed began to burn, and he saw an Indian running away.

Swanee moved to the north window, away from the burning shed, judging that the Cheyennes would avoid outlining themselves in the glare of the fire. He was right. A bullet smashed the glass above his head, and he heard canned goods tumble from a shelf.

Joncie was at his side, and she had the bird gun. Then whooping Indians came riding out of the dawn shadows, charging toward the building. There were no more than a dozen of them, Swanee decided, which meant that only the men from Yellow Jacket's own lodge were involved.

He knocked the broken glass out of the window frame with the barrel of his gun, waited until he was sure of his target, then fired at a pony. The animal went down less than a hundred feet away. Its rider landed on his feet. In the glow of the increasing fire from the shed Swanee recognized Yellow Jacket.

The Cheyenne leaped astride behind another Indian. To Swanee's surprise the quail gun in the hands of the girl exploded then. There was no sign that any of the shot had bothered the Indians, but on top of the killing of the pony it discouraged them. They veered away to a safer distance.

"Where'd you get the shell for that chicken gun?" Swanee asked.

"Found it in Dad's hunting coat," she said. Her voice was shaking.

"How many more shells you got?"

She didn't answer for a moment. "None. That was all I could find."

Swanee crouched there, sweating a little. He didn't tell her his own gun was empty, too. He wondered if the Cheyennes would try another rush. If they did and reached close quarters, they'd learn the defenders had no ammunition.

He waited. The Cheyennes began using rifles again from a distance. The bullets shook dust from the rafters as they tore through the planks, but the besieged four were unhurt as they hugged the floor.

Daylight was strengthening. Swanee showed himself occasionally at the windows, brandishing the six-shooter for moral effect. He also poked the shotgun into view at times.

Then the Indians came riding out of a coulée three hundred yards north of the store. They made a fierce display as they raced toward the building, yelling and hanging on the off side of their ponies, moccasins hooked in the footstraps.

Swanee glanced at Joncie, who was crouching behind him. Back of them Mrs. Parley was praying. Swanee arose, showing himself at the window, his pistol raised menacingly.

The Indians kept coming, yelling frenziedly. Then they quit, just beyond effective six-shooter range. They veered away, shouting insults.

Swanee sank back. He felt suddenly limp. He knew it was over now. He realized that his arm was around Joncie's waist. He finally took it away, but not until he was ready.

The Indians hung around another half hour, then rode away. They had burned the wagon shed, shot up the store, and lost a pony. Their honor was vindicated.

"Let's git out of here," Ancil Parley croaked. "Let's hit fer Stone Corral."

The harness mare had a deep bullet crease on her hip, which Swanee treated with axle grease. His cow pony had escaped damage.

They waited through a long day until dark, then headed for the ranch. Swanee and Parley walked most of the way, although they rode double back of the women over some of the easy stretches. The thirty-mile trip didn't seem so long to Swanee, even though the last hour was made through a driving snow, for Joncie's hand kept reaching out and touching him in the darkness. When they were riding double, she leaned her head on his shoulder and huddled close. It was warmer that way.

They pulled into Stone Corral at daybreak. Charlie Knight and the missus and the two hands who worked the year around aroused and came on the run.

"I'm takin' that offer you mentioned, Charlie," Swanee said, "if it's still open."

Charlie Knight looked at him, sighing for the tumbleweed who would wander no more. "I warned you, Swanee," he said. "I warned you there was a girl over at Parley's."

Joncie colored up considerable. Her eyes peeked at him from under her long lashes, and then Swanee lifted her off the horse and kissed her right there in front of everybody.

He glowered at the ranch hands, daring 'em to say anything. For Joncie was still wearing her britches. She looked mighty nice in 'em, too.

He Knew All About Women

Shan Baxter had already put in more than a month looking for a wife to marry and a couple of good yoke of oxen to buy. He had acquired the oxen at a bargain price without much trouble, along with a stout wagon that would serve many purposes, but, as he drove along the raw, stump-and-a-jump route through the Ohio forest that had grown up near Zane's trace, he was half of a mind to give up the rest of his plan as a waste of time. Womenfolk were scarce in the new Ohio country and what few possibilities he had investigated in the thin scatter of settlements along the Muskingum and Scioto either had been spoken for already or hadn't measured up to his requirements. Therefore, he had decided to make a last try at Wheeling, on the east bank of the Ohio, more than a hundred miles away. There he hoped to find a bigger field of selection. He had been told there were two or three thousand people living in Wheeling now, what with the way settlers were flocking west from the seaboard.

Even here, west of the river, the handwriting was on the wall. Since sunup Shan had passed a dozen new cabins and the beginnings of stump farms in the forest. The trace was churned to dust around the stumps by the wheels of immigrants' wagons. He had encountered three westbound caravans during the morning, and now sounds ahead — the rattle of yoke rings and the snap of whip poppers — told him he was about to meet another.

Rounding a curve, he came upon a string of ten dusty, ox-drawn, canvas-topped wagons halted in the trace. The second vehicle in line was in trouble, and Shan saw that its fore axle was wedged on a high, center stump.

He walked ahead and stood, leaning on his long rifle to watch with critical, pitying tolerance the way these seaboarders handled this situation. Lank and sinewy, with an uncovered shock of thick black hair, he wore a loose hunting shirt of doeskin and high-topped moccasins. He had made one concession to changing times in that he had on store-bought trousers instead of buckskin breeches. It was getting so that people stared at a man in buckskins.

The wagon was hung up solid, and the men who came flocking from the other vehicles had a dozen different ideas as to what to do. Shan had a notion to tell them that in the first place the stalled wagon was plainly loaded beyond all measure of common sense. In the second place. . . . He straightened suddenly, staring. There were four women in sight. One was a grandmother, and two were obviously middle-aged and married. They wore the usual shapeless calico and sunbonnets and had tired, complaining voices.

The fourth was in sunbonnet and calico, also, but on a person who carried herself with such a swing a dress could never be shapeless. She had lively brown eyes, a few sun freckles on a small, straight nose, and a soft, moist underlip, and her hair, where it showed, had tints of rich copper in its auburn depths. Her voice was clear as granite water. "If everyone will give a hand, we may be able to slide it free." She spotted Shan standing idle. "You there," she said impatiently. "You might give us a hand, too."

Shan kept studying her. This one, at least, had looks. Plenty. And it was clear she had mettle. A little too much, most likely. He didn't aim to pick a bossy one. Still, it was obvious she was worthy of further consideration. He was thinking that he might not have to go to Wheeling, after all.

"Grease the stump," he said. "Get pry pokes under the front wheels. Put two yoke on that back axle and drag it off the way it went on. It's wedged ag'in' a saw notch. Any

286

tarnation fool ought to be able to see that."

The girl's nose went up a trifle, and she gave Shan a closer inspection. Then she peered under the wagon. "He may be right," she conceded reluctantly.

Shan leaned his rifle against a tree and supervised the operation. The wagon came free at first try.

The girl thanked him with rigid politeness. She was Miss Felicity Marsh, she said. From Jersey state. And this was her Uncle Toby and her Aunt Martha.

Felicity Marsh stood about five feet one or two, Shan judged. A little on the thin side, maybe. About two hand stretches at the waist, but more adequate above and below.

"We trust we can return the favor, if we should happen to meet again, Mister . . . Mister . . . ?" she said.

"Baxter," Shan informed her. "Shanwell Baxter. Twenty-eight years old, unmarried, an' fancy free. Are you spoken for, miss?"

Felicity Marsh backed off a pace. "Spoken for?"

Shan glanced at the bystanders. There were two or three young bucks in the party who hovered around the girl. One in particular, a husky six-footer with hair the color of new tow, was right at her elbow.

"Are you pledged to marry anyone?" he

questioned the girl. He believed in coming to the point.

Felicity Marsh's back was suddenly as rigid as a rifle bore. Storm gathered in her eyes. "And if I were, I'm sure it would be no concern of yours," she said.

"I figure I've got a right to ask," Shan said. "Fact is, I might wind up by marryin' up with you."

Felicity's cheeks were on fire. She threw back her head, placed her hands on her hips. "I . . . marry the likes of you? I never heard such conceit!" The towhead barged in, his fists knotted, but she pushed him back. "Never mind, George. I can take care of this patronizing woodsman."

"I'm ready to settle down," Shan explained. "Been a hunter an' trapper since I was big enough to notch a sight on game. I was born in the Ohio country. I've seen it change from a wilderness to a frontier, an' I know it's time to change with it. I sat down a month ago an' figured it all out. I've bought me them two yoke of work stock, a wagon, a plow, an' other possibles. I've still got forty-five dollars, cash, in my wallet. I've located the purtiest piece of land a man ever laid eyes on. Plenty of good bottom soil along a branch crick with only sapling growth that will be easy to clear. A running spring higher up, handy to a cabin

288

site that overlooks a mighty pretty view. Plenty of timber in the hills, an' a deer lick not fur away where a man can get meat as long as the deer hold out. All I need. . . ."

"All you need is a wife to go along with your work stock and your plow," Felicity's voice was strained.

"Of course, she'd have to measure up," Shan warned her. "I don't aim to marry up with a pampered female who'd be a burden on a man, tryin' to make a go of farmin'."

"I'm quite sure you can eliminate me from consideration," she said, and turned her back and walked away.

"She's got spunk," Shan remarked approvingly.

"You're lucky F'licity didn't bend a hickory club over your skull," her uncle remarked. He eyed Shan questioningly. "You mentioned findin' some likely land," he went on. "From what we hear, the best locations have been taken."

"You got to know where to look."

Everyone was listening closely, even the big towhead.

"Now there wouldn't be room for more settlers in this place you mentioned?" Uncle Toby asked.

"Could be," Shan nodded. "There's ten, fifteen miles of country along this branch, an' not an axe mark on it. It's in Congress land, at a dollar an acre."

Uncle Toby said breathlessly: "We been lookin' for somethin' like that without much success. You wouldn't want to tell us how to find this place, I reckon?"

Shan sized up the company. They seemed to be honest, God-fearing, although there could always be one rotten apple in a barrel. But then there was the girl. That was the deciding factor. "I might travel along with you folks a day or two while I think it over," Shan decided.

"How far away is this land?" the towhead demanded.

"Three, maybe four days' travel."

"Have you filed on your location yet?"

Shan looked the towhead over closely. "Not yet," he said slowly. "Can't file till it's surveyed." Shan paused a moment. "One thing," he added. "If I guide you people to this place, the claim with the running spring on it is mine. I stepped off my land by foot, placed my corner markers. I wouldn't take it kindly if someone tried to first-claim me to that particular piece of land."

Uncle Toby slapped him on the back. "You can trust us, every one of us." And he turned to the other men. "What do you say, folks?"

A quick rumble of assent arose.

Shan hawed his wagon around and fell in at the end of the line, as the caravan creaked into motion again. Shan made inquiries and learned the towhead's name was George Steen. The three yoke of oxen that Steen drove bore the welts of a hard-laid whip. He wore striped breeches and fancy calico shirt and shouldered lesser men aside when they got in his way. But he treated Felicity Marsh in a very smooth and proprietary manner.

The girl was doing her best with her cattle, but it was evident that she just didn't have the knack. She was afraid of the oxen and stayed at goad's length from them and was no help at all to the animals, who had all they could handle, what with the overload in the wagon.

At the nooning stop Shan walked to Felicity's wagon, climbed a hub, and peered beneath the tilt at the interior. Room had been left for a pallet bed. Otherwise, the vehicle was packed to the hoops with bulky objects. He identified a walnut highboy, a whatnot, a disassembled four-poster bed, spindle-legged chairs, and other furniture, all carefully padded in quilts and sheeting. There were boxes and barrels.

"What's all this foofaraw?" he demanded, astounded.

Felicity did not deign to answer.

"Them's Felicity's belongings, left to her

when her maw and paw passed away," Uncle Toby explained weakly.

"You mean to say you'd wear out two good yoke of cattle to pack prideful possessions over the mountains?" Shan demanded of the girl, outraged. "Why, it'd take a man a year's time to build a cabin to fit such a passel of truck."

Felicity still ignored him. She was bending over the cook fire, flicking flint and steel with angry vigor, endeavoring futilely to spark a pinch of gunpowder in order to ignite the twigs beneath the teapot.

Shan took the flint and steel from her hands. "You got to go at it like you mean it," he told her. "You're holdin' it too fur from the powder. Afeared of gettin' singed. You can't flint fire without gettin' a taste of flame now and then. Watch this." He ignited the powder at first try.

Felicity straightened. "Thank you," she said in a choked voice.

"Another thing," Shan said. "I'd lighten the load. Some o' that spit-an'-polish furniture you're carryin' ain't worth firewood in this country."

Felicity moved fast. A pail of water stood handy. She seized it up, and Shan received its contents right in the face before he could duck. "Firewood!" Felicity panted. "My beautiful furniture! Just you try to make firewood of it, you . . . you barbarian!"

Afterward, Uncle Toby remarked, mildly reprovingly, to Shan: "F'licity thinks a lot of her belongings. She likes to have things nice."

Shan debated it with himself that evening, after they had camped. He decided he'd better cross Felicity Marsh off the list right now and head for Wheeling again. A woman like that would never be content in a cabin. First it'd be a bigger house she'd want, then a bigger one. She'd nag for lace curtains at the windows and a varnished carriage in the barn. There'd be no end to it. *I'll head east again in the morning,* he decided.

Then he saw Felicity working with her Aunt Martha at their cook fire. She had changed from calico to a dress that had considerable swing and flounce and style to it. She had laid aside the sunbonnet, and her hair caught the golden hue of the fire. Worse yet, she had a green ribbon in her hair and a pink wild rose pinned at her breast.

The aroma of browning corn pone and of smoke meat and greens came from the cookware she was tending. George Steen was a guest at the Marsh fireside, sitting with a moonish grin on his face, waiting for Felicity to serve him.

Shan finished his own self-cooked meal of

warmed-over jerky and fried corn cakes sweetened with lick. He drenched his tiny, Indian-type fire, picked up his rifle, and walked out of camp. It was full moon, and there was a chance he might pick up a deer. He was lucky, for his mind was more on a green ribbon in auburn hair than on being quiet, but he surprised a spike buck, drinking at a stream, and dropped it with an offhand shot. He bled and rough-gutted it and carried it back to his wagon, hanging it to cool overnight.

When breakfast came, he carried the carcass to where Felicity was helping start the meal and laid it on a spread tarp that he had brought from his wagon. "Here's prime meat," he said. "A thin steak or two will go mighty good for everybody this morning." He offered Felicity his heavy skinning knife and belt axe.

She stared, then backed away. "Why . . . why, I can't. . . ."

"You never quartered venison?" Shan said pityingly. "I thought so. Well, it's time you learned."

He fell to and with swift strokes skinned, quartered the deer, and cut steaks for the entire company.

"That's how it's done," he told her.

She thanked him rigidly. Afterward, Uncle

294

Toby brought him a heaped-up platter. "F'licity sent it."

There were golden-brown biscuits, wild-blackberry preserve, thin strips of lean bacon, and the venison steaks were fried just right. Shan decided to put off turning back to Wheeling and fell into line.

At mid-afternoon, it clouded over. Soon rain came, persistent and drenching. The trail became a morass, and wagons began to bog occasionally, requiring double-teaming. Felicity's vehicle was the chief offender.

The rain kept up all night and the next day. Even George Steen finally said in exasperation: "Felicity, there must be something you'll part with in that blasted wagon of yours."

Felicity was fighting back tears. "Surely we haven't much farther to go, have we?"

"That's up to Baxter!" Steen snapped. "And I say it's high time he tells us just where we are going!"

A chorus of testy agreement came from other tired men. Shan got a stick and drew a map in the mud. "About ten miles west we'll hit a crosstrail," he said. "It's passable. Turn north, an' in about two days' travel there's a stream called Fawn Creek. You turn downstream. I blazed a route for wagons. Five miles of hard pullin' and the country opens up. That's the valley I mentioned." He made another mark on the mud map. "This is my location," he said. "There's a knoll covered with big maple growth. That's in the center of it."

Felicity turned to the others. "I'm delaying all of you," she said. "I'd rather you'd go on without me. I'll make it after it stops raining and the trails dry out."

Men looked at one another guiltily. Land hunger was upon them now, like a fever. They were thinking that the first to reach this valley would have best choices of location. Shan saw that it wouldn't take much to stampede them into a wild race.

Uncle Toby called for a vote on Felicity's proposal. It was rejected with a rather faint-hearted chorus of "nays." They toiled ahead again through the driving rain with a new impatience. The popper on George Steen's lash was the loudest, and the welts increased on the rumps of his cattle.

"One location will likely be as good as another," Shan finally remonstrated.

"Except the one you claim for yourself," George Steen said, and his whip cracked with a new ferocity.

Felicity's wagon mired down again. Steen climbed into the wagon, glaring at the load. He tested the weight of a barrel. "What's in

296

this blasted thing?" he demanded. "It must weigh half a ton."

"It's my luster tea set and china, packed in cornmeal," Felicity admitted shakily.

Everyone glared at her accusingly. She stood there guilty but unable to make the decision they wanted her to make. So they double-teamed her out of the bog again and drove angrily ahead. Felicity looked at Shan, her eyes daring him to say anything. But Shan kept his mouth shut. He didn't want another pail of water in his face.

They camped at early twilight on a small stream that was muddy and still rising. The rain, however, ended, and the clouds began to break. A chill wind drove through the timber.

As Shan helped put the stock to graze, the wind brought the far, faint rattle of a turkey gobbler. He got his rifle, hoping to find the roost before it became too dark. He didn't spot the roost, but he kept going. Presently in the fading light he saw fresh tree stumps, indicating that there was a settler close by.

Then he came to the rising stream again and sighted a cabin in a clearing on the far bank. Candlelight showed at a window, and Shan raised his voice: "Hello, there!"

That brought a surprising response. The door opened and a woman called: "Judd! Hurry! Hurry!"

There was desperation in that appeal —
and fear. Shan waded the muddy creek. It was
only a dozen yards across, but the chill water
came almost to his armpits. Emerging, dripping, he raced across the clearing and came
into the glow of the candlelight.

The woman, who looked to be about thirty,
peered at him, and said tragically: "Oh, you're
not Judd! I thought. . . ."

She began to weep. A child about two years
old clutched at her skirts and began wailing,
also.

Shan didn't have to be told what was the
trouble. The story was plain enough. The
woman got a grip on herself and said: "I need
help. We didn't expect the baby so soon. Judd
. . . that's my husband, Judd Collins . . . went
to Zanesville to fetch a midwife, but that's
more'n twenty miles away, and . . . and . . .
it'll likely be too late when she gets here."

Shan began to shake at the knees. Here was
something he knew nothing about, a responsibility that brought frigid terror into the pit of
his stomach. He could have fought a bear
single-handed, but he didn't want to face a
thing like this.

"I can have a woman here in less'n an hour,
ma'am," he said hoarsely. "Will that . . . ?"

"A woman? Oh, thank heaven! Yes, I think
that will be in time. But hurry. Please hurry!"

Shan left his rifle there and began running. It was cowardly, he knew. He should have stayed and done what he could. But he ran. He crossed the stream again and made the mile back to the wagon camp faster than he had ever covered ground before. He was sweating in spite of his soaked clothes, and it wasn't from the pace he had set. It was icy sweat, colder than the touch of the night wind.

Cook fires were burning as he raced into camp. "There's a settler woman at a cabin up the country!" he panted. "The baby's arrivin'! Hurry, somebody! She needs a woman's hand!"

Felicity was alone at her wagon, for her Aunt Martha had a touch of the ague and was bedded in the vehicle. Except for herself, there was only Will Dobbs's corpulent wife, who suffered from asthma, and Grandma Jenkins, who was too elderly to undertake a race through the forest.

Felicity realized her responsibility, and Shan saw fear stiffen her face. He guessed she had no experience with such things, either. He expected her to refuse.

Then she shed her apron, seized up a rain cape. "I'll go!" she said breathlessly.

Shan led the way. Darkness had come now, but the moon was rising amid broken clouds. The stream was his guide. He moved at a nervous trot. "Am I travelin' too fast?" he kept asking her over his shoulder.

She kept saying, no, but he could hear her beginning to gasp for breath. Suddenly he picked her up bodily in his arms, as he would a child. Then he really began making distance with his long legs. She wasn't too heavy, but she wasn't a feather, either. The thought came to him that she wasn't so thin as he had imagined under her calico.

Shan was traveling on sheer will when the clearing and the lighted window finally appeared ahead. At the brink of the stream he lifted her to his shoulder, perching her there as he waded the rushing water, holding her clear and dry. He set her down and followed her at an exhausted stumble as she raced to the cabin and entered the door.

He heard Judd Collins's wife say with heartfelt gratitude: "Thank the merciful God! I've got things ready as best I could. It won't be long."

"If there's anything I can do . . . ?" Shan called.

"If there is, I'll let you know," Felicity said.

Shan had never heard such a measure of strength and confidence in a human voice. His own knees suddenly went to sand, and he sat down against the cabin and began to shake uncontrollably.

He flinched at some of the sounds that

came from the cabin. Then he would hear Felicity's voice calm, soothing, and he would begin to breathe again. Judd Collins's two-year-old would wail, also, and Felicity would comfort it, too.

After an eternity, Shan's head lifted, and he listened to a new sound — the first crying of a newborn child. He swallowed hard. All the moisture on his face wasn't from the cold sweat that continued to bead his forehead. He looked back over the events of the past few hours and shriveled inside as he recalled how he had fled like a rabbit and put this responsibility on Felicity's shoulders.

Presently the door opened, and Felicity said: "It's a girl. A beautiful baby. You may come in now, Mister Baxter."

At that moment a man, running on foot beside a woman, who was jolting along saddleback on a plow horse, came panting out of the darkness. It was the husband, Judd Collins, arriving with the midwife.

Shan listened vaguely to the babble of explanations. Felicity and Mrs. Sealover, the midwife, were cooing and exclaiming over the baby. Felicity seemed as proud and happy as if it were her own. Judd Collins wrung Shan's hand a dozen times and kept thanking him.

Shan stayed out of the candlelight. He was still shaking, and his head was swimming.

One instant he'd be hot as fire, and the next he was cold to the marrow. He'd rather have died than let Felicity know how such a little thing as the birth of a baby had upset him.

Then Felicity was putting on her cape and giving the mother a final hug. "I just love that baby," she was saying.

Shan tried to get a grip on himself as he walked with her away from the cabin in the moonlight, but he kept stumbling. Felicity moved along lightly, eagerly. She seemed to have gained strength in the ordeal.

Reaching the creek, Shan said humbly: "I'll have to carry you across again, I reckon."

He touched her reverently, as though she were something infinitely precious. He tried to lift her to his shoulder, but his arms were putty. He released her and staggered. Felicity caught him but wasn't strong enough to support him, and he sagged down at her feet. The world was spinning, and the fever and chills were racing through him.

Felicity's frightened face was close to his own. He mumbled: "There's things to know that are plenty more important than how to quarter a deer or flint a fire."

He heard her calling frantically, heard Judd Collins coming at a run. "He's taken with the fever chills," Felicity was gasping. "It's a spell of malaria, I'm afraid."

After that came a succession of wild dreams, and the worst of them was one in which Felicity was marrying George Steen, and Steen was smashing her cherished furniture for firewood and yoking her with his oxen and swinging the lash on her back. Between these nightmares Shan would drift back to kitten-weak lucidity. He was on a pallet in Judd Collins's cabin, and Felicity and Mrs. Sealover were working over him. Felicity would stroke back his hair and her voice would speak to him encouragingly, soothingly, confidently.

Once he realized that the sun was shining and knew that the night had passed and that Felicity must not have had a wink of rest. At another time he heard her talking to Uncle Toby outside the door.

When she came back into the cabin, he looked at her. She had shadows of weariness under her eyes. "I heard what Uncle Toby said," he croaked. "The others are moving on without you."

"It doesn't matter," she said, placing her hand on his forehead. "Don't worry about it. You're over the worst of it. You'll likely be up and around in a day or two."

Shan didn't say anything. He was thinking that George Steen would get his location in the valley now. Steen would first-claim him, and he was too helpless to do anything about it.

Felicity seemed to read his thoughts. "You put a lot of store in that land you wanted, didn't you?" she said softly.

Shan didn't answer that, either. Then the chills and fever returned, but they weren't so racking. And after a long time they faded. Finally Shan slept, and Felicity was able to get some rest, too.

It was past noon of the second day in Judd Collins's cabin, when Shan awakened. The fever and chills were gone. Judd Collins's wife had her baby, and Mrs. Sealover was busy at the stove. Shan sat up. He was still dizzy but that slowly faded.

Felicity was nowhere around. "Where's Miss Marsh?" he asked.

"She left this morning," Mrs. Sealover said.

"Left?"

"She seemed anxious to catch up with the others," Mrs. Sealover explained. "She wasn't needed here any longer. It was easy to see that you were going to be all right, when you woke up. Judd went down to the trail to help her, and he stayed there to look after your stock and wagon."

Shan sat for a long time, looking at nothing. Of course, he couldn't blame her.

By the following morning he was in shape to travel. He shouldered his rifle, crossed the stream on a foot log that Judd had felled, and walked that lonely mile back to where the company had been camped. Only his wagon stood there, with the wheel marks in the dried mud, and the ashes of the campfires to mark the overnight stop the caravan had made. Judd was there.

"Miss F'licity pulled out yesterday morning," Judd told him. "Her aunt had stayed here to help her."

Judd assisted him in yoking up. Shan was slow-moving, apathetic — a man without aim or purpose. His land was gone. He had seen the envy in George Steen's eyes at the mention of that running spring. He didn't exactly know whether to head east or west. It didn't much matter now. The only thing sure in his mind was that he didn't ever want to see Felicity and George together again.

He was about to set his oxen into their yokes, when he noticed a barrel, standing under a tree, protected by a tarp. It was the same heavy barrel in which Felicity had said her luster tea set and china were packed.

Judd had been watching him. "Miss F'licity had us roll it out to lighten the load," he explained. "She said anybody who wanted it was welcome."

Shan stood, looking at that barrel. "She took a lot of pride in such things," he said apologetically to Judd. "Seems a shame for her to lose her china after hauling it all this way from Jersey."

He got poles for a skidway, and he and Judd loaded the heavy barrel into his nearly empty wagon. He shook hands with Judd and drove west.

After five miles he came to the cut-off. Wagon marks showed that the company had followed his map correctly. And fresher marks showed that Felicity's wagon had passed this way, also.

Shan hadn't driven a hundred yards up the raw wagon trace until he came upon the walnut highboy sitting abandoned alongside the trace, still wrapped in its gay quilts. He loaded this, too. A mile farther on, he found the spindle-legged chairs and carved whatnot and a cedar chest. And not much farther was all the rest of it. Felicity's wagon must be entirely empty.

Shan didn't understand, but he kept accumulating, and his own wagon was groaning with the load now. His pace slowed. He was four days reaching the valley. His cattle were worn, and he was worn, too, but he had every dish and every stick of furnishings that she had given up. This, at least, would be his wedding present to her.

He drove out of the last stand of timber at mid-afternoon, and the valley opened up before him, green, lush, beautiful. He saw that the company had scattered and picked claims. He sighted Will Dobbs's wagon with camp set up and, farther on, was another. The ring of axes sounded in the valley.

What had been his own choice of location was still hidden by a rise of land, and Shan was sure he would find George Steen's wagon there. But it wasn't Steen's wagon that sat on the knoll near the running spring. It was Felicity's vehicle. Then he saw her. She wore the shapely, flouncey dress and had that green, bold ribbon in her hair.

She was beautiful. Shan halted his team, and walked numbly up the knoll. "I . . . I brung along the stuff you shucked off," he said, and his voice was kitten-weak again.

"Thank you," she said. Her eyes kept dropping, avoiding him. And she was pale one moment, pink the next. She just stood there, waiting for him to speak again.

Her Aunt Martha appeared and began to laugh in a knowing way. "F'licity drove night an' day, and got here ahead of everybody," she said. "We passed the rest of them at night while they was asleep. With an empty wagon we made fast time." Aunt Martha added: "You ought to have seen George Steen's face when he came whipping his cattle down the valley so as to be first to this location and found F'licity here ahead of him. She finally had to run him off with a bullwhip." Then Aunt Martha walked away out of sight.

Shan looked at Felicity, and once more fever and chills rushed through him in dizzy succession, but it wasn't the malaria now.

Felicity was pink to her ears and keeping her eyes on the ground. "I saved it for you." Her voice was shaky. "I knew how much this place meant to you. It's beautiful here. Lovely. I'll . . . I'll move off, now that you're here."

She didn't lift her eyes until Shan had his arms around her. Then she looked up at him as a woman looks at the man she has decided to keep forever above all others.

"You're never leaving," Shan was saying wildly. "And we'll have a big house . . . a carriage . . . lace curtains. . . ."

She was laughing, and she was crying a little, too, as she began kissing him.

The Pay-Back Race

Young Philo Clay set the trap for Honest John Sweet, fully aware that for one of his inexperience to challenge the master was equivalent to defying the lightning. The odds were that he would be withered into abject humiliation. The fact that he was taking the risk revealed the chance-taking depths of his nature, inherited, of course, from the maternal side of his family. The Tarbells had always been horse traders and given to wagering on fast animals.

The site of the trap was the old campground alongside the bridge that spanned Big Tawny River. The bait was unfair. It was none other than the aroma of pork chops and other edibles, cooking over an open fire, and coffee coming to boil. These heavenly fragrances drifted on the sundown air from the riverbottom, across the rail fence into Honest John's property, across his cornfield, and onward to his farm house on the knoll. They passed over a girl who lay in a hammock beneath the apple tree, reading a novel about unrequited love. She wrinkled her pretty nose, for she was healthy and hungry and should be helping the housekeeper speed their own supper. But the saga of romance prevailed, and she read breathlessly on.

Not so, Honest John. He aroused from his nap on the porch, sniffing the breeze. He knew whence this bouquet came. Always at this time of mid-August the first of the gypsy horsemen showed up in the campground, traveling the circuit of fairs and rodeos throughout Nebraska and Iowa. For generations they had camped there and sought to outwit each other in matters of horseflesh and other forms of chance. The impromptu race course that had come into existence in the river bottomland had resounded many times to the pound of hard-pushed hoofs, with stakes big and small. In the beginning the itinerants had traveled saddleback or in wagons. Now they rode on rubber tires, their steeds in trailers. But the rules had never changed. Let the buyer beware. Honest John had camped there in his day. He was not like an old fire horse at the sound of the alarm bell.

The pork chops reached a stage of perfection. Philo Clay polished off three of them with side dishes, while his small, leathery companion, Squint Jones, ate sparingly. Squint was a jockey, who must think of his weight, while Philo was a rugged six-footer.

"What I don't see," Squint was saying, "is

what we're doin' here in the tall corn when we've got a horse with so much swift that we could knock over real money on the big wheels."

He quit talking as Honest John rode into view, mounted on a flashy calico horse. Honest John was garbed like a field hand. He was short and rotund. He overflowed the saddle. His eyes, deceptively mild blue, gazed out from a bird's nest of white beard. He was seventy-five years old and had the hidden energy of two men. He rather resembled a poverty-stricken Santa Claus. The fact was that his farm was opulently productive, and his hobby was breeding prize horses.

" 'Evening friends," he said, "I'm John Sweet. Own the place on the knob."

" 'Evening, sir," Philo responded. "Philo Clay. This is Squint Jones. Light down. How about some grub?"

"Don't mind if I do," Honest John said, never one to turn down a free meal. Dismounting, he accepted the filled plate.

He inspected the horse trailer and Philo's dusty station wagon, which bore Wyoming licenses. Philo wore the garb of a working ranch hand. Philo's two horses munched from nose bags. One was a big black which looked dependable, but slow. The other, a blue roan with three white feet, wore a light

311

blanket. It had the smart features and bunchy, powerful coupling of the quarter horse.

"A sprinter," Honest John said. "A real racer. You boys must be headin' for the fair at Dolliver City."

Philo allowed that this was so.

Honest John inspected the blanketed horse. His manner was a trifle disparaging. "Looks like he'd have made a good saddle animal, if he'd growed half a hand higher an' longer in the barrel. I don't hold much with animals with white stockin's. Sign of weakness. Quitters, generally. How fast is he?"

"Ben Blue's pretty fast," Philo said.

"Now, I've got the gosh-dangedest little mare in the barn," Honest John boasted. "Quarter-horse blood in her, too. You ought to see *her* go. I've often thought of takin' her to the fair to run in a real race. I bet she'd win. But I never got around to it."

"You ought to find out what she can do," Philo said.

"I've got no need for race animals. I have to have saddle mounts to get around the place at my age. The mare's too light for me, like your roan. That big black there is more to my fancy. This calico is a good horse, but too small, too, an' too dang much spirit. I've been lookin' around to make a deal with him, but I wouldn't want my granddaughter to know.

She's rode him." The thought seemed to grow on him. He examined the black closely. "A young fellow in our business might prefer that calico. He's got flash. He'd make a pretty lead pony."

"The black's in top shape," Philo shrugged.

"Ride the calico," Honest John urged. "Try him out, boy. See for yourself."

Philo rode the calico. It seemed sound and handled well enough, but deep in its eyes was a glassy look.

"I might deal, if the difference is right," he said, returning.

Honest John looked shocked. "Difference? Why, friend, it's me that'll have to get something to boot. I'd say my calico is worth your horse and at least forty dollars."

A girl's voice spoke entreatingly. "Grandpa! You're not selling Gumdrop? Not *him?* How could you do that?"

Honest John's granddaughter had arrived. She was a sun-tanned, honey blonde who wore a cool, summery dress. She had hazel eyes that were large and clear and pretty, with other features in keeping. She had curves. She was gazing at Honest John as though he had struck her with a blacksnake whip.

Honest John had a hangdog look. "I just can't afford to keep the calico any longer, honey child," he gulped. "You know how things are with us this year."

The girl seemed about to burst into tears. "I know."

Honest John turned to Philo. "This is Mindy, my granddaughter. Next to me, Gumdrop's about all she's had to cling to, now that her ma an' pa are gone. I know what it's like to be an orphan."

"I'll make the difference twenty bucks," Philo said, gazing at Mindy Sweet.

The dicker continued in the classic pattern of horse trading. After a reasonable time, Philo gave in. He forked over thirty dollars. Honest John removed his saddle from the calico and snapped his hackamore strap on the black's headstall.

He eyed Philo's quarter horse and laid the groundwork for further action. "I reckon my mare, Molly Z, would beat the pants off that animal of yours."

"It could be arranged," Philo said.

"I'll fetch the mare over tomorrow," Honest John said.

He led the black away, but his granddaughter remained there, eyeing Philo. There was pity as well as considerable criticism in her gaze. "Where are you from?" she inquired.

"Fremont County, Wyoming," Philo said. "Born there."

"About yesterday, I take it."

"I'm twenty-six," Philo said.

"And you just got skinned in a horse trade."

"Do you mean there's something wrong with the calico?" Philo exclaimed.

"Don't try to saddle him unless there's a doctor handy," Mindy Sweet said.

"But he was just under saddle. I rode him."

"It took grandpa and two grooms and two men from the threshing crew to get it on him," Mindy stated. "Along with a squeezer chute, a blindfold, and plenty of sweat and cussing. It always does. Gumdrop's not so bad after he's saddled, though he has his moments, even then. He just hates to go through the operation. He's a jibber. And how!"

"But your grandpa said. . . ."

"I rode Gumdrop once," Mindy admitted. "I wouldn't go near him again without police protection."

She walked away. Philo watched her mount the stile over the rail fence and ascend the footpath through the corn toward the house. It was a delightful sight.

A spry little man bounced from concealment in the willows. He had a white goatee and wore cow boots, a checked shirt, saddle jeans, and a ten-gallon hat. He whacked Philo on the back. "It cost us thirty dollars an' a horse, but it's bread cast on the waters, nephew," he chortled. "He thinks you're an easy mark."

"You better stay out of sight, Uncle Toby," Philo said absently.

Tobias Tarbell flitted around the campfire, placing more pork chops to broil. "He even et my supper," he snarled. "He ain't changed a bit in thirty years."

Uncle Toby was Philo's grand-uncle and an example of the forebears to whom horse dealing was not a profession but an art. The only person who had ever got the best of him was Honest John Sweet, and that feat had been accomplished by a piece of chicanery in a match race between quarter horses. It had cost Uncle Toby five thousand dollars. It had happened thirty years in the past, but to Uncle Toby it was as yesterday. The humiliation had never faded. It was not the money, although Uncle Toby had made much of that as an excuse. He had fared well during the years and now owned a prosperous cattle ranch in Wyoming. Nor was it the fact that he had been lulled into incaution through the connivance of a pretty widow that mattered, for the fickle widow had married neither him nor Honest John. It was the disgrace of being outwitted at his own game that had rankled. When Philo had proposed a possible way of squaring the account, he had leaped at the chance.

Uncle Toby finished his meal and poured a

fragrant mug of coffee. "What'n tophet's wrong with you, nephew?" he demanded.

Philo was gazing moodily at the window lights of the farm house, twinkling through the dusk in the distance. "She'll probably hate me for this," he said.

"That fluffy-haired gal?" Uncle Toby roared. "Why, she's as bad as her grandpa! She helped him bamboozle you in that horse trade, didn't she?"

"Naturally she'd help her own kin," Philo said, "like I'm doing. But I'd rather be on her side."

As darkness arrived, he shaved and bathed and changed to his best garb. He mounted the path to the house. Mindy had finished assisting the housekeeper with the chores and was sitting in the porch swing, reading the novel. She laid the book aside and made room for him in the swing. "My name is Philo Clay," he said. "I'm afraid I did rather get the worst of that horse deal."

"Philo," she said, "the first thing you've got to learn about horse trading is never to believe what anyone says . . . man or woman."

"You don't think very highly of me, do you?"

"I was disappointed," she admitted. "I really expected more of you."

"Are you an orphan like your grandpa said?"

"He didn't exactly say that," she pointed out. "He said my parents are gone. They're away, visiting my married brother in Illinois. He said he knows what it is to be an orphan. That's true. He was one, but it was more than sixty years ago. You're too gullible, Philo."

She turned on the radio and got soft music. They talked of matters other than horse trading. He held her hand. When he arose to go, she let him kiss her on the cheek. "But only because it's moonlight," she said.

Philo walked happily down the path. At the stile he found Honest John awaiting him. "Sonny," Honest John said, "my granddaughter ain't meant for the passin' fancy of a gyp horseman."

"I'll mention to her your objections," Philo said.

"Good gravy, don't do that! She'd scalp me if she knew I was interferin'."

"Then we understand each other?" Philo queried.

"You got tradin' blood in you at that," Honest John moaned.

"I'm not exactly improvident," Philo said. "I own a few head of cattle in Wyoming. My horse wins prize money each year, and I pick up a little more at the rodeos. I can lay my hands on seven, eight thousand dollars cash if need be."

"Seven, eight thousand!" Honest John marveled. "Now that's a real nice nest egg. You inherited it, I take it?"

"I've got it," Philo said firmly.

"I'll fetch my fast mare down tomorrow, if you're still of a mind to run your horse," Honest John said. "Just for the heck of it, I've got the thirty dollars you paid in the horse trade that says my Molly Z beats your animal."

"Thirty it is," Philo nodded.

When he returned to camp, Uncle Toby emerged from hiding and listened to his account of that part of his talk with Honest John that had to do with horses. "Thirty dollars!" Uncle Toby scoffed. "Pigeon fodder. We'll win tomorrow. He'll act like he's so mad he's lost all judgment an' is ripe for bein' taken. He'll badger you into puttin' up real money for a rematch."

Honest John came into camp the next morning, leading his saddled mare and accompanied by a hard-bitten jockey, introduced only as "Nebraska," who had the earmarks of a professional. They arrived in time for the breakfast Philo was cooking. Honest John ate ten skillet-size flapjacks, plus bacon and eggs. This added new injury to the score held against him by Uncle Toby, who was again forced to stay in hiding while the edibles vanished into Honest John.

"Now, then," Honest John said. "We're ready if you are, sonny." He pointed. "That leanin' sycamore you see beyond that black-berry thicket is a quarter of a mile from this box elder right here beside us, give or take a few yards. Horses have been trained an' worked here for years."

Farm hands and stablemen appeared. Mindy arrived, wearing a big sun hat, pedal pushers, sandals, and a blouse.

"Wish me luck," Philo said to her.

"I'm afraid you'll need more than that," she stated. She again had that pitying look in her eyes.

Honest John singled out one of his stable hands. "Jim, you go down to the sycamore an' start 'em," he ordered.

From the base of the box elder he drew a line in the earth with the toe of his heavy brogan. "This'll be the finish line," he stated. "Jim, you give 'em a fair start now."

Philo saw the pity grow in Mindy at the way he let Honest John arrange things his own way. However, the start seemed fair enough. Honest John's mare broke fast and had a neck on Ben Blue for a hundred yards.

Honest John pounded his legs with his hat. "Come on, Molly Z!" he bellowed. "Come on, gal! You're showin' 'em how to run. You're showin'. . . ."

His voice faded. Squint Jones had turned Ben Blue loose in the final hundred yards. Molly Z's lead vanished. When they flashed past the box elder, Ben Blue had a half-length victory. Honest John played the part of a hard loser. He stamped around, fuming. He ignored the hand Philo offered.

He examined Molly Z's hoofs. He uttered an exultant shout. "I knowed it! I knowed it! Chestnut bur wedged in the frog. No wonder she couldn't run."

Philo was certain the bur had been in Honest John's sleeve all the time, rather than in the mare's foot.

Honest John became offensive in manner. He said: "Well, you won thirty dollars, sonny. You were lucky. That white-legged hack of yours couldn't beat this mare the best day it ever run, everythin' bein' even."

Philo displayed just the right amount of umbrage. "We could race them again, Mister Sweet, if you're not satisfied."

"That's a deal," Honest John snapped.

"For a consideration," Philo said.

"How about a thousand dollars?" Honest John blustered. "I don't reckon you'd risk losin' money like that, though."

Philo bristled. "Two thousand?"

"I don't hear the rustle of real money," Honest John sniffed.

Philo unbuckled a money belt from inside his shirt and produced bills of large denomination. "You hear it now. How about making it three thousand?"

"Four!" Honest John said eagerly.

"Five," Philo shot back.

Mindy spoke. "Stop this. That's too much."

"We don't need advice from a female," her grandfather thundered. "Sonny, you've got a bet."

"My five thousand is cash, not talk," Philo said.

"I'll cover it as soon as we can get to town an' to the bank, sonny," Honest John said. "The banker can hold the stakes."

"When do we race?" Philo asked. "This afternoon?"

"Better make it tomorrow," Honest John demurred. "My mare's a little ouchy from that bur, but she'll likely be all right in the morning. At high noon. Winner take all. No alibi, no crawfishin'. Race or forfeit." They shook on it. "Sonny," Honest John added: "I've taken a likin' to you. After we get the money officially put up, I want you to have supper with me tonight." He lowered an eyelid. "I got a little hard cider, better'n champagne, in the springhouse."

"I'd be delighted," Philo said.

Mindy gazed sadly at Philo. "Five thousand

dollars," she moaned. "You . . . you babe in the woods."

The hard cider that Honest John drew from a barrel in the springhouse that evening was delectable. Also authoritative. When supper was served, Philo gazed through a golden glow at Mindy. She treated him with extreme civility — the sort that has a razor edge. She often addressed him as "Mister Mud" and kept excusing herself. "Clay is so much like mud, I get them mixed up," she explained. Afterward, sitting in the porch swing, with the moon overhead, he tried to hold her hand. She bounced to her feet and into a wicker chair as far away from him as possible.

"Something tells me you're disappointed in me again," he said. "I've been thinking that with what I win tomorrow I can quit being a gyp horseman and settle down. Have you ever been in Fremont County, Wyoming? It's real pretty country."

She glared at him. "Oh! With what you win? Ha! Don't you know that right at this minute . . . ?" She thought better of whatever she was going to say. "Good night. And . . . and good bye!"

She ran into the house. The screen door slammed.

Philo returned to his camp. Squint Jones lay, snoring, on his blankets. Nearby reposed an empty stone jug. It had recently contained hard cider. Honest John's hospitality had extended even to Philo's jockey. Temptation had been placed before Squint, who was never one to refrain from gazing upon the wine when it was red.

The two horses stood in the shadows. The calico jibber was drowsy and hip-shot. The white-stockinged quarter horse was more than drowsy. It was drooping, its head down, and still breathing a little fast. It looked as though it had recently been hard-ridden over hill and dale by one of Honest John's grooms while Squint slept and while Philo was courting Mindy. Which was exactly what had happened. Philo knew this was what Mindy had been on the point of divulging to him until loyalty to family tradition had intervened.

Uncle Toby emerged from his hiding place. He and Philo gazed at the jaded horse. There was almost awe in their faces.

News of the match race had traveled. Neighbors and townspeople began arriving two hours before noon. Philo waited until the assembly reached goodly proportions, and walked up to the house. Honest John had abandoned his rôle as a needy farmer. Wearing a silk shirt, seersucker trousers, and red suspenders, he was the life of the party.

He waited, surrounded by onlookers, as Philo approached. Philo's expression was doleful, his voice meek. "Mister Sweet, I've got to ask a favor," he said. "Something's gone wrong with my horse. He must have got loose from the picket line last night and did some running. Seems tuckered out. I'd like to put the race off another day or two."

Honest John snapped his galluses. "I don't know what sort of a scheme you got up your sleeve, sonny," he said, smiling knowingly. "But it won't work. The terms was that we race at high noon today, or forfeit the bet."

Everybody laughed at Philo, amused at the thought of anyone's attempting to outwit Honest John Sweet.

"I guess I'm stuck," Philo sighed.

Mindy intercepted him as he walked away. "No matter what happens, I want to talk to you tonight," she stated. "I will explain things."

Philo brightened. "The facts of life?"

"Concerning the facts of being a mark for men like my grandfather, at least," she said.

"It's a date," Philo declared.

When high noon approached, Honest John led the stream of visitors down the path to the campground. Mindy followed timidly, as though fearing what she was about to witness but unable to resist the gory sight. Honest John and the others poured over the stile, while a groom escorted the racing mare by the longer route to the stock gate a hundred yards or so farther along the fence.

Honest John came lumbering into the campground. He halted in his tracks, glaring. Uncle Toby Tarbell stood, a foot on a camp box, picking his teeth nonchalantly. His gaze shifted to Philo, who was without expression, then to Philo's horses. There were three animals in camp, instead of two. The calico jibber was on picket. The two others were tethered to trees. Both were blue roans and both quarter horses of about the same size and conformation, for they were full brothers. Both had three white feet. However, in the case of one animal, it was evident in the broad glare of noon that this effect was not the work of nature. Whitewash had been used. This horse still drooped and was plainly not in shape to do much running. The other, which bore a racing saddle and headstall, stood alert, head up, clear-eyed, impatient. It was obviously rested and in the pink of condition. This blue roan was the real Ben Blue.

Honest John knew, then, that he had been caught in a trap of his own making. The horse with the pseudo-white legs had been substituted for the real Ben Blue the previous evening. The wrong horse had been ridden over the hills — an error easy to make in the darkness, in view of their similarity and the white-washed feet. Honest John gazed dolefully. Uncle Toby burst into wild and triumphant laughter. "That's the same piece of skullduggery you run on me thirty years ago, you old varmint," Uncle Toby guffawed. "You got that redheaded widow to make eyes at me. She hornswoggled me into courtin' her the night before my horse was to race that sprint gelding you owned in them days. You got my hostler drunk, rode my horse a couple of miles to wear him out, an' beat the socks off me the next day. You went south with my five thousand dollars. My nephew here got the idea that you'd figure that stunt was worth repeating, if the chance was offered. We put the chance in front of you, an' you fell for it. Hard."

Philo looked at Mindy and saw a rising and warming glow in her eyes — acknowledgment that she had misjudged him. But Honest John was not one to be beaten without a struggle. He reeled, staggered, and sat down. He panted like a wind-broken horse and pawed the air. He clawed at his pockets and made a helpless gesture. "Forgot my pills," he croaked. "They're at the house. Only thing that's kept me alive." He singled out Mindy. "Maybe you can get there an' back in time, honey! Doubt it. Ride! Horseback! You might make it!"

Honest John was pointing to Ben Blue, which was the only means of fast transportation within quick reach at the moment. Before slower masculine minds could react, Mindy raced to Ben Blue, freed the tether, and leaped into the saddle. She gave Philo a look as she wheeled the horse and hurled it into full stride. In that glance were many emotions. Among them was a challenge, as well as pride in her grandfather's reputation as a difficult man to outwit. Philo caught on. But before he could make a move to halt his commandeered horse, it and Mindy had flashed past.

He whirled on Uncle John. "You old fraud!" he raged.

Honest John's mare was now entering the campground, led by the groom and moving at the shambling gait of a walking horse. Mindy and Ben Blue roared past these arrivals, heading for the stock gate. Philo ran in great, ground-covering strides. He reached Molly Z's side in split seconds. He snatched the reins from the startled groom and vaulted into the saddle. Honest John recovered with amazing alacrity. He came to his feet, brandishing a fist, screeching: "Don't you . . . don't you . . . !" But Philo was on his way in angry pursuit of Mindy. She looked back and began working on Ben Blue. Molly Z's groom had dutifully closed the swing gate after him and had also dropped the wooden bar back in place. Reopening the barrier delayed Mindy and Ben Blue enough to cost them the biggest part of the advantage they had gained initially. It was even too late for Mindy to attempt to close the gate in the path of Philo's oncoming steed. All she could do was to put Ben Blue in motion again and incite it to a greater speed by use of voice, heel, and hand.

Ben Blue still had a three-length lead as they headed for the path through the cornfield. But the mare, ears back and running on fright, what with the bellowing of Honest John and the whooping of the onlookers, gained with each stride in spite of the handicap of Philo's greater poundage. They hurtled through the corn with the stalks crashing around them and residue from the tassels blinding them. Philo drew up stirrup to stirrup with Mindy as they emerged into the clear. They had forgotten everything now, except that this was a horse race. He was determined to beat her. But it was not to be. Molly Z pushed her nose in front for a stride or two. Then Ben Blue left her. Philo's weight and the uphill pull were too much.

Philo pulled the mare to a stop to spare her. He dismounted and held her the last few rods to the house, where Mindy had alighted from

Ben Blue and was waiting. She said with meekness: "I'm sorry I underestimated you, Philo. That was real bright of you, riding the mare up here to tire her out, also. Grandpa never had heart trouble in his life."

Philo kissed her. And again. She did not resist. She no longer pitied him. The contingent from the campground came panting up the knoll. Uncle Toby was in the lead, followed by Honest John who unabashedly had abandoned his rôle as a pitifully ailing old man. Philo spoke. "We're ready to race, Mister Sweet. It's just about high noon."

Honest John gazed at his jaded mare, and at Ben Blue, which was lathered but in obviously better shape. He knew when he was beaten. He and Uncle Toby looked at each other. Their eyes began to twinkle. In the next instant they were roaring with laughter and slapping each other on the back. "You old skunk!" Honest John howled. "I always figured you'd try to sandbag me, but after thirty years I decided I was safe an' was beginnin' to look on that five thousand dollars as really mine. You fooled me by usin' that nephew of yours with his honest face. I tabbed him as a mark."

"That widow that helped you hornswoggle me," Uncle Toby chortled, "eloped with a conductor on the Burlington railroad. She always admired brass buttons."

They moved away, arm in arm. "I know where there's a jug of . . . ," Honest John was saying as their voices faded.

The Shining Mountains

Another trail herd was fording the Arkansas and heading for the bedground west of town, and the hurdy-gurdy at the Buffalo Casino across the tracks began rolling it out in greeting to the drovers. That hurdy-gurdy, which was more elegantly referred to as "The Giant Symphonic Mechanical Orchestra," had once graced the texas deck of a Mississippi River packet. It was now built into the front of the casino. Gilded figures of dancing nymphs adorned its façade, and a swamper was sweating at the big wheel as he ground out the strains of "Oh, Susannah." The music carried a long way on this August afternoon which lay still and sultry hot beneath the battlements of thunderheads that towered heaven high above the prairie to the west.

Respectable folk on this side of the Santa Fé tracks let on as if they never heard the hurdy-gurdy, and the Ladies' Aid prayed regularly against it. For its wild cadenzas and brazen tremolos reminded Pike City of a past it wanted to live down. But Ella May couldn't help listening to it. She always listened. Sometimes at night she sat at her window in her nightgown, looking out over the prairie with that gypsy refrain marching beneath the stars, letting her dreams march with it.

She finished measuring out the calico a homesteader's wife was buying, and penciled the sale in the charge-account book. Through the window of her father's mercantile she watched Matt Gore step from the jail building which stood at the corner, fronting on the railroad tracks. Thick-set, with loose, unshaven jowls, his heavy face glinted sweatily in the sun, as he tilted back his sun-rusted derby and stood there a moment speculatively studying the arriving herd and the drovers. Ella May was glad when he retreated again into the dimness of his marshal's office. There was nothing about Matt Gore that marched with music.

She walked to the door and looked up the length of Custer Street to where false fronts left off and the prairie began. She watched the herd drift by with riders, small and distant, enforcing their will on the cattle. Dust out there spurted like golden spindrift beneath the ponies' hoofs. The hurdy-gurdy at the casino was now playing "Dixie," and the towering clouds, their fringes brocaded in molten gold by the hidden sun, were like shimmering mountains.

Drovers single-footed their horses as they

threw the dusty herd out to graze, and the triumphant abandon in their attitudes struck a deep and yearning response in the amber depths of her eyes. For within her was the capacity to understand what it meant to a Texas man to bed his herd safely north of the Arkansas. Then she recognized one of those horsemen. It was a frightening thing to realize that after a year's time she would single him out so unerringly at that distance from among a dozen similarly garbed men. Shaken, she turned to retreat into the security of the store, but a voice peremptorily called her name.

It was Harvey Johns, coming from his land-agency office, crossing the dusty street toward her. As he approached, she was keenly aware of the way he appraised her good points. In his eyes was the satisfaction of a man who had at last made up his mind and was sure of his bargain. "Be ready at seven sharp," he told her, pulling a gilt-banded cigar, holding his Panama hat under his arm. She knew that Pike City was watching and accepting this as further evidence that Harvey Johns had finally made up his mind, after everyone had decided he wouldn't pick out a town girl, after all. He hadn't popped the question yet, but he had been taking her driving regularly on Sunday afternoons back of his matched span of bay pacers. Every Wednesday night he escorted her to sodality meeting and, afterward, sat with her in Charlie Lampton's parlor. He had bought twenty tickets from her for the chicken supper and dance the Missionary Society was holding at the schoolhouse on this night.

There likely were broken hearts in Pike City. Harvey Johns was a catch. Still in his middle thirties, he was making his mark. As land agent for the railroad he hobnobbed with bigwigs and made monthly business trips to Leavenworth and St. Louis. He had got his start dealing in hides, tallow, and buffalo bones, but that was past now, and he wore pleated linen shirts and broadcloth. A solid, pink-fleshed man with a bristly corn-colored mustache and incisive blue eyes, his stomach was beginning to develop a prosperous front. He carried the Republican vote of Pike County right in his vest pocket, beneath his elktooth watch-charm, and men like Matt Gore and Mayor Jim Ellison listened respectfully when he spoke.

"Wear the same outfit tonight that you had on at church, Sunday," he instructed. "The gray one with the jacket. I like that costume. It gives you dignity and modesty. We'll dine at the head table, of course."

Harvey Johns was building a ten-room mansion of brownstone on the knoll north of

335

town. It would have a reception hall and servants' quarters, and beyond the house would be a stable for blooded horses. Ella May could picture herself presiding at his table, wearing a jewel or two, and a low-necked evening gown.

Her father came out of the store lugging a bushel of Illinois apples that had come by freight. He sat the basket on a tripod amid the sidewalk display. "Howdy, Harvey," he said with the deference of a man who knows his daughter is a lucky girl. "Another cattle herd, hey? Are they shippin' from here?"

"No," Harvey Johns said indifferently. "It's a stock herd, bound for Montana."

"Montana," Charlie Lampton marveled, "is a long ways. What do fellows like them Texas drovers see in that kind of life?"

"About all they see is the inside of every barroom and jail from here to Miles City," Harvey Johns shrugged. "They'll be flat broke, when they head back to Texas in the fall. A year gone out of their lives and nothing to show for it."

"There'll be little sleep for any of us after they get lit up across the tracks tonight," Charlie Lampton predicted.

Harvey Johns removed his cigar. "You'll get your sleep. Matt Gore will take care of 'em."

"At three dollars a head," Charlie Lampton nodded. They both chuckled knowingly. "Here they come," said Ella May's father, pointing. "Look at 'em ride! Wilder'n Comanche Indians."

Ella May retreated into the store which always had the musty, cool smell of stored potatoes.

The Texans were coming at a long lope, five of them. And the hurdy-gurdy was playing "The Girl I Left Behind Me" in double time. Town women cleared the sidewalks, and men led harness rigs around back of the buildings.

Ella May fought a cold dread. She wanted to go to her room and hide there, but sterner fiber prevailed. He rode with those five who thundered past the store, sounding the Rebel yell. He was a year older. He looked even taller, leaner, and more deeply tanned, and she saw a new responsibility, a new purpose in his demeanor. But he still laughed with the joy of a man to whom laughter is important.

One of them snatched a red apple from the basket her father had just placed on the sidewalk. The drover tossed the apple in the air, and two of them blew it to fragments with bullets from their six-shooters. The reports thundered against the false fronts. A woman screamed somewhere, and a buggy horse ran away up the street.

They crossed the tracks, and pulled up before the casino. They quit yelling, and their laughter mingled with the crescendo from the hurdy-gurdy. Four of them dismounted and entered the casino, but he wheeled his horse and came cantering back across the tracks into Custer Street, and rode directly to the mercantile. Ella May felt her knees shaking. She watched him swing to the ground at the tie rail. She was conscious of a definite parting as he turned away from his horse. He was not at home on his feet.

He ducked beneath the rail, straightened, and started to smile at Harvey Johns and her father, but they studiously looked away into the distance. An unease and a caution fell upon him as he stepped beneath a roof and hemming walls after weeks in the open. Against the deep bronze of his skin his eyes were powder gray. Thick, dark hair, bleached at the ends by the sun, curled thickly from under his round-brimmed, black felt hat sitting carelessly at the back of his head. She saw the shape of a holster gun beneath his frayed brush jacket.

He brought to her the substance of her dreams, for stamped upon him were his memories of those distant horizons she had never crossed, the mud of the Brazos, and the alkali and the rains and the hailstorms of The

Nations, and the knowledge of a thousand miles of sagebrush and mesquite and buffalo grass. He came to the counter, resting his saddle-browned hands flat upon it, facing her. "I'll have another of the same," he said. "But just stand there some more before you move . . . so I can look at you."

She felt empty, cheerless. She turned, lifted a tin of peaches from a shelf, handed him an opener and a spoon from the tray that was kept there for the cowboy trade. "How are you, San'tone?" her voice said.

She felt a twinge of resentment as she remembered that she knew him only by that name. That was all he had given her when he first came into the store the previous season to buy and eat a tin of canned peaches — luxury to a man who had been many weeks from such delicacies.

"Is that all you've got to say to me?" he asked slowly. "I told you I'd be back. Remember?"

Again it was only her voice talking. "Yes. And now you're back."

"Headin' for country beyond the Yellowstone River," he said. "I'm drivin' into Montana with a stock herd. Part of the drive belongs to me, Ella May. I'll cross big rivers . . . see tall, white mountains." She wanted to stop him, wanted to tell him about Harvey

Johns and that brownstone house, and that stable for blooded horses which was building out there on high ground overlooking Pike City. But, like an old song, she was recalling his answer to a question she had put to him that day a year ago, when he had first come into this store.

"A mountain?" he had pondered her query. "Haven't you ever seen a mountain, ma'am . . . miss? Why, they're not easy to describe. Sorta like clouds when you look at 'em from a distance. Then again, mostly under a noon sun, they don't seem such as much. But at sunrise and sundown mountains shore rear up. They make you pull up your horse an' set there takin' it all in."

That had been a year ago. That had been before Harvey Johns made up his mind he would marry a town girl. San'tone had stayed in Pike City a week on that occasion while the herd was being sold. He had been a faithful customer at the tinned peach shelf in Charlie Lampton's mercantile.

Ella May remembered that hilarious afternoon when she had danced a Virginia reel with him there in the store to the rhythm of the casino hurdy-gurdy, and two other cowboys had joined in with sacks of potatoes as partners. And she remembered the moonlit night, with the prairie drenched in still, white beauty when she had ridden with him out to the herd and sided him as he stood first trick on the bedground. That was the night he had told her he would return to Pike City. And now he was asking her if she remembered. He had ridden away a year ago, and no word had ever come back from him. And now she was a lady, learning to carry herself decorously in the way that Harvey Johns approved and with her chestnut hair massed primly high on her head. It gave her a feeling of maturity that helped place her more at ease among Harvey's friends. She saw San'tone draw into himself as he watched her. She knew he was reflecting on these changes a year had made upon her — and upon the town itself.

"I'm stayin' in Montana, when I get there," he said musingly. "Stockin' new range with cattle in my own brand. The trail days are about over."

Ella May saw Matt Gore come striding from the jail and head toward the mercantile. "Give me your gun, San'tone," she said hastily. "Here comes the marshal. It's a twenty-five dollar fine and fees to carry a gun in town limits."

He hesitated. Then he shrugged, unbuckled his gun belt, wrapped it around the holster, and passed it to her. She thrust the leathery weight beneath the counter.

Harvey Johns joined Matt Gore, and they entered the store together. Gore walked directly to San'tone and flipped aside the skirts of his brush jacket. He scowled at finding the drover unarmed.

"You lose three dollars, mister," San'tone said, faintly amused.

"Don't get gay with me, fellow," Gore said.

The marshal had killed a drunken drover a few weeks previously, when the man had resisted arrest. That memory was working in him now, making him dangerous, unpredictable.

Harvey Johns took a hand. "Better go back across the tracks and stay there," he advised San'tone. "But even across the tracks there's a limit. The old hurrah days are gone. Tell your pals that."

San'tone stared at them, and Ella May saw pity in his face, a pity they could not understand. He tossed a dollar on the counter, paying for the peaches, and picked up his change. "Do you know Ella May?" he remarked. "Some folks never even take time to stop an' look at a mountain."

He headed for the door, then paused, attracted by a big, hand-printed placard which Ella May had made and hung on the wall beside the door.

"Chicken supper an' dance at the schoolhouse," San'tone murmured aloud. "An' the shindig is tonight. Fifty cents a person for the benefit o' the heathen Chinese. Buy your tickets here." He turned to Ella May. "Heathen Chinee?" he marveled. "Do you know, Ella May, I never yet danced with a Chinee girl. It'll be somethin' to remark, I'll tell a man. I'm buyin' into that dance." And he produced another dollar.

Matt Gore spoke. "Stay away from that dance, drover."

Harvey Johns added: "Give him back his money, Ella May."

Ella heard them only remotely, for she was seeing only that challenge in his eyes and remembering the pity and scorn that he entertained for this town. She produced the tickets, and he put them in his pocket.

"Maybe, if there's no Chinee gals handy, you'd save a dance for me, Ella May?" he suggested.

He turned and went out. He mounted his horse and rode across the tracks and walked into the casino. The hurdy-gurdy was playing "La Golondrina."

Ella May looked at Harvey Johns, and now she knew what she had done.

"You have a headstrong and reckless streak in you, my dear," Harvey said, and his voice was like the breaking of glass. "You will learn to control it in time. That was a brazen thing to do."

Ella May suddenly went to her mother, who had been listening at the rear door which led to their living quarters. "They can't . . . ," she said shakily. "Harvey won't let Matt Gore . . . ?"

"The drover won't come to the dance," Jennie Lampton soothed her.

But neither of them believed that. For they had seen San'tone's face, and they had seen Harvey Johns's face. And they knew, because they were women, that before this was ended, Ella May would have to make her choice.

Ella May sat in her room, using her hairbrush. Within a quarter of an hour Harvey Johns, who said that punctuality was a virtue, would arrive to drive her with a flourish back of his bay pacers to the schoolhouse. Then she stood, inspecting her wardrobe. She let her fingers travel longingly over the crisp coolness of a light and gay party dress that she had bought by mail order just for this occasion. Then she took down the mature, dove-gray long skirt and mutton-sleeved jacket, and finished dressing. This was the costume Harvey Johns preferred, but it was not the one intended for dancing the night away. She put on her bonnet, pinched color into her cheeks, and was ready when Harvey Johns drove up.

He inspected her in the lamplight at the door and nodded approval. "Very good," he said. "I'm proud of you."

She sat with Harvey at the head table while supper was served. The talk was mainly of crops and politics, for at this table were Mr. and Mrs. Uriah Baker, and Sam Bartlett and his spinster daughter, and the minister and Jim Ellison, and a few of the other more important men of the community and their ladies. There was none of the noisy buffoonery here that went on at the other crowded tables down the room.

Matt Gore appeared in the door, looked the assemblage over, and moved to stand just inside where he could pass judgment on all arrivals. The tables were cleared away, and the fiddlers tuned up. Uriah Baker, who owned the Fidelity Trust Bank, led the grand march. Ella May on Harvey's arm was next in line back of the banker and ahead of even the Mayor and Sarah Bartlett.

A square dance was called next, and Harvey led her to a chair, for he danced only waltzes. Afterward she waltzed with him, with the loop of her train hung over her wrist, smiling brightly in response to the smiles of the better people on the floor. According to custom she danced next with Uriah Baker, enduring with fortitude his spade beard which tickled her neck.

She went back to her chair on Uriah Baker's arm. She looked up and framed in the door was San'tone! He stepped into the room, and then he was walking directly down its length toward her. He wore a store coat and dark trousers over his spurred, high-heeled boots, and a white, soft-collared shirt with a black string tie. He wore no hat, and his hair, freshly barbered, was dark and Indian-straight in the lamplight. He had passed Matt Gore before the marshal discovered him. Gore now hastily followed him down the room, looking at Harvey Johns for new instructions.

Ella May heard a few women giggle nervously, for word of what had taken place in the mercantile had gone by gossip-route through Pike City. She was aware of the silence that moved ahead of San'tone. There was now only the thud of his boot heels and the soft jingle of his spur chains — that and a faint, half-heard strain of hurdy-gurdy music from far away.

He bowed to her, and he was entirely self-possessed. "I would consider it a high honor, Miss Lampton," he spoke, "for the favor of dancin' with you . . . if all your card hasn't been spoken for."

She was aware of the chill, ruthless anger of Harvey Johns who stood a pace back of the drover. And she was aware of the capacity for violence in Matt Gore who stood there, also, with the killing lust humming inside of him. She felt the isolation of San'tone as she sought for her answer. And she knew that, if she danced with him, it would only go the harder with him when Gore confronted him afterward.

She met his gaze. She shook her head. "I'm sorry," she said. "I'm sorry, San'tone."

She steeled herself, waiting for the pity and scorn to rise in his eyes. But his gaze remained only level and challenging.

"Mountains," he said, "are a sight to see. And worth the trouble, too, Ella May."

He turned then and walked easily toward the door.

Harvey Johns flicked a thumb, and Ella May saw Matt Gore move eagerly to follow the drover.

"Gore!" she spoke.

The marshal turned, and the blaze of fury in her eyes amazed him. She looked up at Harvey Johns then who had started to frown impatiently. The reprimand he was framing remained unspoken. He shrugged, and with the air of a man catering to a whim he shook his head at Gore. The marshal reluctantly relaxed and strolled back to his former position at the door.

Ella May arranged her skirts and seated herself. After a moment she heard the slow pad of hoofs as San'tone rode away from the schoolhouse, heading back to the casino — back across the tracks where she was sending him. The fiddlers swung into another waltz, and Harvey was offering his arm. She danced, following his heavy, insistent lead mechanically.

"I will present you in a moment to Mister and Missus Daniel Ramsbottom," Harvey Johns said. "You will oblige me by going out of your way tonight to be gracious to them. Ramsbottom is in the market for wheat land. He has ready cash. I aim to close a deal with him no later than tomorrow."

This, Ella May perceived, was her future, and its name was Harvey Johns. There would always be other Ramsbottoms in the years ahead to be nice to — for business reasons — other land to be sold by one means or another. Harvey Johns did not dance with his heart.

She left him, when the music ended. She went to the cloakroom but did not pause there. She left the schoolhouse by the rear door. And then she was hurrying through the cooling darkness beneath the locust trees and into Custer Street. The music of the fiddles thinned and faded out behind her as she hurried along beneath the shadows of the false fronts and wooden awnings.

The mercantile was dark as she passed it, but she could picture her mother at her knitting in the living room, and her father dozing over his beloved Illinois newspaper. She reached the dark dépôt corner, with the tracks before her, the tracery of steel glinting faintly in the lights from the colored window glass in the swing doors of the casino over there. She could still turn back, but she knew now that this was the way life was calling her. For a dismounted man, standing by his horse, was waiting there in the shadow of the dark dépôt. He came to her, and she heard the soft jingle of his spur chains. The hurdy-gurdy across the tracks aroused to life then, playing something she could not name, but it had a deep, compelling rhythm.

"I will dance with you, San'tone," she said, and lifted her arms.

His laughter was like that music, and she understood that he had known this all along — known that she would dance with him. His hand lay lightly on her waist, and her hand was in his. They swung with that music, dancing there on that hard-clay railroad platform with only the prairie stars overhead. The

year that had passed since they had danced in
the store was now no more, and they were
again dancing with their hearts — and their
hearts were young and gay.

The music ended, and not until San'tone
thrust her away did she see the intruders.
Harvey Johns and Matt Gore had stepped
around the dépôt corner and stood there
twenty paces away.

"Come here, Ella!" Harvey Johns said, and
his tone was the same he used when he ordered his pointer to heel.

She shook her head. "This is good bye,
Harvey," she said.

She saw him nudge Matt Gore. She tried to
move in front of San'tone to stop this, for she
was thinking of the six-shooter San'tone had
given her and which she had placed beneath
the counter of the mercantile. But San'tone
had moved far out of her reach, and his voice
spoke imperatively, halting her, warning her.
She had danced with him, and now Gore was
there to kill him for it. She could not stop it.
Gore was jerking out his black-handled gun.
Red powder flame etched out the scene vividly. She saw Gore jerk queerly. Gore's gun
exploded downward into the clay platform,
and she felt the heat of it, felt the sting of particles thrown by the concussion.

Gore, a blurred shape in the darkness,

slumped down on his knees, all the lust torn suddenly out of him. And Harvey Johns turned and began to run in clumsy panic up Custer Street.

San'tone had a gun in his hand, and Ella May understood that it was his bullet that had struck Matt Gore before the marshal could fire. San'tone did not even glance at the retreating Harvey Johns. He walked to the huddled marshal, bent over him. Then he came back. "He'll have an arm in a sling for a long time," he said, "that's about all." He lifted her on his horse, mounted in front of her. "Your mother gave me back my gun," he explained. "She was waitin' at the store. She seemed to know I would need it. And she seems to know your mind, Ella May. For she said she'd have all your clothes packed and will be waiting for us with the top buggy up the trail. She's going with us for a ways. She allowed she wanted to be on hand, when her only daughter was married. Your mother, I reckon, never saw a mountain, either."

The horse surged forward.

"Know what they call the Rockies up in the country where we're headin'?" he asked her as he pulled her arms around him. "They call 'em the Shinin' Mountains. That's what they look like, Ella. They sort of shine like big, green-gray jewels in an early mornin' sun."

Ella could hear that hurdy-gurdy music growing fainter and fainter behind them as they rode away from Pike City. Even after her ears could no longer hear it, her heart continued to keep tune with that rhythm.

Desperate Journey

A rider brought the word after midnight that the Comanches were down off the Staked Plains again, raiding south of the San Saba, and the Parkers wasted no time hooking the team to the wagon to head for Blaine's station, which was the strong point in the Round Prairie country. Bide Parker kept the rifle, and his son, Eli, carried the shotgun, an old flintlock muzzle-loader, charged with buckshot.

"But make blamed sure you know what you're shootin' at, Eli, if you cut loose," Bide Parker admonished.

Eli took that in silence, although it seemed to him his father ought to be willing to forget that mistake of two months in the past. However, he rebelled when his twelve-year-old sister put in her usual word: "We ain't finished paying for Amos Russell's mule yet, have we, Daddy? Remember that, Eli. You better be careful."

Eli gave her a freezing glare. "Mom," he said stiffly, "make Kathy keep her mouth shut."

"Let Eli alone," his mother complied.

353

"Anyway, he didn't mean to kill that mule." She dabbed at her eyes as she spoke and looked at their cabin. If the Indians passed this way, they'd burn it sure. She and Kathy were on the wagon, enthroned on the three featherbeds which she had thought of first when they were trying to decide what to take with them. She carefully held in her hands the fancy new kerosene lamp with the pink, hand-decorated china shade that Eli's father had brought back from his trip to San Antonio the previous year. The churn, a few cooking utensils, and clothes were all that Bide Parker would take the time to add to the load, for Blaine's was twelve miles away, and they had only two scant hours between moondown and daybreak.

Eli climbed up on the load, taking painful care of the shotgun, for he was acutely aware that his father was in no mood for mistakes. And, of course, in his anxiety he bumped into the lamp his mother was holding in the dark. The china shade with its hand-painted roses went tumbling down and shattered on a wheel hub.

There was a momentary silence. "Eli . . . ," Bide said in a strained voice. Then, as though that covered the subject, he closed up with a snap of his jaws.

Miserably, Eli rode on the creaking wagon

through the darkness. He was nearly eighteen, and already half an inch taller than his father. He was still a little self-conscious of his lankiness and plagued by an annoying surplus of elbows and knees and feet when he was trying to appear at ease in the presence of his elders. He was able to shave twice a week now, in spite of the fact that he had unfortunately inherited the fair hair and complexion of his mother's side of the family, but it seemed to him his father became more critical of him the older he got.

Bide Parker was a solid, efficient man who never wasted the stroke of an axe or spilled a grain of powder, and he made a habit of pointing out the mistakes Eli made and instructing him in better ways of doing things. Eli guessed he was a disappointment to his father. Other settlers were always boasting about the ability of their offspring, but Bide Parker never said anything like that — at least, when Eli was around. Eli wished his father would realize he was old enough to do his own thinking.

For instance, Eli didn't want to go to Blaine's. He had suggested that he stay home with the shotgun and plenty of powder to keep an eye on the place. His father had told him tersely that they would all go to Blaine's together and seemed so upset about the idea that Eli dropped the subject. His father didn't seem to understand just what an ordeal Eli would face at Blaine's. Everybody from Round Prairie who could make it would be at the station for safety, and all of them had heard about Eli's killing Amos Russell's harness mule. A thing like that didn't happen every day in a new, thinly settled country where even the tiniest item of gossip was repeated for months. Bide Parker had taken a sock at a freight-wagon swamper only a week in the past for referring to Eli as "Mule" Parker.

It had been an easy mistake, but one hard to live down. Eli's father had gone up on the ridge to kick out any deer that happened to be bushed up that hot afternoon. Eli waited below with the rifle. Something came crashing downhill through the thickets, and his father had yelled at him. Anxious not to disappoint his daddy, Eli had fired at first glimpse. It was a good shot for offhand shooting at long range through the brush. The only trouble was that it was Amos Russell's mule he killed. The mule had no business there, having wandered half a dozen miles from his home pasture, but Eli was still working out the debt by hiring out as a wood chopper or helping the freighters whenever his father could spare him from the farm work.

Just before dawn they saw the far, sullen

glow of a burning cabin off in the direction of Pilot Ridge and knew for sure then that the Comanches had reached Round Prairie, but they made it to Blaine's shortly after sunup without meeting trouble. Eli cringed a little, when he saw the activity. Women and kids swarmed around the station. It was a double building of post-oak logs, connected by a gallery, and stood in open ground beyond arrow shot of the creek brush. The freight trail passed close by the door, and the main house was flanked by a grass-roofed barn, a corncrib, and a corral.

The Mattinglys, Ketchums, and Simpsons from Plum Creek and the Caldwells from the North Fork had arrived, along with a scattering of other families. Open breakfast fires were in operation to take care of the overflow. It looked like a picnic scene, except that only the smallest children were lighthearted.

The Russells with their five children were present. Eli glimpsed Angelina Russell, and he was careful not to look again in that direction. She was the daughter of the settler whose mule he had killed, and he had no desire to have her look down her nose at him. She had the right kind of little nose for putting people in their place, along with lively dark eyes and an independent way of carrying herself. She was younger than Eli, but she was right in the midst of it with the married women, getting breakfast and bossing the smaller children around.

The men were gathered at the corral where Tom Mattingly, who had been a Confederate captain, was drawing a map in the dust. The news was bad. Two families near Red Hill had been wiped out. Several others were telling of losing stock.

"We've got enough men now to go out," Mr. Mattingly said. "It looks like the Indians are in small bunches so far, but they'll join together soon. We've got to hit 'em before that happens. Maybe we can get back some of the stock they're runnin' off. There's twelve of us here. Three men will be enough to leave at Blaine's. This place is built to stand a siege, and the Indians know better'n to bother it." Mr. Mattingly looked around, singling out those who were to stay. Eli tried to make himself as small as possible, but it wasn't any use. "You stand guard here, Eli," he said. "And Jonas Ketchum and Sim Wickens."

Mr. Ketchum and Sim Wickens were gray-headed men well up in years. Eli was the youngest in the group. Even so, he believed he wouldn't have been condemned to stay with the women and kids if it hadn't been for that dead mule.

"Don't kill no more mules, Eli," big Jake

Singleton joshed him. "Save your powder for Injuns."

Eli's father wheeled around, glaring at Jake Singleton. For an instant, Eli believed there was going to be a fight. Then Bide Parker decided to let it pass. He looked at Eli. "Somebody's got to stay, Son," he said gruffly.

Eli stood there with the old muzzle-loader in his hands and watched the scouting party saddle up and ride away, heading west. They aimed to go as far as the San Saba.

"Eli," his mother called from the house, "the water barrel is empty."

Eli walked slowly to the house. It was Angelina Russell who handed him a noggin tub at the door. "And we could use some firewood, too," she said. She wore calico with short sleeves, and she was flushed with the heat of the crowded kitchen. "You'll find it handier if you put down the shotgun, while you fetch the water," she added. "If any Comanches show up, I'll let you know in time to get your gun."

She put her hands on her hips as though expecting him to talk back to her, but Eli only performed the chores in listless silence. Afterward, he took up a post in an empty wagon whose position commanded all the flat. He sat with his long legs dangling over the dropped tailgate, the shotgun, powderhorn, and shot pouch handy.

The day turned hot, and the flat drowsed beneath the sun. The trail remained empty, and the two old men who shared with him the task of guarding the women and children nodded sleepily over their pipes in the shade of the grape arbor.

Two wood choppers arrived at the station during the afternoon, having kept their scalps intact in their flight to sanctuary. That made five armed men at the station, which reduced Eli's responsibility almost to zero.

The fretting voice of a child drifted at intervals from the house. Angelina Russell's six-year-old sister was ill, suffering from a high fever. Eli's mother and Mrs. Russell doctored the child, and the other women gave advice, but Eli noticed Angelina brushing at her eyes once when she thought nobody was watching. He guessed that little Jody was not responding.

The afternoon waned, and the trail remained empty. Eli's thoughts were with his father and the others, riding toward the headwaters of the San Saba, and the hurt was vast and bitter within him. He realized that the women, too, were waiting and watching for their men. That tension grew as sundown came, and there was no longer any pretense of cheer at Blaine's station. Early twilight had come, and the strain of the long day was upon Eli. He was standing at the corner of the house, when he saw something. He kept his gaze fixed on the shadowy brush near the creek more than a hundred yards across the road. No wind was stirring, but he was sure he had seen the plum brush quiver at one point. Then it came again. The fronds stirred slightly. Eli convinced himself he saw something lurking there, spying on the station. The range was too great for his shotgun, but Sim Wickens had just stood his rifle against the house and had gone inside to light his pipe at the open fireplace.

Eli lifted the rifle and sent a bullet into the brush low enough to catch any lurking Comanche who might be crouching there. The report broke the evening silence with a jar, and he heard little Jody Russell suddenly begin wailing again. With a pang of regret, he realized she must have finally fallen asleep. That gunshot had aroused her.

He stood staring, numb and aghast, watching a razorback sow stampede off across the creek through the brush, followed by a litter of pigs. Women were crying out. The men came racing. They watched the sow vanish into the thickets. Then they looked critically at Eli.

"You almost got yourself a hog that time,

Eli," Sim Wickens finally remarked. "An' with my gun."

Sick at heart, Eli handed the gun over to its owner. "I thought . . . ," he began. Then he turned and walked away.

He could still hear little Jody Russell. She was wailing that she wanted her dolly. She sounded delirious. She had been asking for her doll all day, but it appeared that it had been left at home in the excitement of the family's hurried departure the previous night.

Eli walked around back of the corral and stood there, while twilight faded into darkness and the moon brightened. He was remembering with the devastating clarity of youth all the blunders, both big and small, he had made. He wheeled around suddenly, realizing he was not alone. It was Angelina Russell. She had a scarf over her dark hair to ward off the quick chill of evening.

"You haven't had any supper, Eli," she said.

"I'm not hungry, thanks."

She eyed him thoughtfully. "It might have been an Indian," she remarked.

"But it wasn't," Eli said stonily.

"Maybe, if the other man had been keeping a sharp watch, they might have shot at that sow, too," she said slowly. "But they didn't, because they had got careless. They wouldn't even have known it if it had really been a Comanche. But you were watching. Don't forget that."

"I woke up Jody," Eli said. "She'd maybe have been better if she had been allowed to sleep."

"She might have awakened, anyway," Angelina pointed out. "You mustn't blame yourself for that."

She waited for him to talk again, and, when he stayed silent, there was nothing for her to do but leave him. "People who never make mistakes," she said as she turned to go, "never amount to much, Eli."

Eli wanted her to stay but didn't know how to ask her. He watched her enter the house. Against the glow of the dim light she was straight and shapely. In the house, little Jody was still plaintively wailing for her lost dolly.

Eli waited until nobody would sight him as he left. He kept the barn between him and the house until he had reached the brush along the creek upstream. He had the shotgun slung in his arm and carried the horn and pouch and his sheath knife. Leaving the creek, he headed across country for Little Branch, which was a dozen miles to the southwest. With the moon hanging like a silver lantern in a cloudless sky, every shadow was a menace. As he skirted Pilot Ridge, the dead, stale smoke of smoldering cabin embers drifted through the mesquite. Farther on, a doe and fawn, running steadily away from some alarm, crossed a swell ahead of him and kept going west.

It was nearly midnight when he crossed Little Branch Creek. A gunshot sounded, so faintly he could only guess at the direction, and he kept to the shelter of a run of scrub-oak brush until he struck the wagon trace that led to Amos Russell's cabin. He followed this until he sighted the place, then lay in cover for a time, studying it. In the moonlight, the cabin stood silent and unmolested, flanked by a patch of waist-high corn and a garden. The Comanches had not passed this way — yet.

He arose finally and ran across the cleared ground to the cabin, lifted the catch, and went in. Moonlight streaming through the small windows showed the disorder of the family's hasty departure. He searched for minutes before he found the doll. He thrust it inside his shirt for safekeeping and moved to the door to leave. He stepped back, just out of reach of the moonlight, then half raised the shotgun.

Four Indians on foot were crossing the clearing, moving with their peculiar loping trot. They had come from the mesquite south of the house. One carried an ancient bell-muzzled Spanish *escopeta*, which was said to fire a slug as big as a pullet egg, while another held what looked like a Sharps rifle. All had bows and war axes slung on them.

Eli held his fire, for the manner of their approach indicated they did not know he was there. He glanced at the windows but heard them scattering to surround the place, and knew it was too late to escape by that route. He did not have time to think further, for two of them were at the door. They paused there an instant, listening. Then they came charging in. Their strong animal smell was like a blow. They had tomahawks in their hands, but they evidently were confident the place was abandoned. Their rush carried them past Eli as he flattened alongside the door. He drove the butt of his shotgun against the head of the nearest, sending the Comanche plunging against a wall.

He leaped through the door as the tomahawk thrown by the other buried itself in the wall. Startled screeching was in his ears. He made it to the corner of the cabin and turned, lifting the shotgun as the Indian appeared in the door. The Comanche looked into the muzzle of the gun and expected to die, but Eli did not pull the trigger, knowing that a loaded muzzle gun was the best insurance against close attack. The Indian seized that chance to dart back into the cabin.

Eli heard the two Comanches yelling from the opposite side. He turned and raced through the corn patch. It was like a nightmare, with him running his heart out and the shadows of the creek timber seeming to recede from him. He heard the thin whisper of a passing arrow. The Sharps roared behind him, but he was not hit. Then an arrow struck the calf of his left leg, its force whirling him. He fell, rolled over, and came to his feet, running ahead. He reached the shelter of young pecans and willows along the small stream.

He saw three of them coming, but they dropped to cover among the corn. They were still respectful of that loaded shotgun, although Eli was wondering about the priming after his race for life. He broke off the shaft of the arrow, leaving the barbed head in his leg. He retreated downstream through the brush. Then he heard the movement of horses, and he ran in that direction, realizing the Comanches had come here mounted in the moon-dappled timber. He ran among the roaring horses, severing the picket thongs with his sheath knife, and leaped astride a roan which he recognized as having belonged to one of the Red Hill settlers.

A Comanche came charging at him from the shadows, lifting the Sharps to fire. Eli swung the shotgun around and tripped the hammer. The priming flashed true, and he felt the solid impact of the recoil. When he looked through the smoke again, the Indian was down, the Sharps still unfired.

Then Eli was riding, following the released horses, which were crashing through the thickets. After a time, he overtook three of the loose animals and drove them ahead of him. He finally caught up their dangling neck ropes and led them by hand. He recognized all the animals as stock belonging to settlers in the vicinity. Looking back, he saw no glow of fire and guessed the Comanches had cleared out without wasting time.

Finally reaching a small stream, he pulled up and steeled himself to take a look at his leg. The arrowhead had skewered the muscles of the calf of his leg, but the head had pushed entirely through. He pulled the broken shaft clear, and wondered if the head had been poisoned. Tearing the sleeve from his shirt, he washed and bound the injury.

He felt a little discouraged with himself because of the way he was trembling. He could hardly pull himself back astride the pad saddle on the roan, but he finally made it. He quit shaking after a mile or two and felt only tired. He reloaded the shotgun, condemning himself for overlooking that matter so long. His father, he reflected, would not have forgotten to reload at the earliest opportunity.

The first glimmer of daylight was in the sky, when he tied up the horses in the brush near Blaine's. He went in on foot, calling his name, so that the men on guard wouldn't take a shot at him. He explained he had been out scouting around and sent them to bring in the recovered horses.

The faint light of a tallow dip showed in the cabin where little Jody lay. He went to the open door. Angelina and her mother were awake, using turkey-feather fans over the patient, who was murmuring feverishly. Eli's mother lay asleep on a pallet.

Angelina saw him at the door and came tiptoeing.

"How is Jody?" Eli whispered.

"She's no worse, at least," Angelina murmured.

Eli produced the doll. "Maybe it'll help soothe her," he said hopefully. "This is what she was asking for, I reckon."

He didn't feel like answering any questions. He turned and walked away, managing to move without limping. He walked around the house and made his way to the creek, where he rolled up the leg of his breeches and studied his injury in the strengthening light. He heard shouts and saw tired riders coming into the station, his father among them. It was the

368

party that had gone out the previous day to ride toward the San Saba, but Eli saw that they brought nothing back with them, and their attitudes told they had not found any Comanches.

Eli moved out of sight in the brush and used cold water on his wound. He decided the arrow had not been poisoned or he would have been dead by this time. It wasn't a serious injury, but it was no mere scratch, either. He'd have to favor that leg for a week or two, and he was wondering how he could keep the family from finding out that he had nearly lost his scalp.

He presently turned. Angelina was standing there, looking at him. Her dark eyes were wide, and her mouth was in the shape of a circle. She came with a rush and knelt beside him, staring at his leg, which he was clumsily bandaging. Her gaze lifted to him searchingly, and he knew that she didn't have to be told how he had gotten that jab in his leg.

"J-Jody's asleep," she began shakily. "With the doll cuddled in her arms."

She was near, and she was breathtaking, with her eyes like stars and sudden tears shining on her cheeks. Eli said: "Angie. . . ." And then he was kissing her.

He heard his father calling: "Eli!"

Bide Parker's voice was not demanding or

369

critical. It carried the deep and quiet pride of a man who did not need to boast of the ability of his son. It was the voice of one man calling to another, and Eli suddenly understood why his father had whipped that freight swamper and had almost socked Jake Singleton.

Eli didn't answer at once. He was telling Angelina that in another year he would build a cabin of his own. By that time he would have accumulated enough to set up housekeeping. And she was saying that she guessed they'd have to wait that long, being as they were still so young, but that at least it would give her time to get some things made for their house, too.

About the Author

Cliff Farrell was born in Zanesville, Ohio, where earlier Zane Grey had been born. Following graduation from high school, Farrell became a newspaper reporter. His first Western stories were written for *Cowboy Stories* in 1926. In 1933 Farrell was invited to contribute a story for the first issue of *Dime Western*. He soon became a regular contributor to this magazine and to *Star Western* as well. FOLLOW THE NEW GRASS (1954) was Farrell's first Western novel. Among the best of Farrell's later novels are FORT DECEPTION (1960), RIDE THE WILD COUNTRY (1963), THE RENEGADE (1970), and THE DEVIL'S PLAYGROUND (1976).

About the Editor

Robert E. Briney was born in Benton Harbor, Michigan, and grew up there and in Muskegon, Michigan. His essays, reviews, and author profiles have appeared in a number of periodicals including *American Bookman*, *Views and Reviews*, *Journal of Popular Culture*, and *The Armchair Detective*. He has contributed to reference works and popular survey volumes such as THE MYSTERY WRITER'S ART (1970), THE MYSTERY STORY (1976), TWENTIETH CENTURY CRIME AND MYSTERY WRITERS, TWENTIETH CENTURY WESTERN WRITERS, TWENTIETH CENTURY SCIENCE FICTION WRITERS, 1001 MIDNIGHTS (1986) edited by Bill Pronzini and Marcia Muller, and the MYSTERY WRITERS volume in the Scribner's Writers Series (1998). He served as a Contributing Editor for the ENCYCLOPEDIA OF MYSTERY AND DETECTION (1976) and for the first edition of ENCYCLOPEDIA OF FRONTIER AND WESTERN FICTION (1983). He has written introductions for several books, including

THE BEST WESTERN STORIES OF LEWIS B. PATTEN (1987) and THE BEST WESTERN STORIES OF BILL PRONZINI (1990). Mr. Briney is a graduate of Northwestern University and of M.I.T. and is a Professor of Computer Science at Salem State College in Salem, Massachusetts. He is currently assembling a second collection of Cliff Farrell's stories.

We hope you have enjoyed this Large Print book. Other Thorndike Press or Chivers Press Large Print books are available at your library or directly from the publishers.

For more information about current and upcoming titles, please call or write, without obligation, to:

Thorndike Press
P.O. Box 159
Thorndike, Maine 04986 USA
Tel. (800) 257-5157

OR

Chivers Press Limited
Windsor Bridge Road
Bath BA2 3AX
England
Tel. (0225) 335336

All our Large Print titles are designed for easy reading, and all our books are made to last.